The Right Kind of Love

The Right Kind of Love

A Novel

Jeanne McCann

iUniverse, Inc.
New York Lincoln Shanghai

The Right Kind of Love

iUniverse books may be ordered through booksellers or by contacting:

iUniverse
2021 Pine Lake Road, Suite 100
Lincoln, NE 68512
www.iuniverse.com
1-800-Authors (1-800-288-4677)

Because of the dynamic nature of the Internet, any Web addresses or links contained in this book may have changed since publication and may no longer be valid.

This is a work of fiction. All of the characters, names, incidents, organizations, and dialogue in this novel are either the products of the author's imagination or are used fictitiously.

ISBN: 978-0-595-47642-8 (pbk)
ISBN: 978-0-595-91906-2 (ebk)

Printed in the United States of America

I dedicate this book to the many men and women who selflessly devote their lives to protect and support the victims of the type of crime depicted in this novel. It takes a community of supportive, aware people who are vigilant in their protection of women and children who are subjected to inhumane treatment. Without them, many victims would go unaided and be forced to live with horrific behavior. All of us should, at some point in our lives, volunteer time or money to support these worthy advocates for justice.

Acknowledgements

To my partner and family who continue to support my writing efforts with encouragement and love ...

To my friends, the LLL group—laughter, loyalty, and most important of all, love ...

To my editor and friend who continues to help me improve my craft with her careful and thorough revisions.

Chapter One

Jack Robinson spoke confidently to his management team. His well-cut business suit was appropriate for an owner of a thriving business. His investment company was doing well, and he credited his small but talented work force for the success. He felt proud knowing he had hired every one of them.

"Alicia, what is our record on new accounts this year?"

Alicia smiled as she began to speak. She didn't have to refer to the report in front of her. She knew the numbers by heart. "Sixteen new client contracts signed through last week with a combined total of eight hundred and sixty-three million in assets. Five new possibilities are being worked right now, and another six are still on the list as high potentials."

"What is your prediction?"

Alicia felt Jack's confidence in her work and she grinned. "I think we can count on another four, maybe five, by year end."

"Excellent work! You and your team have done a stellar job. If my numbers are correct, that is thirty-five percent higher than last year."

"Everyone worked hard this year." Alicia never forgot the members of her team. Without them she wouldn't be nearly as successful. "I'd like to suggest some bonuses for their performances. I have some preliminary numbers worked up."

Jack chuckled as he took the report from Alicia. "I'm going to have to give you another promotion with all this success."

Alicia basked in the comment as she sat back in her chair. Jack wasn't stingy with his praise, but Alicia enjoyed hearing it at all the same.

"Stephen, do you have the international numbers?"

"We haven't finished compiling all of them. We'll have them ready by end of the week, but we're doing very well." Stephen's voice echoed over the conference line from Paris, where he was in charge of their small international office.

Alicia watched a frown cross Jack's face. He didn't like it when people weren't prepared for the monthly updates, and this was the second month in a row that Stephen hadn't provided his numbers. "I expect them on my desk by week end, and Stephen ..."

"Yes, Jack?"

"Don't be late next month."

"Yes, sir."

"That's it then. Monique, schedule an hour with me later this week to discuss our recruiting efforts, and Alicia, would you stay for a moment?"

"Sure, Jack."

Alicia sat quietly waiting until everyone had vacated the conference room. Jack stood up and looked out the large picture window that overlooked downtown Seattle. "Alicia, do you know how much annual revenue your new accounts will bring in this year?"

"My team and I are calculating something close to eighty-six million without any more new accounts. We're hoping to top one hundred."

"That would be a new record for us."

"We know." Alicia couldn't keep the glee out of her voice. She and her team had set the goal earlier in the year, and they all were working diligently to meet it.

Jack turned and faced the highest earner in his firm. "I am serious about the promotion. I'd like to make you a senior vice-president with a substantial raise later this year during our annual salary review."

"I'd like that, Jack."

"Alicia, you're a talented woman. Are you enjoying your work?"

"I am—very much."

"Good, we'll talk more about your promotion later this month."

"Thanks, Jack. Let me know about the bonuses." Alicia walked back to her office, feeling very good about her career. Her personal life, on the other hand, wasn't so great.

Three hours later, Alicia Towers stretched in her soft, expensive, brown leather chair, raising her tired eyes from her computer screen for the first time in over an hour. Glancing at the stylish and costly gold watch on her left wrist, she was surprised to see it was after seven o'clock in the evening. The last thing she remembered was her secretary, Julie Pollan, poking her head in to say goodnight around five-thirty. She had been deeply engrossed in a file and had barely acknowledged Julie's goodnight with a wave of her hand. Alicia was a workaholic, and on many late nights she could be found in her office in front of her computer. Work was the one place that Alicia felt assured of her self worth. She was comfortable with her job, having developed the skills to do it exceptionally well. Alicia knew she was talented at investing. She protected her clients and built a strong foundation that would increase their net worth. She treated their investments like they were her own, and that was one of the keys to her success. It didn't matter if her client was a pension fund or a wealthy individual investor. Everyone got the same diligent attention from Alicia. She was very successful at gaining a client's trust and keeping it, because each one recognized that she did care. Because she respected the owner and the company ethics, she had chosen to work for this small investment firm. Jack had built his company on strong fundamentals, honor and trust for their clients. Alicia agreed with his business ethics and lived them in her daily work.

No one complained about Alicia Towers' work ethic. She was one of the first to arrive and usually the last to leave the office at night. She had worked there for over ten years and had been promoted to vice-president of new accounts several years earlier. She was expected to spend whatever time it took to stay on top of her job and she did. Since her promotion two years earlier, she had worked diligently to bring new accounts into the business, and she had done this well. She had a solid stable of clients and was the top earner at the firm. Diligence and skill earned her clients money, and Alicia's attention and ethics kept them loyal and made Alicia and the members of her small team successful.

Sighing aloud in her darkened office she pushed away from her desk and stood up, stretching her aching back after the hours of sitting hunched over her computer. She would need to put some time in at Pilates to loosen up her neck and back. Glancing around her tastefully decorated office on the twelfth floor of the downtown Columbia Towers, she should have felt satisfied with her life and her career. Not many people reached the level she had aspired to, and Alicia should have been proud and satisfied. She was completely and utterly bored out of her mind.

Watching her reflection in the floor length window, she unemotionally reviewed her own attributes. She was fairly intelligent, with an MBA from the University of Washington. She made a very good living, and the few people who knew her well would say she had a sharp wit and a wonderful sense of humor. She was tall, a little over five feet nine, and slender due to a healthy diet and three nights a week at the gym working out. Her figure would be considered by most as well endowed, and many a man had commented on her assets. Her light blond hair, luxurious and shiny, hung straight to her shoulders, but it was her eyes that most people remarked upon. They were pale, ice blue eyes that were an exact match to her late father's. They completed a package that could easily have graced the cover of a fashion magazine. Alicia was aware of her looks but didn't rely on them because they were due to genetics, not talent. It was her work that she wanted to be respected for.

She had been called drop dead gorgeous by some, stunningly beautiful by others, but her outstanding looks hadn't kept her husband of four years interested enough to keep him from sleeping around. In fact, his interest had waned within months of their quietly elegant marriage ceremony, and he had looked elsewhere for entertainment that included another woman at their firm. Not that Alicia had minded. Within weeks of their marriage she had known she had made a horrible mistake by marrying Stephen. She couldn't stand to have him touch her let alone have sex with him, and she had been at a loss as to what to do about it. Stephen was another vice-president in charge of international accounts at the same firm, and had made it an art form to screw around on his initially unsuspecting but very unhappy wife. Stephen was not anything like his outward image, and he had hidden this from Alicia while they dated. Once married, however, his behavior had degenerated to the point where Alicia couldn't stand to be in the same room with him.

She couldn't forget the night she had stumbled upon one of Stephen's dark secrets.

"Damn!" Alicia swore as her computer locked up for the third time while trying to access her work e-mail from home. She was expecting an important document she needed to review. She headed into the study where Stephen's computer sat silent. She booted it up and prepared to log on to her e-mail account at work.

She opened the web mail program and watched as a strange e-mail account filled the screen with messages. It wasn't Stephen's work account. Puzzled, she opened the first e-mail and was stunned into silence. The picture of a naked young girl filled the screen. Shocked, she opened another e-mail and her gasp of outrage echoed through the empty room. It was another picture of a prepubescent girl, completely naked, who was obviously being held down while a man was having sex with her. She was a child!

Alicia's stomach rebelled, and she fled from the room barely making it to the bathroom before vomiting in the toilet until her stomach was completely empty. "Oh my God, what should I do?"

Alicia wept as she realized the type of man she had married. She cried until she was numb, and then she took action. She was through living with Stephen. First she copied all of the e-mails and pictures on Stephen's computer, burning everything to CDs and placed them in her briefcase. Then she packed all of Stephen's clothes from the bedroom closet that she could cram into a suitcase. She would make Stephen leave tonight. He was due home around ten, and she was not going to let him stay one minute longer.

Alicia's plans that night hadn't worked out quite the way she had expected. Instead of being surprised, Stephen was quite smug at being found out.

"I want you to leave!"

"Alicia, get real. I'm not leaving until I am damn good and ready." Stephen laughed as he began to unpack his suitcase. "How would it look if people found out that you enjoyed looking at pornography with your husband? No one will believe you didn't know about all of my predilections. That revelation will ruin your career and your stellar reputation."

Alicia stared at the stranger she had married. Stephen terrified her. "I want you to leave."

"I don't give a fuck what you want, dear wife. I'm not leaving unless it's on my terms. And don't you even think about telling your dyke sister about any of this. I'll destroy both of you."

Alicia turned and fled the bedroom in shock. She had seen a frightening part of Stephen he had kept hidden from her. At that moment, he seemed very capable of hurting her and her sister. She gathered her briefcase and her keys and left the condominium, heading to her office. She couldn't go to her sister's yet. She had to keep her safe and to do that, she had to keep Stephen's horrifying secrets. But she would get away from him some way. She had to.

Feeling trapped in a loveless marriage, she endured months with silent stoicism, never admitting to anyone but herself that she had made a huge mistake. She had failed at the one thing she had wanted in life, a lifelong relationship with someone who would love her unconditionally. She had settled for the absence of passion, replacing it with the semblance of stability. Stephen coldly ignored his beautiful wife in private, expecting her to maintain the façade of a happy relationship at work functions. Neither had gotten what each one had wanted. It wasn't until after catching Stephen in a compromising situation in his office late one night that the couple had parted company as quietly as they had married and with mutual agreement. Many in the office had known about Stephen's dalliance with a secretary, and Alicia had at last felt safe enough to demand a divorce. Alicia had been relieved to have the marriage over with after months of living in a passionless relationship that made her miserable and physically ill. She was again single and still as incredibly lonely as ever. She also harbored deep in her soul the thought that her relationship had failed because of something inherently wrong with her.

She blamed herself for her failed marriage because, no matter what anyone else said, she had chosen Stephen as a spouse. Finding out he was so horribly wrong for her, and so sick, made Alicia question everything about herself—her judgment, her appeal and most of all her own worth. Being an extremely private person, Alicia grieved quietly and resigned herself to being alone for the rest of her life. Work and family were all she had, and now her family consisted of just two people.

Her cell phone vibrated on her desk startling her from her musings. She pulled herself back from her memories and picked up the insistent instrument. Caller ID told her it was her only sister Madeline—Maddy, as she liked to be called.

"Hi, what's up sis?" Alicia smiled as she answered her cell phone. She loved her sister without reservation. Maddy was one of the few people she could count on in her life. She was always there, supportive and returning her love unconditionally. She was also honorable and honest to a fault. She was a loyal friend who would do anything for her sibling.

"Le Le, what are you doing tonight?" Maddy had called her older sister Le Le from the time she could speak, and the name had stuck. From an early age Maddy had been a precocious and busy little girl. She began gabbing with her older sister when she was tiny and because she had difficulty pronouncing Alicia, the name Le Le was born. The girls had been inseparable while they were growing up, never experiencing any of the usual sibling rivalry that some sisters suffered through. They were best friends and each other's biggest supporter.

To her family, Alicia was still Le Le. Stephen thought it was a silly nickname and refused to call her anything but Alicia. He felt it detracted from her image to be called by a silly childhood nickname. He had been disdainful of a lot of her family's traditions and particularly of Maddy. He didn't like Maddy for many reasons, among them her lesbianism and her honesty, but most of all because she saw through his artificiality. The feeling was mutual because Maddy disliked Stephen's disrespectful treatment of her sister. The more she was exposed to Stephen's behavior, the angrier she became. Alicia had finally confided in her when she was completely distraught and scared that she wanted a divorce. Months before they separated, Maddy had begged and pleaded with her sister to leave her unfaithful husband. Alicia deserved someone who would love her and care for her, and she couldn't understand why Alicia wouldn't dump her husband and get on with her life. She felt Stephen was a horrible excuse for a human being.

"Working, what are you up to?" Alicia's depression lifted as she talked to her sister.

"Honey, you work too hard. Come over to the house. Bet and I are having a spontaneous barbeque since our kitchen is being remodeled."

"When did you decide to remodel your kitchen?" Alicia asked as she turned her computer off.

"When Reed moved into our place and decided we needed to remodel."

"Who's Reed?"

"She's an old friend of Bet's and an incredible carpenter. She needed a place to live for a while, and in exchange for room and board she's working on our kitchen. Come on, we're barbequing burgers and vegetables and we have tons of food. We have wine and beer and crusty French bread."

Alicia smiled as she listened to her sister. Maddy was a year and a half younger and had been her best friend and loyal sister since the day she came home from the hospital thirty-one years ago. Alicia had loved her from that very first day. Maddy had been a free spirit all her life and as different as night and day from Alicia. She was a research chemist at Fred Hutchinson Cancer Center and had a brilliant talent for mathematics. She was also a lesbian who celebrated her life every single day by living it with passion and enthusiasm. Alicia loved her madly and wished every day that she could find the type of love and supportive relationship that her sister had found with her lover and partner, Betty Larson, a firefighter and lieutenant at Station Forty-Seven in downtown Seattle. They had been together for over five years, and Alicia found that spending time with the two women helped rejuvenate her worn out spirit.

"What can I bring?"

"You're badass self, and hurry up. I have a cold beer waiting just for you."

"Twenty minutes."

"Make it ten."

Alicia laughed as her sister hung up the telephone. Maddy could do that with her at the oddest times—make her laugh. She treasured that part of their relationship very much. Maddy always knew what to say. The night Alicia had found her husband at the office with his pants literally down around his knees she had fled to Maddy's house for solace and had found the courage to finally kick him out of her home. But Maddy was so infuriated that Stephen was, in her words, '*boinking his secretary,*' she had roared off on her motorcycle before Alicia could stop her, hell bent on making him pay. Alicia had never heard the whole story of what Maddy had done to Stephen and his secretary, but two things had happened the very next day. Stephen had packed all his clothing and moved out of their loft apartment, and the secretary had quit without giving any notice. Maddy's words to Alicia when she returned to her house could still make Alicia laugh.

"His extremely small dick just shriveled up and died when I told him you were suing him for divorce. Alicia, how could you marry such a pitiful excuse for an adult male?"

Alicia had first stared at her sister and then burst into laughter. "He is a poor excuse for a man, isn't he? Come on, let's get drunk." And she and Maddy had proceeded to do just that.

What Maddy hadn't told Alicia about was the filthy language Stephen had used to demean his soon-to-be ex-wife and her lesbian sister. He had gotten in Maddy's face while the frightened secretary had cowered in her office. No one got in Maddy's face, especially some spiny-assed prick that screwed around on her sister. She'd flattened Stephen so fast he was incredulous as he looked up at her from his inelegant position on the floor.

"You will pack your clothes tonight and move out of your loft by tomorrow morning. If I find out you've said anything to Le Le, I will rip your prick off and stuff it in that dirty mouth of yours!" Maddy stood up straight and turned on the terrified secretary. "You will leave this job and these premises immediately. Both of you make me sick!"

After that dramatic incident, Alicia spent at least one night a week at Maddy and Bet's house, enjoying their company and their support. Her place no longer appealed to her even though she had loved it before Stephen had moved in with her. She had owned it for several years before Stephen settled in, but now it was tainted with bad memories. Often, she couldn't shake her utter loneliness except when she was spending time with Maddy and Bet.

Alicia filed all of her documents and locked her office door, heading down the darkened hallway and into the main elevator for the trip down to the parking garage. Some of the nice things about being a vice-president were a large salary and a prime parking spot. In a city the size of Seattle, parking places were at a premium and exorbitantly expensive. Shortly after her separation, she had indulged herself by buying a very expensive Mercedes convertible, her one incidence of out-of-character behavior. She normally didn't spend money unwisely, buying her high-end clothing when there were sales and researching long and hard before purchasing almost anything else. Her loft was now paid for, thanks to a publicly guilty ex-husband and a good lawyer.

Her one huge indulgence was the single thing that gave her enormous pleasure, her sailboat. She had purchased a single-masted, forty-three foot long sloop before she and Stephen started dating. She had dreamed all her life about one day owning a sailboat, and she had searched for a long time before she found exactly the one she wanted. While they were dating, Stephen had acted like it was wonderful to go out for a day of sailing, especially when he invited people he wanted to impress from the office. It wasn't until after they married that he complained that the boat was a huge waste of money and refused to spend any time at all on board. He had regularly tried to get her to sell her boat, and he never missed an opportunity to whine about how expensive it was to own. Alicia now spent almost every Sunday on it. Her one real passion in her life was sailing, and she loved to be out on the water, flying across the Puget Sound in front of the wind. Sailing had literally saved her sanity as she healed from her horrible marriage. Whenever she could talk Bet and Maddy into joining her, they would sail up to the San Juan Islands. Fishing, eating, drinking, and laughter were a large part of the trip.

"Goodnight, Ms. Powers."

"Goodnight, Eric. How is your daughter doing at college?" Alicia smiled at the security guard she had known for almost eight years. She knew he worked two jobs to pay for his daughter's college education. His daughter wanted to be a lawyer, and her father was going to provide as much support as he could. He was very proud of his child with good reason. Alicia considered Eric a very honorable, hardworking parent.

"Good—she's doing real good. I can't thank you enough for writing a recommendation for her." Eric had brought his daughter to her office to meet her, and Alicia had enjoyed their conversation. She was a very motivated young woman.

"It was no problem." Alicia smiled back at the heavyset man. He was a dedicated family man with two more daughters heading for high school. "Have a quiet evening."

"Do you need me to walk with you to your car?"

"No thanks, Eric, I'll be fine."

Alicia unlocked her car and dumped her full briefcase on the passenger seat and pushed the button letting the top down. There was nothing better than driving in a convertible on a balmy night. Reaching into her dash she pulled out her well-used Mariners' baseball cap and tucked her blond hair up, pulling the brim down as she started her powerful car. She quickly maneuvered out of the parking lot and zipped down Fourth Avenue. The small sports car handled like a dream, and she turned south toward the West Seattle Bridge. She made it to Maddy and Bet's home in ten minutes, almost a personal best. Her mind was at ease, and her stress melted away as she pulled into her sister's driveway.

Chapter Two

Reed finished leveling the bottom kitchen cabinet and nailed it into place, running her hand over the smooth natural cherry wood trim. She loved beautiful wood and enjoyed creating a pleasing and usable space for people to work in. She had been a master carpenter for almost fourteen years, having spent the first five years working with her father to learn the skills. He was an artist when it came to carpentry and from the time Reed was old enough to help, she wanted to be just like him. She had spent many a night and weekend in his workroom sanding wood and watching her father create works of art with his hands and a piece of wood. When he passed away eight years ago, he left her in charge of his business, a family owned and run construction firm. He had also instilled in her a strong code of ethics and encouraged her innate business sense. He had been a loving and supportive father, mentor and friend. She missed him dearly. They had bonded early in Reed's life when her mother passed away while Reed was still in high school. She had died of an aneurism of the brain. It was unexpected and terribly devastating for both husband and daughter, and they had both taken refuge in the business while Reed learned the craft of carpentry. They had healed from their grief while working side by side on numerous projects. Her father had been an excellent teacher, and his daughter had learned her lessons well.

The Thomas Company was now in its twenty-eighth year of business. And business was very good due to a boom in home reconstruction and the company's reputation as a high quality and honest construction firm. They had more business than they could handle, and Reed made a good living. Now, if only she could get her personal life in order. Reed took a big breath and concentrated on the work in front of her.

She was a successful business owner, a talented carpenter, a loyal friend, and an idiot when it came to choosing girlfriends. Her last one was a case in point.

Sheri was now living with another woman she had been seeing behind Reed's back for the last year. Her explanation for staying with Reed was that she liked the lifestyle. In other words, she liked the fact that Reed paid for everything. This last infidelity had been the straw that broke the camel's back. Reed was tired of living in a house that she didn't like, decorated with furniture that she had not chosen, and tired of paying for vacations that she didn't enjoy. She finally signed the house over to Sheri, closed out all of their joint credit cards and checking accounts, and moved out, thanks to the kind invitation of her best friend Bet, Maddy's girlfriend.

"Sheri, why did you stay with me if you didn't love me?" Reed needed to know.

"I love the house and, let's face it Reed, we live very well. I'm sorry we didn't click, but I needed more than just a nice quiet relationship. To be brutally honest, Reed, you're boring. You never want to do anything but stay home. I need more passion in my life."

Reed felt the blow as if she had been hit. She was boring and not passionate. Maybe there was something wrong with her. "I'll sign the house over to you and move my things out this weekend." Reed turned to leave.

"Reed, I'm sorry."

Reed looked at Sheri and saw nothing but disinterest. "Yeah, I'm sorry too."

That was the last time Reed and Sheri had spoken to each other. Everything had been handled efficiently by Reed's lawyer. Reed hadn't been crushed by Sheri's defection, but her faith in her own ability to make good decisions was deeply shaken. She had taken Bet up on her offer of a place to stay until she could make some decisions about what she wanted to do with the rest of her life.

Bet and Reed had known each other for years and when Bet and Maddy had become partners, Reed had developed a strong friendship with Maddy too. She respected and liked both of them very much. To thank them for giving her a place to live in peace, she was going to complete their kitchen remodel and do what she did best—carpentry.

Reed was a powerfully built woman who stood almost five feet ten. Her hair was solid black, thick and healthy, and trimmed to just above her shoulders. She had dark, almost black eyes with long eyelashes. Her face had been called striking by some, and many a woman had commented on her lush mouth and the deep dimples in her cheeks. Her good looks and her extremely well-muscled body made her a popular and appealing woman.

Reed loved what she did and smiled as she worked, lost in her own world. She hummed a song as she centered the new stainless steel sink in the newly installed kitchen countertop. She was interrupted by the roar of a high-powered car and looked out of the large kitchen window as a newer model navy blue Mercedes convertible zipped into the driveway and parked next to her large black Dodge truck. A woman stepped out of the car after putting up the top on the convertible. She was tall with long legs, and she was wearing a fashionable pantsuit in mint green. The baseball cap on her head made Reed smile because it was so incongruous with the outfit. Then she pulled it off her head and shook out her shiny long hair which fell straight to her shoulders. Reed's eyes were locked on the stranger, and she felt her heart shudder in her chest as she watched the woman stretch and then toss her hat into the car. Alicia looked up, and her eyes connected with Reed's. She stared back at the unfamiliar woman who was watching her so intently from the new window in her sister's house.

"Le Le, get in here!" Maddy yelled from the back door.

Alicia walked quickly toward her sister and was met with a vigorous hug and a big smile. She grinned back at her sister and followed her into the house. Maddy was dressed in a pair of threadbare 501s that were hanging off her slim hips, a ragged tee shirt, and no bra. Her ash brown hair was short and spiked on top. She wore a single earring in her right ear and sported a tattoo of a Celtic cross around her left wrist. She was one of a kind, her eyes a bright blue and wide with humor and love. She looked happy and healthy, and she was. She loved her partner, her job, and her life. Nothing kept Maddy down for long and she made everyone around her feel well loved.

"Come on in and get out of those clothes. Have a beer."

Maddy flung her arm around her sister's waist and turned to face Reed who stood quietly watching the two women. She didn't have to be told they loved each other. It was very obvious by the way they looked at each other. She could see the resemblance in their faces, the same long legs and height, but Maddy's hair was darker than her older sister's. Maddy was casual, spontaneous, open about her sexuality, and her sister was elegant, feminine, and much more reserved.

"Reed, this is my older sister, Le Le. Le Le, this is one of my best friends, Reed Thomas."

"Hello." Alicia reached out and offered her hand to the woman who stood silently watching them, her large dark eyes locked on Alicia's face. "It's Alicia."

"Hi, it's nice to finally meet you." Reed's voice was low, melodic, and a surprise to Alicia. The hand that gripped hers was strong, her long fingers wrapping around Alicia's smaller hand.

Alicia couldn't help but stare at the woman. She was incredibly compelling, her black hair held back by a faded bandanna wrapped around the top of her head. She was almost the same height as Alicia, but her body was more muscular, her arms solidly defined. She was wearing old faded painter's pants that sat low on her slender hips, and her stomach was flat. She wore a faded tee shirt that had seen better days, and it was very obvious she wasn't wearing anything underneath it. Her breasts were full, her nipples prominent. Alicia couldn't keep from look-ing, and she glanced back up at Reed to find her following her gaze, a slight dim-ple playing in her cheek.

God, she saw me checking her out. Alicia felt her face flush with embarrassment that she had been caught. Alicia wasn't quite sure why she found that a little bit sexy. She'd never found herself in this kind of predicament before.

The dimple grew deeper in Reed's cheek as she watched Alicia grow even more embarrassed. Reed was used to gay women looking her over, but rarely did a straight woman look at Reed in quite that way. It made Reed's body ripple with attraction. *Jesus, Reed, cut it out! She's straight—what the hell is wrong with you?*

"Le Le, look at what Reed has done with the kitchen. Isn't it incredible?" Maddy was unaware of the byplay between her sister and Reed as she twirled in the middle of her new kitchen space. She was obviously pleased with the transfor-mation.

Alicia turned and focused her gaze at the newly remodeled space and was astounded at the change. She knew high end woodworking when she saw it. "This is beautiful. Is it cherry?"

"Yes, with a natural stain on it. It matches well with the granite counters that Bet and Maddy chose." Reed turned and ran her hand along the upper cabinet. "It will look very nice with the new stainless steel appliances."

Alicia's eyes moved over the custom cabinetry, the matching molding around the window, and up at the crown molding around the high ceiling. Stainless steel light pendants hung over the sink and canister lighting illuminated the rest of the kitchen. "What kind of flooring are you going to put in?"

"It's going to be stone tile to match the granite counters, just a lighter shade. There's a center counter and stove going right here to give them more working space. I should be ready to have the granite installed on the island counter by tomorrow afternoon. The floor will go in next week. It should all be done by next weekend," Reed responded as Maddy grinned at her sister in delight.

"I like it. It's very welcoming and fits the rest of your home." Alicia thought the kitchen was stunning and elegant.

"It's Reed's design, and she's done all the work. She's amazing."

Alicia looked up into the dark brown eyes that hadn't left her face, and she smiled. "You've created a beautiful kitchen."

Reed smiled in return and watched the smile transform Alicia's face. Her eyes were such a pale blue. They were almost the color of ice but they glowed in her remarkable face. Again, she felt the tug of attraction in the center of her body and tried to ignore it as she watched all sorts of emotions play across Alicia's face. It wouldn't be smart to look at Maddy's straight sister with anything but friendship. "Thanks, it's a pleasure to work for people who like natural woods and stone work."

"Reed, wrap it up! It's time to eat dinner and drink beer. Come on sis, Bet's due back from the station any minute, and I have the barbeque going. You can put on a pair of my jeans and a tee shirt."

Alicia allowed Maddy to drag her by the hand out of the kitchen and give her a playful shove up the stairs. Alicia glanced quickly back at her sister and Reed and found Reed standing motionless, still watching her, her eyes dark, full of humor … and something more. She was very impressive as she stood silently watchful.

Reed watched as Alicia climbed the stairs and then turned and started putting her tools away. She needed to settle her heart before Maddy caught her lusting after her sister. She didn't want to cross the line when it came to her friendship with Maddy and Bet. She loaded her tool chest and carried it out to her truck, placing it in the back of her cab. She carried a broom back in and started to sweep up the wood shavings from her work. She liked to clean up after she worked. She was just sweeping up the last of the sawdust when Bet came through the front door in her blue uniform.

"Hey, Reed, it looks great!" Bet's eyes lit up with pleasure as Maddy entered through the back door. "Hey, honey."

"Hi, baby, welcome home." Maddy's arms slid around her lover's shoulders and her lips met Bet's with a kiss, one full of love and passion for the woman who had captured her heart five years earlier. "How was your shift?"

"Long." Bet sighed as she hugged her girlfriend.

"Come on, baby, let's get you out of your uniform and into something comfortable. I'm going to barbeque burgers, and you're going to put your feet up on a lounge chair and relax."

"Is Alicia here?"

"Yep, she's upstairs changing into a pair of jeans."

"Good. I'll go take a quick shower and meet you outside in five minutes."

"Love you, baby." Maddy ran her fingers across her girlfriend's cheek and then turned and headed for the old refrigerator that had been moved out to their garage, along with their microwave oven and everything else they might need while the kitchen was being remodeled. The extra trips to the garage were an inconvenience that was well worth it. The kitchen was turning out better than either woman had envisioned.

"Love you, honey." Bet turned to climb the stairs in time to meet Alicia coming back down, her slender legs covered in a pair of faded, torn jeans. She wore a yellow tee shirt tucked in, and her feet were bare.

"Hey, sis."

Alicia smiled at Bet and hugged her tightly. "You look beat, Bet."

"It was a long shift, but I'll be good as new as soon as I can get a shower and some comfortable clothes on."

"Go. I'll get a cold beer for you."

Bet grinned and loped up the stairs as Alicia headed out the back door to help Maddy with dinner. Reed was already outside sitting on a patio chair next to Maddy's. Both women held cold beers in their hands. Maddy held a full one up to her sister as she sat down on a chair near Maddy's.

Maddy and Bet had done a nice job with their backyard. It was edged with flowerbeds and included a large patio with a hot tub to one side. It was secluded and quiet, perfect for relaxing and enjoying a nice late spring night. They had purchased their home in West Seattle two years after moving in together. It was their safe haven, and they were enjoying slowly remodeling every square inch of it.

Bet joined them ten minutes later, wearing her usual baggy shorts and tee shirt. She regaled their guests with stories about her day while Maddy finished barbequing. As the sun was setting, they ate dinner on the back patio. Alicia was surprised to find she could totally relax and enjoy the evening. Reed was a welcome addition to the group with her quick humor and intelligent comments. She and Bet carried on an animated conversation about music, politics and, of all things, art, before Bet began to run out of energy after being on shift for forty-eight hours. She and Maddy lay together on the chaise lounge, and Alicia and Reed sat across from them on patio chairs. Bet dozed, and Maddy cradled her protectively in her arms.

"I need to get my baby upstairs." Maddy spoke softly as she eased herself up.

"I'll clean up out here," Alicia responded as she stood up collecting glasses and plates.

"I'll help." Reed rose from her chair and began to close up the barbeque.

"Hey, sis, are you taking the boat out this weekend?" Maddy asked quietly as she nuzzled her girlfriend awake.

"I thought I would. You want to come out and do some fishing?"

"Bet has to work tomorrow and Sunday but Reed and I could come."

Reed was surprised that Maddy had included her. She was planning to work on the kitchen Saturday. Alicia smiled up at Reed as they walked into the house together. "Reed, do you like to fish?"

"I do."

"Great, we can troll for salmon early in the afternoon and have fresh fish for dinner."

"You guys should leave tomorrow afternoon and go to Blake Island and spend the night. You can collect clams and mussels, maybe some oysters for dinner, and you can get an early start fishing on Sunday. I expect some fresh salmon for dinner when I get home." Bet grinned as she preceded her girlfriend up the stairs.

"Sounds good. What time can you and Reed get to the marina?"

"How about by three? I've got some chores to run in the morning," Maddy responded, following Bet up the stairs.

"Perfect. I'll go in to work for a while and then get the boat ready." Alicia smiled as she thought of spending the night on the water. It was one of her favorite things to do. She found sailing rejuvenated her flagging spirit.

"You should do that more often." Reed's voice was low and husky so close to her.

"Do what?" Alicia turned to find the woman right behind her.

"Smile—it lights up your whole face." Reed spoke softly as she reached out and took the dishes from Alicia. "Here, let me take the dishes. We have to wash them in the garage until I get the kitchen done."

"I can help." Alicia followed Reed out into the garage and watched as she turned hot water on in the large industrial sink and added dish soap.

"Okay. I'll wash, you dry." Reed grinned as she began to load dishes and glasses into the sink.

"Reed, what made you become a carpenter?" Alicia had wanted to ask her that all evening.

"My dad was one and I wanted to grow up and do the same thing."

"He must be very proud of you."

"I was proud of him. He ran a very successful contracting company until he retired and turned the business over to his only child."

"Is he still with you?"

"No, he and Mom both passed away, my mom while I was in high school and my dad several years ago. What about you?"

"What about me?"

"Did you always want to be an investment banker?" Reed handed Alicia a dripping plate.

"No, actually, I wanted to be a pirate until I was about ten."

Reed laughed as she saw the grin on Alicia's face. "What changed your mind?"

"I realized that I couldn't afford a pirate ship unless I had a good job." Alicia's pale eyes sparkled with humor and a little flirtation.

"So you did become a pirate after all." Reed's dark eyes flashed with delight as she handed another plate to Alicia.

"I guess I did." Alicia's laughter filled the garage.

"So do you sail the high seas a lot?"

"As much as possible—it's my favorite thing to do."

"Everyone should do their favorite thing as much as possible."

Alicia took a glass from Reed and spoke softly. "What is your favorite thing to do?"

"I love building things. I'm taking my time building a house and I really enjoy that. It's incredible when all the work is done and you have this great feeling of accomplishment. I also like spending a quiet day reading or just enjoying the day with a little music.

"What about a relationship?"

"Are you asking me if I'm seeing anyone?" Reed's dark eyes locked onto Alicia's face, her heart pounding in her chest. Something about Alicia appealed to her enormously.

"Yes."

"I'm single. What about you?"

"I'm also single. I was married for a short while and went through a divorce a little less than a year ago." Reed didn't have to be told that Alicia found it painful to admit. Her amazing eyes clouded up and revealed how very hurt she was.

"I'm sorry."

"I'm not. I should never have married Stephen."

"It's still hard when a relationship ends."

"How long have you been single?"

"About four months. We broke up almost a year ago but it took us a while to figure out all of the financial stuff. Now, I'm going to focus on completing the building of my house and keeping my business stable."

"Where is your home?"

"It's on the east side of Lake Sammamish. My dad bought the property a long time ago, but I didn't start building my house until last year."

"I'd like to see your house."

Reed was startled. She was having a hard time not thinking of Alicia as anything other than Maddy's sister, and she was surprised at her unconcealed interest. Alicia was so compelling, intelligent, and downright gorgeous. "Sure, I can take you out there some day."

"Le Le, why don't you just stay the night? Your room is ready, and Bet will wake you up when she leaves for work," Maddy asked, coming into the garage.

"I can go home. There's no reason I should stay."

"You're family, you've been working all day, and we want you to." Maddy hugged her sister and then Reed. "Goodnight, ladies. We'll be at the marina by three."

"Goodnight." Alicia watched her sister head back into the house unaware that Reed's eyes were on her.

"She loves you very much," Reed commented as she rinsed out the sink.

"I love her very much and Bet, too. They have what I want in a relationship."

"What's that?"

"Love, passion, humor, and respect—the same things that everyone wants."

"Hard to find." Reed picked up a towel and dried her hands.

"Yes, but worth it when you do." Alicia placed the dried glass on the shelf.

"Have you found it?"

"No."

"And you still believe you will?"

"I hope I do," Alicia sighed, her face soft as she responded. "Don't you?"

"Oh, I want that and more," Reed spoke, her heart once again pounding in her chest.

"More?" Alicia looked directly into dark brown eyes that held her captive.

"I want dreams to come true."

"Dreams to come true?"

"Yes, like you wanting to be a pirate and me wanting to build a house. I want to believe I can make someone else's dreams come true."

Alicia's smile was brilliant, her icy blue eyes locked onto Reed's face. "That's a wonderful goal."

Reed's body ached to touch Alicia, she was so incredibly sexy. "I had better go climb into bed. I've got to get up early and do some work in the kitchen before we sail."

"I've enjoyed meeting you, Reed." Alicia's smile lit up her incredibly expressive face.

"It's been a pleasure. I'll see you tomorrow afternoon. Can I bring anything?"

"No, I have everything covered."

"Are you staying here?"

"Maybe I will. I don't relish going home to my empty place."

"Well then, I'll lock up and I'll see you tomorrow."

"Goodnight." Alicia climbed the stairs to the second bedroom.

Reed waited until she disappeared and then turned out the lights after locking all of the doors. She headed for the downstairs bedroom where she was staying. Most of her things were in storage at the warehouse where she kept all of her work supplies and larger equipment. Reed quickly washed her face and stripped down to a pair of briefs. She crawled under the covers and then let her mind wander over her evening with Maddy's sister. Under the cover of darkness she could admit that she was wildly attracted to her, and she also knew nothing could come of it. Her feelings would have to remain hidden from everyone, especially Alicia. She couldn't risk losing the friendship or trust of Maddy and Bet. She depended on them. They were her family. But that didn't stop the erotic dreams from keeping her on the razor's edge of attraction. Reed had never felt like this around any woman, the need to touch her so huge it made it hard to stay in the same room with Alicia. Maybe she should decline from going on the boat. Being around Alicia for that length of time could drive her crazy.

Chapter Three

Alicia slept restlessly until seven the next morning, her mind active and her thoughts jumbled. She couldn't articulate what was actually bothering her but something wasn't quite right. She felt a little odd, just a tad bit off center. She was up, showered, and dressed by seven-thirty. She had some work to do before she went to ready the boat. She couldn't wait to get out on the water and relax. She was in need of a break. She had been working nonstop for several weeks. As Maddy would say, "Alicia you need to recharge your batteries more often. Working all the time is not healthy."

Gathering up her work clothes, she slipped through the quiet house intending to get to her car and head home without disturbing anyone. The smell of freshly brewed coffee caught her attention as it wafted from the kitchen. She stuck her head in the open doorway and was amazed at the work that Reed had accomplished overnight. The kitchen was completely painted!

"How long have you been up working?" Alicia inquired, as she stepped into the room and looked at the glowing walls. Reed was standing on a ladder adjusting one of the cabinet doors. She was wearing old, ripped jeans and a faded blue shirt with the sleeves torn off. Her hair was tied back from her face, and she looked down at Alicia, a slight smile on her face. Alicia thought she looked beautiful with her ready smile and dimples winking in both cheeks.

"Not too long. I want to get the walls fully painted before they install the granite countertop later today."

"You put all their things in the new cupboards." Alicia was astounded at how meticulous Reed was with her work. This was a clue to the type of person Reed was.

"They've been without a kitchen for over two weeks. I want to get it done so they can use it again." Reed couldn't help but react to the beautiful woman looking up at her with such admiration. She was overcome by those pale blue eyes.

Alicia had to turn away from the dark eyes that stared at her with such intensity. She felt like she could almost find answers if she stared at her long enough. "I like the color you chose for the walls. How did you get that golden yellow with red undertones? The color glows with light."

Reed climbed down off the ladder and watched the slender blond woman twirl in the kitchen, her pale eyes taking everything in. "It's a glaze, a mixture of colors that aren't completely opaque. The undercoat is a cherry red and the overcoat is goldenrod. I need to paint one more coat to finish it."

"Are you doing this same kind of work at your house?" Alicia was curious as to what kind of house Reed would design. If this kitchen was an indication of the kind of work she did, it would be incredible. Reed put her heart and soul into her work.

"I haven't started on my kitchen yet. I've just finished the shell, the roof, and the windows. I'm starting on the interior next week."

"I'd really like to see it."

"Maybe next weekend you can come out and take a look." Reed really wanted to share her house with Alicia. It had been her longtime dream, and she felt Alicia would understand when she saw it how much it meant to her.

"I'd like that." Alicia smiled at the compelling woman. The dimples winked in Reed's cheeks as her face broke into another grin. "Hey, do I smell coffee?"

"A full pot of French Roast—would you like a cup?"

"I'd love one, thanks."

Reed poured a cup of coffee for Alicia and handed it to her, then filled her own cup before leaning up against the ladder and taking a sip. The two women remained silent just enjoying the coffee and the company. Reed had felt comfortable around Alicia from the first moment she met her. Alicia couldn't explain her feelings, but she felt right at home quietly sharing the morning with Reed. It was rare that Alicia felt so open with someone other than Maddy or Bet.

"I should get going otherwise you and Maddy are going to find a dirty boat this afternoon," Alicia admitted with a quick grin.

"Can I help with anything?" Reed's voice was soft and low, almost intimate.

Alicia smiled as she placed her empty coffee cup on a cardboard box. "Nope, I'll have everything ready by the time you get there. I'll see you and Maddy around three at the Marina."

"We'll be there."

Alicia turned and headed out the front door, her clothes in her hand. Reed watched her slender figure walk to her car, climb into the Mercedes, and pull out of the driveway before she turned back to hanging the cupboard doors. Although she was alone now, her body still vibrated with attraction as she allowed herself to respond to Alicia. She really had no other choice but to let her feelings go. She had never felt this type of overwhelming emotion before. Reed was a very sexual woman and enjoyed an active sex life, but this felt different. For the first time in her life, Reed wanted someone to share her every experience, to live with her in her home, and to take care of her for the rest of her life. That someone apparently was the straight sister of her very best friend. Sighing audibly, she shook her head and focused on her work.

"Reed, you are a piece of work," she muttered, as she pulled her level out of her belt.

Chapter Four

After changing clothes at her loft, Alicia arrived at her office a little after eight-thirty and prepared to get a couple hours of work done. She wasn't the only one who was working on Saturday, and the office hummed with quiet conversation. Alicia usually worked on Saturdays, but for some reason she was having a difficult time concentrating today, which was unusual for her. Normally, nothing distracted Alicia from her work. She felt vaguely agitated and found it very difficult to pay attention. She stared at the open file on her desk trying to make sense of it as she fiddled with her pen.

"Alicia, do you have the Barstow file?" Alex Stone entered her office, a grin on his handsome face. He was a thirty-eight year old account manager who was newly single and had set his sights on dating Alicia. He was always stylishly dressed and even on Saturday he was dressed in an Italian suit that fit him perfectly, and his pale gold tie was knotted perfectly. Most women would find him good looking and charming. Alicia felt absolutely nothing when she looked at him.

"It's in the file cabinet." Alicia looked up at Alex as he slid his hip onto the corner of her desk. She recognized his predatory look and prepared to rebuff his advances.

"Hey, how about having a bite to eat with me tonight? I know a place that has great food and hot jazz." Alex had been hitting on Alicia since word had spread of her separation and divorce.

"I'm sorry, Alex, but I already have plans," Alicia responded, as she put his request out of her mind.

"Maybe some other time?" Alex wasn't easily discouraged, and he wanted Alicia badly. She was smart, beautiful, and well off—a perfect woman to date. Besides, she was sexy as hell, and he was intrigued with her.

"That would be nice." Alicia smiled distractedly, as she handed the file to Alex. She didn't have anything against him. In fact, he was a very funny and charming man. Alicia just wasn't interested in dating anyone. Besides, Alicia felt no physical attraction to Alex. She was completely ambivalent toward him.

"Thanks for the file. I'll drop it off when I'm done with it."

"Thanks, Alex."

"Are you sure I can't change your mind about tonight?" Alex grinned at her, his hazel eyes sparkling.

"Sorry, not tonight. I really do have plans."

"Maybe next weekend we can get together?"

"Maybe—it depends on my workload. Why don't you check with me later next week?" Alicia was very careful to be non-committal. She worked with Alex and wanted to be polite, but dating him was out of the question. Alicia would keep her private life and her work life separate. She had learned a very tough but valuable lesson and would never make the same mistake again.

"I'll do that." Alex flashed his trademark grin and strode out of Alicia's office.

Alicia sat back in her chair and rubbed her neck. She really didn't want to be at the office, and she wasn't getting much work done. Shutting down her computer, she packed her briefcase and prepared to leave. She could do some work at home Sunday night. She stood up and threw her briefcase strap over her shoulder, turned out her light, and moved to her office door.

"Alicia, do you have a minute?"

"Stephen, I thought you were in Paris!" Alicia was very surprised to see her ex-husband in the office. He had taken a new job several months after they had separated. He was based abroad in Paris and rarely had a reason for coming to the Seattle office. They seldom ran into each other and when they did, they were coldly polite. To be honest, Stephen made Alicia's skin crawl, and she didn't trust him in any way.

"Jack wanted me to meet with him and update him on our European activities. I'm here for a week, and then I'm back in Paris for at least another year. How are you, Alicia?" Stephen asked with cold deliberation.

"Fine, and you?" Alicia cared nothing about Stephen, but good manners were ingrained in her. She also knew that the numbers for the European branch were way down, and Jack was extremely concerned. No wonder Jack had called Stephen to the home office.

"I'm good. I needed to talk to you for a minute, if you don't mind." Stephen had always been a polite man, too polite. She couldn't help but notice that his hair was thinning and graying on the sides. She also hadn't noticed how much heavier his face appeared. He'd been a handsome man with close cut pale brown hair and a slender six feet tall frame. He dressed impeccably, buying only the most expensive Italian suits and dress shoes. Maddy had joked that even his boxers were snobby. He had very expensive tastes and indulged them. Alicia was startled to realize that she now found his nose to be a little too large and his eyes too small for his face. He'd also cut one of his sideburns slightly shorter than the other, a small chink in his seemingly flawless image, one that Alicia knew first-hand was faulty. She alone knew a lot of Stephen's deep, dark secrets. Underneath his polished exterior, he was an evil man.

"Sure." Alicia flicked the light switch, backed up, and leaned against her desk as Stephen entered her office and closed the door.

"I wanted to tell you before you heard it from anyone else. I'm getting married again," Stephen announced, his eyes cold as he watched his ex-wife's face.

Alicia was shocked. She hadn't expected that news. She also didn't envy the woman that married Stephen. She was in for a rude awakening. Alicia wouldn't wish that on any unsuspecting woman. She felt sad for her. "Well, congratulations."

"Thanks, I also need to tell you that I'm going to be a father."

Alicia felt the pain hit right in her heart. No one but her sister knew that she really wanted to have a child. Stephen had not wanted children, at least not with her! It reminded her again of what a failure she was. She was also horrified that someone like Stephen would have children.

"Congratulations again."

"Thank you. I didn't want someone else in the office to tell you." Actually, Stephen had wanted to be the one to tell his ex-wife the news. He felt superior now that he had moved on with his new life.

"I appreciate your telling me, and I wish you all the best." Alicia smiled briefly, as she looked back at the stranger that stood in her office. She had never really known the man she had been married to for several years. The silence stretched out as Stephen waited for her to say something else, but Alicia was through talking. She just wanted to leave and not waste one more minute talking to him.

"Well, I won't keep you." Stephen turned and left her office confident that he had upset his ex-wife with his announcement. His look of arrogant pleasure went unnoticed by Alicia.

Alicia waited until he disappeared and then closed up her office and headed for home. She kept her emotions bottled up until she entered her loft. She felt raw inside as she leaned against the closed door of what had been her sanctuary, hot tears rolling down her face. How could she have ever been with him? How could she have been so mistaken about the type of person he was? Why couldn't she find someone who would love her unconditionally, passionately? Was she asking too much? What was wrong with her? Now her ex-husband was going to have a child. He was a sick and depraved individual who was having a baby—something Alicia had yearned for most of her adult life.

Chapter Five

"Right there, drop the countertop straight down," Reed directed, as her crew set the final piece of marble in place.

The stone mason grinned as he looked at the perfect fit of the countertop to the space. He couldn't help but land a playful punch to Reed's shoulder. "Boy, are we good!"

"Yes, you are!" Reed laughed as she acknowledged the beautiful job. The fit was perfect, the coloration of the marble an exact match. "And you can finish it. I have to get out of here and get some chores done."

"We have about thirty minutes of work left. Then it should sit overnight before you use it. I'll leave some cleaner for the homeowner."

"Thanks, Russ. Can you lock the door when you leave? I might not get back before you head out." Reed had a list of things to pick up before she met Alicia and Maddy at the marina.

"I can do that. We're at the Capital Hill place on Tuesday, right?"

"Yes, the bathroom is all plumbed and the green board is up, so we're ready for you to do the stone work. I'll be at the site when you arrive."

"Good. We appreciate all the work, Reed."

Russ's dad had worked for years for Reed's family-owned business, and Reed had continued the tradition with Russ. Not only did he have some of the best tile and stone workers, but she knew the quality of their work was exceptional. She used them for all of her tile, stone, and marble installations. She had plans for them to do the kitchen in her own home. "You do great work."

"Thanks."

"I've got to go, so I'll catch up with you guys on Tuesday." Reed took a moment to look at the counters in the kitchen. The center island was covered with granite. Everything was coming together nicely. Reed should have the floor laid by Monday evening, and the kitchen should be completed by the end of the week when the appliances arrived. She grinned as she glanced about the room. It always pleased her to see a room come together. She never got tired of her job. She found the transformation of a room or home exceptionally gratifying.

Reed strode down the hall to her bedroom and grabbed her wallet. She needed to get some shopping done before she drove to the marina. Maddy was going to meet her there. She'd had a minor emergency at work and was running a little late. Reed hurriedly washed her face, brushed her teeth, and ran a comb through her hair. She slipped out of her work pants and grabbed a pair of shorts, sliding her feet into leather sandals. She stuffed a pair of clean jeans and a sweatshirt into her pack, along with underwear, her toothbrush, and a few other personal items and headed for the garage.

"Russ, I'm leaving. Make sure you lock everything up and go out the garage door, please."

"Will do."

Reed climbed into her truck and struck out for the QFC down the street. She wasn't going empty handed overnight on the boat. She had a plan.

Alicia had a plan of her own. After her initial tears, she had become royally pissed and vented her anger while preparing and cleaning her boat. She had only the outside deck and hull to scrub and *The Wind Warrior* would be shipshape. One thing Alicia prided herself on was keeping her boat in good repair. Glancing around the small galley area, she nodded her head. She had fresh fruit and vegetables in an ice chest on deck, along with lots of beer, wine, pop, and bottled water. She had steaks in the refrigerator in case they got a craving for meat along with their seafood. Fresh French bread sat in the cupboard, along with chips and dip. Clean towels hung in the head, and the one bed was made up with clean sheets. She had another set for the bed stored under the table. She also had two hammocks that could be hung out on deck in case someone was interested in sleeping outside.

She climbed up on deck lugging with her a bucket of warm water and a scrub brush. Working her way across the deck, she methodically washed the decking, periodically rinsing off the suds with a hose. Alicia was so completely intent upon her work as she moved to the hull and hung over the side with her long-handled scrub brush in her hand that she didn't see Reed arrive until she was standing right next to the boat.

"Permission to come aboard, Captain?" Reed's voice was low and full of humor as she stood grinning up at Alicia.

"Hi, please come on up. What have you got?" Alicia put down her brush and went over to the stern where Reed stood, her arms full of bags, a pack hanging off her shoulder.

"I brought some stuff." Reed laughed, as she stepped up on to the boat and grinned at Alicia. She looked so cute in her faded shorts and grimy tee shirt, her feet bare. She looked nothing like the woman who had arrived the night before in a business suit. Reed didn't have to be told that this was the real Alicia. She looked completely relaxed and at home on her boat. Reed liked what she saw more than before because Alicia was even more approachable.

"Stuff, huh, what kind of stuff?" Alicia chuckled, as she reached out and took one of the three bags.

"I brought lots of things. Where do you want them? Maddy is running a little late. She had an emergency at work this morning. A cryogenic freezer stopped functioning, and she went in to handle the clean up. She should be here in a little while. She said she'd get here by three-thirty, no later."

"No problem. Let's see what you brought with you."

Alicia led the way down into the galley and placed the bag on the counter. She stepped away to let Reed set down her bags. Alicia couldn't help but notice the long, muscular legs that were revealed by her shorts. Reed's healthy body was largely exposed, and Alicia had to admit she had rarely seen a woman who was in such good shape. The muscles of her legs rippled as she moved around the kitchen. She moved gracefully, her strength obvious but not overwhelming.

Reed had to keep her eyes away from Alicia she was too damned appealing in her shorts and tee shirt. "Okay, let's see what I brought. Here are a couple of bottles of wine I thought you might like, and some fresh strawberries and chocolate to dip them in. I also threw in some cheese and crackers and a couple other treats. I thought I'd offer to cook breakfast, if you don't mind. I have a little surprise, if you're game."

"I'd be nuts not to let you make breakfast. Thanks, Reed."

"No problem." Reed could see the turmoil in Alicia's eyes, and it tugged at her heart. She sensed that something was bothering Alicia, and Reed didn't know what to do about it. Reed hesitated briefly and then just forged ahead. "Alicia, what's going on?"

Alicia's eyes jerked back to Reed's, her face pale. "What do you mean?"

"Honey, I can see it in your eyes. Something is going on. I'm a really good listener."

Alicia's eyes filled with tears as she realized that Reed meant what she said. Her dark eyes were full of compassion, her voice soft and gentle. Without further hesitation, Alicia blurted out, "I'm mad at myself for being an idiot!"

Reed knew Alicia was using anger to control her emotions. Something had hurt her deeply. "Why do you think you're an idiot?"

"Oh, I don't know. I married a man I didn't love. Within three weeks we were sick to death of each other, and Stephen chose to look for entertainment elsewhere. We finally separated after over two years in a passionless marriage. His many mistresses worked at my office." Alicia grew more agitated as she spoke. She couldn't tell Reed the whole story, it was too horrifying.

Reed didn't say a word but she moved closer to Alicia and placed her hand against Alicia's back rubbing gently in circles as she continued to speak. "He stopped in my office this morning to tell me he and his current mistress are getting married. They live in Paris."

"I'm sorry." Reed spoke softly, her eyes locked on Alicia's face as her hand continued gently rubbing her back.

Alicia moved closer to Reed, placing her hand on her arm and looked up into dark gentle eyes. "I'm not sorry he's getting married. I've had no feelings for him for a long time. His girlfriend is pregnant."

Alicia started to cry, her pale eyes glossy as she fought the emotion. Reed gently wrapped her arms around Alicia and held her as she wept. She was heartbroken, and Reed wanted more than anything to take away her pain. Alicia slowly stopped weeping and stayed within Reed's arms, needing the comfort that had been missing in her life for so long. She breathed deeply calming herself as she relaxed in Reed's embrace. She breathed in the unique scent that wafted from Reed's shirt—a combination of citrus and soap, clean and sexy.

"I always wanted to have a child and Stephen never did, at least not with me." Alicia's voice was so soft Reed could barely hear her. She bent over to speak.

"Would you have wanted to have a child with Stephen?"

"God, no!" Alicia responded with a snort. "He's going to make a horrible parent. He's the last person in the world that should have a child."

"Then I suggest you have a child of your own," Reed remarked, as she stroked Alicia's back.

Alicia leaned back until she could look directly into Reed's eyes. "Now that's an idea. Do you want to have children?"

Reed's face lit up with a smile, the dimples on her cheeks pronounced. "Hell no, but I thought I might find a woman who wanted to have children with me. I'd like to be a parent."

Alicia relaxed and chuckled as she smiled up at the charming woman. "I can just see you teaching your child how to be a carpenter. That would be so cute."

Reed blushed with embarrassment and then stepped away from Alicia. She was finding their proximity way too enjoyable. "Hey, I brought you a present."

"A present?" Alicia was pleased with how thoughtful Reed was and how easy it was to talk to her.

"Yep." Reed turned and rummaged through her bag until she found what she was looking for. It was a folded piece of cloth, and she proudly handed it to Alicia, shaking it out with a flourish.

"What is this? Oh my God, it's a pirate flag! Where did you find it?"

"Toys'R'Us. I even got an eye patch." Reed grinned, enjoying Alicia's delight in her gift.

"I can't believe you went out and found a pirate flag. That is so sweet. Thank you." Alicia reached out and hugged Reed tightly. Reed thought she was going to jump out of her skin as she felt Alicia's body press against her own. "You'll have to help me hang it."

Reed pulled away and lifted the eye patch to her right eye. "Arrr, me fine Captain."

Alicia cracked up with laughter, hugging Reed once more. "Reed, thanks for listening."

"No problem, how about I put these things away for you? Is there anything I can do to help you with the boat?"

"Nope, all I need to do is put my scrub bucket away, and when Maddy arrives we can set sail." Alicia no longer felt the least bit unhappy. A small, thoughtful gift and an understanding new friend had raised her spirits. Thoughts of Stephen had been forgotten as she felt all her worries slide away.

"I haven't been fishing for a couple of years," Reed admitted, as she finished putting away all of the food.

"Do you like fishing?"

"Yes, I do. I just haven't taken the time to do any."

"Then I'm glad you're here."

Reed was very glad herself, for all the wrong reasons. Every minute she spent with Alicia made her want to spend even more time with her. Reed was rapidly losing her heart to Alicia—not a very smart thing to do especially since she was straight and her best friend's sister.

"Hey guys, anyone around?" Maddy called, climbing onto the boat.

"We're down here putting things away."

"Hey, sis, Reed, are we ready to rock and roll?" Maddy grinned as she stepped down into the galley and slipped her arm around her sister's waist, hugging her.

"Absolutely! How about you and Reed hang up my new flag while I get us out of the marina?" Alicia's face was free of worry, here eyes alight with happiness.

"A skull and crossbones flag, how cool." Maddy trooped up the stairs behind her sister, with Reed bringing up the rear, after dropping her pack on the table.

Within minutes they were underway and sailed slowly out into the Sound. Reed couldn't keep her eyes off of Alicia, her blond hair snagged up under a baseball cap, her bare feet tucked under her on the Captain's chair. She looked like she belonged just where she was, as she smiled while expertly piloting the boat out of the marina. Once they cleared the buoys, she unfurled the sails and they were under way, the wind moving them along at a fast clip. The pirate flag flapped gaily in the brisk wind, the skull and crossbones standing out against the black background. Maddy and Reed found spots on the deck and watched West Seattle slide past as they moved quickly south toward Blake Island.

"Arr, it should be a good day," Reed growled as Maddy turned and grinned at her.

"An eye patch—how cool!" She and Reed laughed loudly, and Alicia turned and smiled as she saw the grins on their faces while Maddy slid the eye patch on. It tickled her that Reed had cared enough to remember Alicia's dream of being a pirate. Her thoughtfulness told her so much about the type of person Reed was.

Chapter Six

"Let's get the poles ready," Maddy suggested, reaching into a storage cabinet and pulling out a tackle box. She reached up and unhooked one of four poles that were hanging on hooks in the cabinet. "Here's a pole for you and one for Alicia."

"There's some fresh herring in the small ice chest by the ladder," Alicia announced, as she corrected the boat's course.

"Do you want to cut herring into plugs or do you want to troll with whole herring?" Reed asked.

"We usually troll with full herring."

Reed reached into the ice chest and pulled out a large bag of fresh bait fish. She efficiently baited two poles and laid them down before glancing up to find Alicia watching her. The smile Alicia flashed at her was enough to make Reed flush with attraction, her body reacting without thought. She turned away so that Maddy wouldn't catch her coveting her sister.

"Hey, did you get the countertop installed today?" Maddy sat down with her pole in her hand.

"Yep, it looks good. The guys did a great job with the installation. I should be able to get the floor laid down by mid-week and have everything ready for the appliances to be installed. You'll be cooking in a new kitchen by next weekend."

"Cool, Bet's going to love that. You do beautiful work, Reed."

Reed blushed with embarrassment, her grin quick. "Thanks."

"So when are you going to tell me you have a crush on my sister?" Reed was so shocked, her mouth dropped open as Maddy grinned back at her. "What, you didn't think I could see how you can't keep from looking at her?"

"I wouldn't do anything, Maddy." Reed's eyes filled with trepidation as she began to panic. She would never put their friendship in jeopardy.

"That's too bad, because if there was anyone I'd like to see Alicia with it would be someone as loving and honorable as you." Maddy placed her hand on Reed's arm. "Reed, my sister is intrigued by you. She could do worse than fall in love with someone like you."

"But, Maddy, she's straight." Reed was very uncomfortable talking about Maddy's sister. She also felt a little vulnerable knowing she was so easy to read.

"Honey, I'm not worried about my sister. I'm worried about you. I know you. You love deeply and seriously. My sister is still recovering from her disastrous marriage to that asshole. I don't want to see you get hurt. Please be careful." Maddy's eyes were compassionate and full of love.

"I would never do anything to hurt your sister or you. It's just a little crush. I can handle it." Reed was hoping she could handle her feelings, especially since they were so transparent to Maddy. She should stay away from Alicia, at least until she got a handle on her crush. That's what it was, a silly crush!

"Sweetie, I know you wouldn't hurt my sister."

"I'm sorry, Maddy." Reed was appalled that Maddy had been able to pick up on her feelings.

"Reed, there's nothing for you to apologize for." Maddy smiled at her best friend and reached out to squeeze her hand. Maddy was aware of more than just Reed's feelings. She knew her sister well, and she also saw the attraction for Reed in Alicia's eyes. She wondered how long it would be before Alicia figured things out. It wouldn't bother Maddy if Alicia pursued a relationship with Reed. In fact, she thought it might provide Alicia with the passion she was missing in her life. She wanted Alicia to be happy and well loved. Reed was someone who would provide those things and more. Maddy had enormous respect for Reed. She had had such bad luck in her relationships. Reed was one of those people who believed what she was told and trusted completely. Her last girlfriend had taken unfair advantage of that and almost stolen her blind. Maddy had wanted to get even with her in some way. Only a promise extracted by Bet, had kept her from making Sheri pay for the shabby way she had treated Reed. Maddy had a quick and ferocious temper and protected those she loved. Bet was much more controlled and level-headed, keeping Maddy from barreling into trouble, something she did quite regularly.

"Don't say anything to Alicia, please!" Reed would be devastated if Maddy said something to her sister.

"I'm not going to say a word."

"Thanks, Maddy." Reed felt like her heart was going to jump out of her chest.

"I love you, buddy." Maddy smiled and squeezed her hand again with affection.

"I love you."

"Hey guys, I'm going to take the sails down and get the trolling motor going," Alicia called out, as she moved to lower the sails. "As soon as I get the trolling motor started you can throw your lines out. This is a good spot for silvers."

"I never would have guessed your sister liked to fish," Reed commented, as she and Maddy stood up.

"She loves to fish, but her ex didn't like to sail or own a boat. For about three years she barely took the boat out. I think she would live on her boat if she could."

Alicia went to the back of the boat and started the trolling motor then turned to the two women and grinned. "Get your lines in the water."

"Here's your pole. Reed baited it for you."

"Thanks, Reed. Okay, first one to catch a fish gets out of dinner dishes!" Alicia's grin was contagious, and Reed felt her heart catch in her chest. She couldn't believe how much Alicia affected her.

"You're on!" Maddy laughed and cast her line out. Reed launched her line, and Alicia expertly flipped her line over the port side of the boat.

The three women allowed their lines to play out and then lounged on the padded bench enjoying the fresh air and the gentle movement of the boat. Forty minutes later, after re-baiting her hook, Reed felt the jerk of a fish. Her line began to play out as the fish was firmly hooked.

"Got one," Reed announced, standing up to begin landing her fish.

"I'll get the net." Alicia rapidly reeled her line in and grabbed the net, preparing to help bring Reed's fish in.

Maddy pulled her line in and watched the battle as Reed slowly brought the fish closer to the boat. "There it is! It's a good-sized fish."

Alicia grinned as Reed concentrated on reeling in her catch. She wasn't about to lose it. This was dinner for the three of them! Alicia couldn't help but admire Reed's thighs. Her muscles flexed as she stood with her legs planted, her arms tight, working her pole and reel. Alicia felt herself flush with feeling as she watched Reed's amazing body. Alicia turned away from Reed and focused her attention on the fighting fish. Alicia couldn't remember ever feeling this kind of attraction before, not even for her ex-husband.

Maddy's observant eyes didn't miss a thing. She noticed her sister's reaction and smiled as she watched Alicia gaping at Reed. There was definite attraction there. She couldn't wait to tell Bet! Maddy wasn't the least bit worried about the idea of Alicia being attracted to Reed. Maddy knew that sexuality had as much to do with respect as with attraction to either the male or female of the species. It was the whole person that was the appeal, and Maddy was hoping and praying that Alicia was smart enough to know that.

"Reed, bring it in just a little bit closer and I can net it. It's a nice one! Look at that fish!" Alicia couldn't contain her excitement when a fish was caught.

Reed remained calm as she brought the fish up to the side of the boat. Alicia bent over the side and in one graceful swoop had the fish in the net. "All right! It looks like you caught a very nice silver, about fourteen pounds or so. Nice job, Reed."

Reed breathed deeply, releasing an audible sigh as she looked at the fish in the net. "Well, I'd better put this guy out of his misery. And I might point out that I am not doing the dishes tonight."

"Yep, but another rule we have on the boat is the first person who catches a fish gets everyone else a beer," Alicia teased, grinning up at Reed.

"As soon as I take care of this bad boy, I'll gladly get beers for everyone," Reed chuckled, taking the fish out of the net.

She quickly dispatched the fish and placed it in the ice chest along with the bait fish. She headed into the cabin and washed her hands before coming back out and grabbing three beers from the ice chest. Alicia and Maddy were leaning against each other laughing as they both watched their lines. Reed smiled at the sisters. It was obvious that they were very close. She liked it that they were so supportive of each other. Reed didn't have any siblings and thought that it would have been nice to have a sister or brother to share her life with. Reed admitted to herself that she felt lonely a lot of the time.

"Here are your beers."

"Thanks, Reed. How are you at cooking salmon?"

"I can figure it out," she replied, as she baited her line and once more cast it out behind the boat.

"Good, 'cause you're cooking tonight." Maddy grinned as she poked her sister in the arm. "We decided for you."

"What makes you think I can cook?" Reed teased her.

"Because you are a single gay woman who is very popular with the ladies, and I've heard a rumor that you fix nice romantic meals." Maddy almost choked with laughter at the look on Reed's face. Reed may have been a very popular woman, but she was also quite shy. Discussing her dating habits in front of Alicia was bound to get a strong reaction from Reed.

Alicia watched as Reed's face turned bright red. Reed wouldn't even look at her. "I don't date."

"What's wrong with you? A beautiful gay woman and you don't date?" Maddy couldn't help but continue to tease her. She wasn't sure who was more bothered by her comments, Reed or Alicia. Alicia's face had frozen at Maddy's comment.

"I haven't met anyone I'd like to date yet," Reed mumbled, fussing with her reel.

"What are you waiting for?" Maddy again stifled her laughter as she continued to harass her best friend and tweak her sister.

"Oh, got one!" Alicia cried excitedly as her pole bent toward the water. Reed was relieved that she was interrupted before she had a chance to respond to Maddy.

"I've got the net." Maddy handed her pole to Reed and grabbed the net. "We're going to eat well tonight!"

And eat well they did. After Alicia caught a nice ten-pounder, Reed brought in another good-sized silver, and then Maddy caught an eighteen pound salmon. By six o'clock, they called it a day and anchored off the south end of Blake Island. Reed and Alicia cleaned the salmon while Maddy prepared a tossed green salad.

Alicia almost whistled as she and Reed worked side by side cleaning the fish. She was enjoying herself very much.

"You love being out here," Reed commented with a smile, her dark eyes twinkling.

"Very much, I didn't realize how much I missed being out on the water until about a year ago. Now it's something I do to relax. I'm usually not very good at relaxing. I tend to be a workaholic."

"Everyone needs to take time for themselves. I think too often people forget about that when they're in a relationship and concentrating on the other person."

"I have to admit I wasn't good at it when I was with Stephen. If I'd been thinking about myself I would never have gotten married."

"We all make mistakes."

"Yes, but at least you didn't marry yours," Alicia remarked, as she efficiently filleted her salmon.

"No—I let my last girlfriend run through almost all of my savings and put my business in jeopardy before I cut her off. She really didn't want to be with me. She wanted access to the money."

"I'm sorry, Reed." Alicia accurately read the hurt on Reed's face and in her voice.

"It's okay." Reed was becoming resigned to the fact that she had made bad choices in girlfriends.

Alicia looked over at Reed and nodded her head. "Well, let's go cook one of these incredible beauties. I'll put the rest of the fish in the freezer. You and Maddy can take them home. Bet loves fresh salmon."

The rest of the evening passed quickly. Reed grilled the salmon filets and prepared salad, corn on the cob, and fresh French bread. The three women ate dinner on the deck under the stars. Reed opened a bottle of white wine, and they shared it while they ate. Then Maddy and Alicia washed the dishes and cleaned the galley, talking quietly as they worked. Reed sat out on the deck listening to the slap of the water as the tide moved in. She felt at peace sitting there, all serious thoughts set aside for the moment.

Maddy and Alicia finished cleaning up and joined Reed for some quiet conversation about the remodel, Maddy's project at work, and Alicia's job. It was after ten o'clock before Maddy began to yawn and decided to call it a night. She and Alicia were sharing the bunk, and the table bed was to be made up for Reed.

"Goodnight, you two, I'll see you in the morning," Maddy called, as she headed down the stairs and through the galley. She was hoping that Alicia and Reed would do more than just stare at each other. They had been doing that for most of the evening, their eyes eating each other up.

"Goodnight," Reed responded as she stretched her legs and got more comfortable on the bench she was lounging on.

"I think this is my favorite time on the boat—when everything is quiet and dark, just the sounds of the water."

"It's very soothing."

"Reed, can I ask you something private?" Reed could see Alicia's pale eyes glowing in the dark as she turned toward where she sat in a deck chair.

"Of course."

"Your last relationship—were you in love with her?"

Reed hesitated a moment before answering.

"I wanted to be, but no, I wasn't in love with her."

"Why were you with her?" Alicia spoke softly, her pale eyes intent on Reed's face.

"Let me ask you a question first."

"Okay."

"Have you ever done something because it's what everyone else thinks you should be doing, even though you know it's not what you want?"

It was Alicia's turn to consider. "Yes, I got married."

"Because everyone else thought you should?"

"Everyone but Maddy, I'm at the age where everyone asks, *Why aren't you married?*"

"That's pretty much what happened to me. I started a relationship that I really didn't need or want because everyone told me it was time. After I got out of it, I promised myself that I would never again be with someone unless it would be forever."

"I sometimes think I'll be alone for the rest of my life." Alicia's voice was low, her tone full of regret.

"You don't believe you can find your soul mate, the one person that accepts you for who you are?"

"I'd like to believe I will. Do you?"

"Yes." Reed's dark eyes were intent on Alicia.

"That's nice."

"Yes, it is. I think sometimes we miss our soul mate because we let others decide for us. I think everyone should search for passion and find that one person that makes your heart pound and your body tingle every time you're around them."

Alicia absorbed her comment with a smile. "Here's to soul mates." Alicia touched her wine glass against Reed's and finished the last bit of wine in her glass.

"Soul mates."

"Thanks for the nice evening, Reed. I'm going to go make up your bed and call it a day."

"I can help." They both entered the cabin and placed their wine glasses in the sink.

Alicia unlatched the table and flipped it over, placing a foam pad flat on top of the platform and then added a mattress pad on top before shaking out the bottom sheet. Reed gathered her end and started tucking it in.

"I'm sorry. This bed isn't the most comfortable place to sleep." Alicia smiled in the darkened galley.

"It'll be fine." Reed and Alicia finished tucking the sheets in and then Alicia unfolded a blanket and spread it over the sheet.

Reed tucked a pillow into a pillow case and tossed it onto the bed. Alicia reached out and plumped up the pillow before looking up at Reed. Reed's eyes were dark and gazed back at Alicia. Alicia felt heat erupt in her body. Her eyes focused on Reed's generous mouth, and she ached with something she had never felt before. She wanted to know what kissing Reed would feel like.

"Well, I'm going to pop into the bathroom for a minute and then it's yours." Alicia had to turn away from Reed.

"Thanks, Alicia, I enjoyed today very much."

Alicia's smile was huge, and she saw Reed's dimples peek out as she grinned back at her. "It was fun. I'm glad you came. Goodnight."

"Goodnight." Reed sat down on the bed and leaned back, closing her eyes as Alicia stepped into the tiny bathroom. Reed was in serious trouble. She probably should stay away from Alicia from now on. She didn't seem to have any control over her reactions to her. The fact that Maddy had figured it out so quickly was bothersome. Reed didn't want Alicia to know what she was feeling. It would make her very uncomfortable and Reed would never want that to happen. She wanted to be friends with Alicia.

"Reed, it's all yours." Alicia's soft voice called to her.

"Thanks." Out of the corner of her eye Reed saw Alicia enter her bedroom in a tee shirt and bikini panties, her long slender legs naked. Reed almost groaned as she felt her body clench. Jesus, she needed to get laid or something—anything to get her mind off Alicia.

Alicia chuckled as she slipped into the bed next to her sleeping sister. Maddy lay flat on her back, her covers kicked down around her ankles. She had on crazy plaid boxers and a white tank top. Maddy had slept like that since she was a tiny child and the sisters shared a room. Alicia pulled the covers up around her shoulders and closed her eyes. Her thoughts immediately went to Reed. Something was so compelling about the woman that Alicia found herself observing her constantly. She enjoyed talking to her because she knew that Reed actually listened to her. She trusted her already, and Alicia had trusted only a couple of other people in her life. It was interesting that the only people she seemed to be able to trust were women.

Chapter Seven

Reed was wide awake by six in the morning and up enjoying the sunrise. She sat on the bench and relished the quiet. Reed had always been someone who enjoyed some alone time, but lately her life had turned into almost complete solitude. She hadn't been interested in dating anyone for so long. Now, all she could think about was Alicia—beautiful, straight Alicia. She was so incredibly lovely, genuine, and open.

"Did you make the coffee?" Maddy asked as she snuck up behind Reed.

"Yep. What are you doing up so early?"

"I'm always up this early, what's your excuse?"

"I couldn't sleep."

"What's going on, honey?" Maddy asked concern in her voice.

"Nothing."

"Reed, what's going on?"

"I'm just lonely." Reed found it hard to say it out loud.

"Honey, I'm sorry. I know this last year has been very tough on you." Maddy slipped her arm around Reed's shoulders.

"You were right when you told me she was out for my money."

"I didn't want to be right. Reed, I want to see you happy. I could kill Sheri for what she did to you."

"I let her do it, Maddy. I knew something was wrong. We stopped sleeping with each other within months of moving in together. Maybe I'm meant to be alone."

"Reed, you are the most honest, loving woman I know. There is someone out there who's waiting just for you."

Reed's brown eyes met Maddy's and she smiled. "You think so?"

"Honey, I know so. Now, what are you going to do about Alicia?"

"Nothing." Reed turned away from Maddy.

"Why not?"

"She's straight and she's your sister."

"So."

41

"She's still recuperating from her divorce and finding out about her ex's upcoming marriage and baby hasn't helped."

"His what?" Maddy bounced up, anger flaring from her. This information made her immediately livid.

"Her ex—he's getting married, and his girlfriend is going to have a baby."

"Damn that ass! I should have castrated him when I had the chance. He should not be allowed to reproduce!"

"She's pretty hurt."

"She never loved Stephen."

"It doesn't matter, she's still very hurt."

"God, I could kill him. He was such a pansy ass!"

"Who's a pansy ass?" Alicia stepped up on to the deck, still wearing a tee shirt that hung just past her hips.

"Stephen."

"Why are you talking about Stephen?" Alicia asked, looking uncomfortably at the two women.

"We were talking about ex's we don't like." Maddy tugged her sister down on the bench next to her. "Remember Elise, my first relationship?"

Alicia laughed and hugged her sister. "Elise—isn't she the one with the motor-cycle and the chains and the tattoo on her neck?"

"Yep, she dumped me two days after I moved in with her. I was heartbroken." Maddy grinned as she remembered. "You let me move in with you until I could find another place."

"Hey, you and Bet came and stayed with me after Stephen left."

"She and Bet came and packed all my stuff up and moved me out of my last place." Reed added with a smile.

"That's 'cause you were living with your ex and her new girlfriend."

"I didn't know it was her new girlfriend," Reed retorted, her eyes flashing with humor, her dimples deepening.

"Yeah, women share a bed all the time," Maddy admitted with a sly grin.

Alicia snorted with laughter at the look on Reed's face as she responded while Maddy laughed. "Hey, I've shared a bed with you."

"Well yeah, but you're my best friend."

"You two are so funny." Alicia stood up and headed for the galley. "Who wants more coffee?"

"I'd like some more." Reed tried not to look at Alicia's long legs as she walked away.

The rest of the day was full of fun. The three women bantered back and forth while fishing, enjoying each other's company. Alicia caught three more fish and Maddy and Reed one each. Sunburned and tired, they pulled into the marina a little after four that afternoon.

After they cleaned the boat and packed up the leftover food, Maddy took off for home. Reed helped Alicia carry her things to her car. "Don't forget you're cooking fish Tuesday night for dinner."

Reed smiled as she loaded the last box into Alicia's trunk. "I won't."

"Tell Maddy and Bet I'll be there sometime after six."

"I will. Thanks for taking me out on your boat."

"You're welcome. We'll have to do it again."

"I'd like that."

"Reed, thanks for listening to me. I really appreciate being able to talk to you." Reed couldn't turn away from Alicia's pale blue eyes.

"No problem. Alicia, please don't let Stephen ruin your life. You're a smart, beautiful woman."

Alicia turned bright red, unbelievably moved by Reed's comment. "Thanks."

"I should get going."

"Thanks, Reed."

Reed turned and looked back at Alicia. "You're welcome."

Alicia climbed into her car with a smile on her face. She really did like Reed.

Reed jogged over to her truck and climbed in the cab. She was missing Alicia's company already.

"Damn it, Reed, what the hell is wrong with you?" she growled, pulling out of the parking lot.

Chapter Eight

By Tuesday evening Reed had the floor slate cut and in place, ready for grouting. Checking her watch, she groaned. It was a little after three, and she was fixing dinner that night. Alicia was coming over at six, and Reed was nervous.

"Come on, Reed get your ass in gear!"

"Do you always talk to yourself when you work?"

"Jesus!" Reed jerked her head around to find Alicia grinning at her from the open doorway. She was wearing a slim yellow dress and matching jacket. She looked beautiful.

"Sorry, I didn't mean to startle you."

Reed flashed a grin at her as she stood up. "I didn't hear you come in."

"That's because you were too busy yelling at yourself," Alicia teased, as she gazed around the kitchen. "It's stunning, Reed."

"It's turning out very nicely. I just need to grout the floor, and then the appliances can be installed. You're here early."

"I know. I just needed to get away from the office."

"What's going on?" Reed accurately read the turmoil in Alicia's eyes.

"They had a wedding shower and party for Stephen at the office, and I felt like I shouldn't be there."

Reed gazed silently back as Alicia spoke. Her pale eyes were full of hurt. "Do you have a change of clothes with you?

"Yes, I have some jeans and a shirt, why?"

"Go change. You're going to help me grout the floor."

Alicia gaped in astonishment at Reed. "I don't know how."

"No time like the present to learn." Reed turned her around and shoved her gently. "Go change."

Alicia didn't think to argue. She went to her car and grabbed her bag, then changed in the upstairs back bedroom before rushing down the stairs to find Reed bending over a large bucket of what looked like tan cement.

"Okay, what do you want me to do?"

Reed turned around and felt her breath leave her chest in one big gasp. Alicia had on a pair of faded 501s, her slim long legs and slender waist well defined. The shirt she had on though, wouldn't do. It was too clean and too nice. "Wait a minute."

Reed rushed out of the kitchen in the direction of her bedroom. After rummaging through her drawers, she came back out to find Alicia looking at her with puzzlement and a little humor. "Here, take your shirt off and put this tee shirt on."

"What's wrong with my shirt?"

"It's too nice to work in."

Alicia grinned, grabbed the tee shirt and turned, pulling her shirt over her head. Reed all but choked, turning at the last minute when she caught a glimpse of Alicia's slender back and pale blue bra.

"Jesus." Reed muttered to herself.

Alicia turned and couldn't miss the blush on Reed's face. "Okay, I've changed."

"Good," Reed sighed as she saw Alicia standing next to her wearing her favorite old sleeping shirt. She didn't know what was worse. Seeing Alicia in her shirt or wearing a sexy bra.

"Okay, boss, what do you want me to do?"

Reed snorted and then led Alicia over to the bucket and handed her a pointed tool. "Okay, this is your trowel."

Bet stepped in the front door of her house and heard laughter coming from the kitchen area. She knew Reed was finishing the kitchen floor but she wasn't prepared for what she found. Alicia and Reed were kneeling in the center of the kitchen wiping the slate floor clean with sponges. Alicia's hair was tied back with one of Reed's bandannas, her face streaked with something tan. Reed's wasn't looking much better streaks of brown grit were on her chin and left cheek.

"You two are having too much fun to be working," Bet commented, grinning at the twosome. They both glanced up and the look on their faces was one of complete pleasure.

"We just finished grouting the floor. Reed taught me how to grout." You'd think Alicia had been given a pair of diamond earrings, she sounded so pleased with herself.

Bet looked at the floor and flashed a smile their way. "It looks fantastic."

"Alicia has a talent for tile work," Reed admitted as she stood up and then helped Alicia to her feet. "It's done. I just need to wash out this bucket and take a shower, and then I'm barbequing salmon. We need to stay of the floor as much as possible for the next twenty-four hours or so until the grout sets up."

"You both need a shower. Have you looked at yourselves? I should just hose you two down." Bet started laughing. Reed had streaks of grout down both thighs and both muscular arms. Alicia's tee shirt was covered with grout, and the back of her jeans had a hand print on her butt. Bet wasn't sure whose hand it was or how it got there.

Reed and Alicia took a look at each other and burst into laughter. "You go first, Alicia, and get cleaned up. I'll wash out the bucket and take a shower when you're done."

"Bet, can I borrow a pair of jeans from Maddy?"

"Sure, you know where they are."

Alicia walked down the hall and headed upstairs to the bathroom. Both Reed and Bet's eyes followed her. "Okay, Reed, what's going on?"

"What do you mean what's going on?" Reed's face grew pale as she waited for Bet to speak.

"Is Alicia hitting on you?" Bet reached out and placed her hand on Reed's arm. "I don't want you to get hurt."

"She's not hitting on me."

"Oh, honey, I think she is and I don't think you would say no to her."

"Bet, nothing's going on."

"But you like her." Bet hadn't missed the dynamics between the two.

"Of course I like her. She's a nice woman." Reed backed up from Bet. She didn't want to be having this conversation.

"Reed, honey, look at me." Bet's voice was gentle.

Reed's dark eyes met Bet's hazel ones, and she saw nothing but love from her best friend. "Okay, I like her. She's sexy, funny, and she gets me."

"But she's straight."

"I know that, and I'm not doing anything inappropriate."

"Oh honey, if I thought she could make you happy and love you, I'd do everything I could to make this happen."

"Can we drop this discussion?" Reed started to turn away from Bet.

"Honey …"

Reed's eyes filled with tears as she looked down at Bet. "I think I'm falling in love with her."

"Reed …"

"I know I must be out of my mind."

"Not at all, I …"

"Shush, she's coming." Reed turned and fled to the garage before Alicia could see her face.

"Is Reed okay?" Alicia inquired, as she watched Reed stride out of the house. Her face was pale, and she didn't look very happy.

"She's fine. How are *you* doing?"

"I'm good. I never thought I could do something like grout a slate floor. Your kitchen looks great."

"Reed is very talented." Bet watched Alicia's face and didn't miss the hint of color that bloomed on her face. "Come on outside and sit with me."

Reed waited until the two women went outside and then headed for the bathroom and a quick shower. She needed to settle her nerves before being around Alicia one more minute. There was nothing sexier than watching Alicia grin with delight as she spread grout over the floor tiles. They had laughed and joked for over an hour as they finished the kitchen floor. Reed couldn't remember enjoying a job more. She was in deep, deep trouble.

Maddy arrived home from work coming through the door with a huge burst of energy and began to get dinner together while Reed finished cleaning up. Reed had prepared the salad earlier in the day, and the fish was ready to barbeque. Reed rummaged around in the garage avoiding going outside until Maddy came to find her.

"Hey, are you going to hide out in the garage all night?" Maddy teased, poking Reed in the stomach.

"I'm not hiding out," Reed snapped, as she coated the fish fillet with olive oil.

"Yes you are, and if you really have feelings for my sister don't hide from them. I know you very well, and I know if you are in love with my sister you mean it."

"Have you forgotten that she's straight and isn't interested in me as anything more than a friend? Besides, who said anything about love?"

"So tell me why she has talked about you and working on the kitchen floor for the last half an hour. She may not know it yet, but I think my sister is developing feelings for you."

"She's not gay." Reed stated what she thought was obvious.

"Reed, it's not that simple and you know it."

"If I let her know how I feel and she gets offended, how will you deal with that?" Reed responded, her face full of feeling.

"She's not going to be offended."

"I don't know if I can handle another rejection right now."

"Oh, honey. I'm sorry. The last thing in the world I want to have happen is for you to be hurt again." Maddy hugged her best friend tightly.

"I'd better start this salmon if we want to eat tonight." Reed pulled away, her eyes glassy with emotion.

"Reed, just think about it."

Reed couldn't think about anything else. Every waking minute she was thinking about Alicia and her feelings.

Reed followed Maddy out to the patio and the waiting grill. While Maddy turned the gas on and started the burners, Reed finished preparing the salmon and potatoes she planned on roasting.

"Here's a cold beer." Alicia's voice caught Reed off guard, and she smiled back at the lovely woman who could turn her inside out with the sound of her voice. Reed found herself wanting just to be in the same room with Alicia.

"Thanks, I could use a cold one."

"Thanks for letting me help with the floor. I've never done anything like that before. I enjoyed it."

"Maybe I can hire you to grout the floors at my house," Reed teased, as she placed the fish on the grill.

"I'd love to help you on your house."

Reed couldn't help but stare at the face that kept her awake long into the night, her ice blue eyes touching her very soul. "I'm going out there on Saturday if you'd like to see it."

"I'd love to."

"Great. I can pick you up around nine, and we can take the grand tour."

"I'll look forward to it." Alicia turned back to where her sister and Bet sat talking on a chaise lounge. She would rather have stayed and talked to Reed, but Reed seemed a little more reserved than usual. Alicia couldn't help but notice what she was wearing—a pair of shorts and a tank top. God, Alicia couldn't remember ever looking at Stephen's body and finding it as sexy as she found Reed's. The realization that she was attracted to Reed hit her right between the eyes. Oh my God, she was attracted to Reed! She needed to talk to Maddy. She began to panic, her heart pounding loudly in her chest.

"Alicia, are you okay?" Bet asked quietly, noticing Alicia's pale face.

"I'm fine Bet—just thinking."

"I'm going inside to help Reed with the rest of the dinner." Bet stood up giving Maddy a look and followed Reed into the house.

Maddy turned to her sister and watched her eyes trail after Reed as she went through the patio door. "Le Le, are you attracted to Reed?"

Alicia's head snapped around, and then she blushed, her eyes wide with surprise. "Yes, I think I am."

"When did you realize you were attracted to her?"

"Out on the boat."

"Do you want to do something about it?"

"Like what? It's not like I have a lot of experience with this kind of thing."

"Then you're in luck, because I do."

"Maddy, I'm not sure I want to do anything." Alicia spoke quietly, her eyes serious.

"Why not?"

"Because Reed is a very nice woman who wants a long-term relationship, not a fling with a straight woman who's going through some sort of midlife crisis."

"And you think that's what this is, a midlife crisis?"

"I don't know what it is!" Alicia snapped, glaring at her sister.

"Maybe Reed is the passion you've been looking for! She's the most honorable and loving woman I know. She's also incredibly sexy."

"I know all that!" Alicia bit her words off. She was terribly confused.

"What if she's interested in you?"

Alicia turned and stared at Maddy for a minute. "Is she? Has she said something, Oh, God, could she tell I'm attracted to her?"

"I wouldn't know. That's for you to find out. Why don't you talk to her about it?"

"But I couldn't!" Alicia felt panic set in again.

"Why not?"

"I'm horrible at relationships."

"You are not! You just happened to choose a jerk for a husband. That doesn't mean you're horrible at relationships."

"Reed and I are becoming good friends, and I'd hate to lose that."

"That would be fine if you really had only friend feelings for her."

"God, my life is a mess," Alicia whined, leaning back in her chair.

"I'd say your life is looking up. You've met someone who loves to fish and sail on a boat. This same person wants more than anything to find the one woman who will love her unconditionally and accept her for who and what she is. She wants to build her dream home and share it with this same woman for the rest of her life."

"But what if I'm not really attracted to a woman?"

"Reed isn't just any woman. I've always said it's not about someone being male or female. It has everything to do with the person you fall in love with."

"Fall in love with, who said I was in love with her?" Maddy just grinned at her sister and waited for the panic to subside. "Maddy, what if I say something to Reed and she's not interested?"

Maddy wanted to tell Alicia that Reed was falling in love with her but she had promised, and she wouldn't break a promise. She could only encourage her sister to be honest and allow fate to take over. "I think you need to spend more time with Reed, let her know that you're interested in seeing her as more than a friend. Even if she is attracted to you she wouldn't tell you."

"Why not?"

"Because you're a straight woman and her best friend's sister. Reed would consider that a breach of trust on her part. You'll have to be the one to let her know you're interested."

"Maddy, I don't know what to do!"

"Le Le, I love you, and the only thing I know is you have a wonderful heart and are full of passion. Let your heart tell you what to do."

"Hey, do either of you need another beer?" Bet yelled from the doorway.

"Yes, please." Maddy held her empty beer bottle up in the air.

Reed's eyes met Alicia's as she exited the house carrying a bowl of salad and a plate of bread. Alicia's ice blue eyes glowed hotly as she held Reed's gaze. Alicia stood up and went over to the picnic table, her eyes still steady on Reed's face.

"Can I help with dinner?"

"No, I think I have it covered. Thanks for asking."

"Can I talk to you for a minute?"

"Sure, is everything okay?" Reed turned to face Alicia.

"Everything's fine." Alicia placed her hand on Reed's arm and watched her carefully. Reed's eyes dilated and her breath caught in her throat. Alicia didn't miss her reaction and felt her body heat up with attraction. "I just wanted to know if you would like to go out on the boat with me tomorrow night. I thought we could take it out for an evening sail, maybe drop anchor for a late dinner."

"I'd like to do that." Reed could barely speak. Her heart was pounding loudly in her ears. God, being around Alicia was driving her crazy.

"Good, can you meet me at the marina around six?"

"I'll be there. Can I bring anything?"

"Nope." Alicia's smile was brilliant. She turned away leaving Reed standing helplessly next to the table. Maddy and Bet watched the interaction with amusement. They looked forward to being entertained some more watching Reed and Alicia figure things out.

Dinner was delicious, and the company was fun as the four visited about the kitchen and Bet's job. She always had some amusing stories to share about fire-fighting and the personalities of her crew. It was after ten before Alicia decided to leave. She didn't want to, but she needed to go in to work early if she was going to have enough time to get the boat ready for an evening sail. It was important that she make the evening perfect, especially if she was going to tell Reed she wanted to be more than just friends. All evening long she had been overly aware that Reed was watching her every move. Alicia found that surprisingly sexy, and she returned Reed's stares.

Chapter Nine

Reed groaned as the doctor manipulated her fingers, checking for broken bones. "Hurts, huh? I think you have a broken finger, maybe a cracked knuckle joint. I need x-rays to confirm. You're also going to need stitches to close this tear on the top of your hand. What the hell did you do?" the doctor inquired as he continued to feel the joints of Reed's swollen hand.

"A big ass beam was dropped on my hand," Reed responded, her tone disgusted. She should have paid closer attention.

She had been helping Hank and Tim place a wooden open beam at one of their remodeling jobs. They had successfully placed six out of eight beams when the one they were lowering into place had gotten hung up. Reed had reached out from her precarious perch straddling a ladder to move it back. "Hold on, Hank, while I get it back in line."

Hank had thought she said to lower it further, and he loosened his hold on the pulley rope dropping the beam into place.

"Stop!" Tim yelled, as he saw Reed's hand get pinned. "Jesus, Reed! Hank, bring it up quick!"

"Fuck, that hurt," Reed gasped, as she moved unsteadily down the ladder.

"Reed, Christ, you need to get to the hospital. Come on, I'll drive."

"God, Reed, I'm sorry." Hank rushed up to his boss, his face starkly white.

"Hank, it's okay. It was an accident. I'll be okay." Reed was about to lose her lunch on Hank's feet. "You stay and get the job done. Tim will drop me off at the hospital and come back to help. I probably just need a few stitches."

She gritted her teeth the whole way to the hospital, especially when they placed a bag of ice on her hand in the emergency room.

"Well, you're lucky you didn't crush it completely. Let's get some x-rays and some sutures to close this tear and get you home in bed with an ice bag."

"Sounds good, doc." Reed lay back on the emergency room bed and closed her eyes. Shit, she was supposed to go on the boat with Alicia and she wanted to very much. Now she had to cancel. "Shit!"

"Can I get you anything?" the nurse asked as she prepared a suture tray for the doctor. Her eyes drank in the exceptionally good looking woman who was currently residing in her emergency room.

"No thanks. Is it okay if I use my cell phone in here?"

"Go ahead, I won't tell anyone." The nurse grinned flirtatiously at Reed. Reed was completely oblivious to the woman's attentions. Her mind was on one thing—making sure that Alicia knew she would have to miss dinner with her on the boat.

"Thanks." Reed quickly dialed Maddy's work number. "Maddy, it's Reed. There's been a little accident, and I'm at the emergency room at Swedish Hospital."

"Are you okay?"

"I'm fine. My left hand took a beating, but everything else is okay. I need you to let Alicia know I can't go out on the boat with her tonight."

"I'd come and be with you but I'm in the middle of a test that I can't leave unattended. It'll take me an hour to shut things down and then I can get there."

"That's all right. I have one of the guys driving my truck to the house. I'll take a taxi home."

"No you won't. I'm calling Alicia."

"Maddy don't ..." But Maddy had hung up before Reed could stop her.

"Alicia, it's Maddy. Reed is at Swedish Hospital. Her hand was injured at work."

"Is she okay? What's wrong with her hand? Did she say what happened?" Alicia's heart raced, her voice rising in panic.

"I don't know everything, and I can't leave right this minute."

"I'll go right now. Swedish Emergency Room?"

"Yes, she has her cell phone with her. Here's the number."

Alicia was out of her office at a dead run before she hung up the telephone. "I have a family emergency to attend to. Handle everything."

Alicia's secretary watched as the normally placid woman shot by her. "I will."

Alicia made it to Swedish in under twenty minutes, a feat at any time of the day in the city of Seattle. She streaked up to the emergency room desk and blurted out her question.

"Reed Thomas, what room?"

"She's in room three, down there on the right."

Alicia darted down the hall and charged into the room to find Reed lying flat on the bed, her left hand being worked on by a doctor and a nurse. "Reed, honey, what happened?"

Reed's eyes snapped opened when Alicia's voice penetrated through the fog of pain. "One of my guys dropped a big beam on my hand. It was an accident."

Alicia moved up to the side of the bed and placed her hand on Reed's shoulder, massaging her gently. Reed's tee shirt was spotted with blood, and her face was white and sweaty. Alicia could see the pain in her eyes. "Oh honey, I'm sorry."

Alicia bent over and hugged Reed, placing her face against Reed's, needing to make physical contact with her to keep from crying. Reed's arm reached up and slid around Alicia's neck gently holding her. "It's okay. Just a few stitches and a broken finger, I'll be back to work in a couple of days. I was looking forward to going out on the boat tonight."

"We'll do it another night." Alicia kept her face next to Reed's while the doctor finished stitching her hand. She couldn't watch him working. It was killing her to think of Reed being hurt. She kept her eyes on Reed's face. "I'm taking you home and putting you to bed."

"You'll miss work." Reed couldn't look away from Alicia's face. She was mesmerized by her ice blue eyes that mirrored concern for her.

"They'll get over it," Alicia responded, rubbing her hand in circles on Reed's shoulder while they spoke softly to each other.

"I'm glad you're here," Reed admitted, reaching up and clasping Alicia's hand in her right one.

"So am I, honey."

"Ms. Thomas, I'm going to go get the x-rays and check them, and then I'll come back and see what we've got. Don't go anywhere." The doctor spoke as he stood up, pulling his gloves off as he strode out of the room.

"Okay, doctor."

Alicia sat down in the chair next to Reed's bed, holding tightly to her hand. Reed turned to face her, her eyes dark and watchful. Alicia scooted closer, placing her other hand on Reed's thigh. Reed just about levitated off the bed, when Alicia's hand came to rest on her leg. She felt her touch all through her body.

"Reed, is there anything that needs to be taken care of for your company?"

"No, my job foreman will handle everything. Someone is driving my truck home, so all I need to do is get out of here."

"As soon as you're done, I'll drive you home."

"I really appreciate this …"

"Reed, I want to be here." Alicia bent closer to Reed until their faces were inches apart. "I need to be here."

Reed's eyes lit up as she stared into pale blue eyes that glowed back at her. She wanted to kiss Alicia so badly it was painful. Her mouth was so inviting, moist, her lips slightly parted. Reed caught her perfume and almost moaned she was so turned on. Alicia glanced down and stared at Reed's mouth, her hand trembling in Reed's. Alicia moved slowly closer, her eyes drifting shut as she bent and placed a soft kiss on Reed's beautiful mouth. Reed groaned, responding to Alicia's gentle kiss, her lips parting as she tasted Alicia for the first time. The kiss was slow, soft, and perfect.

"Ms. Thomas … I'm sorry, uh, excuse me." The doctor entered the room startling Alicia and Reed apart.

"No problem, doctor." Reed was too shocked to say much of anything else. Alicia still clasped her hand, her other hand rested on her thigh. Reed was surprised the doctor couldn't hear her heart pounding. It was thumping loudly in her chest.

"Okay, let's show you what we have going on." The doctor held the x-ray up against the light box as he spoke. "You have fairly bad fractures of your ring finger and your little finger. You have some major trauma going on. I don't want to use a cast. Instead, I'm going to put your hand in a brace and tape your fingers down. You need to leave the brace on for about a week. Then I want you to go to your regular doctor and have him check your fingers to see if they're staying in alignment. I'm going to give you a prescription for pain pills and an anti-inflammatory to keep the swelling down. You need to go right home, get in bed and put a big ice bag on your hand. Let's get the nurse in here and get you taped up so you can get out of here."

"Sounds good." Reed glanced over at Alicia and found her smiling sweetly at her. Reed paid little attention to the doctor.

"Okay, I'll be right back." The doctor headed back out of the room. Reed turned and found Alicia watching her closely.

"Is it hurting very much?" Alicia asked, leaning closer to Reed.

"Not bad at all," Reed responded, her eyes dropping once more to Alicia's lips. Alicia didn't hesitate as she leaned up and kissed Reed again. "Actually, I can't feel a thing when you kiss me."

Alicia chuckled and kissed her softly once more then leaned against her watching Reed's face. "We'll see if it works as well later on."

"I'd like that," Reed whispered, her dimples appearing deep in her cheeks.

"So would I." Alicia sighed as she looked into dark eyes that hid nothing from her. She couldn't believe how wonderful kissing Reed made her feel, and she wanted to do it again very soon.

By the time Reed's hand was completely taped up, the anesthesia she had received during her stitches was beginning to wear off. In a short time, Alicia was back at her bedside with the prescriptions she had filled at the hospital pharmacy. She helped Reed out of the hospital, and Reed made it out to Alicia's car, sweating profusely her face pale. Alicia could see how much pain she was in by her clouded eyes and the way she cradled her hand against her chest. "Come on honey, we need to get you into bed with a pain pill."

"I think that's a good idea." Reed swallowed carefully, her stomach roiling.

Reed settled into the passenger seat of the Mercedes, her hand resting in her lap. Alicia climbed in the driver's side and glanced at her. "Hold on sweetie, we'll be home shortly."

Alicia started her car and drove down Madison to the freeway, her eyes glancing nervously at Reed as she drove. Reed's eyes were closed, her head rested against the seatback, and her breathing seemed shallow. It killed Alicia to see her hurting. All she wanted to do was reach out and hold her and try and give her some measure of comfort. She placed her hand on Reed's leg, squeezing gently. Reed reached over with her right hand and covered Alicia's hand holding it against her leg. It helped her relax a little bit to feel a connection to Alicia.

Alicia pulled up into the driveway and almost vaulted out of the car, getting to the passenger door before Reed could open it. "Come on, honey, let me help you into the house."

It didn't take more than a few minutes before Reed was sitting on her bed, but her stomach revolted, and her hand screamed with pain. "I think I'm going to be sick," she muttered as she bent over her legs trying to keep from vomiting.

Alicia ran into the bathroom and grabbed the wastebasket and a towel. She set the wastebasket on the floor in front of Reed and placed the towel on her lap. "Let me get a warm washcloth."

Reed struggled not to vomit, her head swimming. "I just need to lie down, I think."

"Okay, honey, let's get some of these clothes off. But first, you need to take one of these pain pills and get the medication into your system."

After swallowing the medicine, Reed remained totally docile as Alicia kneeled in front of her and unlaced her work boots, pulling them off. Then she reached up and quickly unbuttoned Reed's jeans so she could pull them down her legs. "Come on, honey, scoot back on the bed, and I'll take your pants off, then I'll get you a clean shirt."

Reed rolled onto her back, her eyes closing immediately when her head hit the pillow. Her headache was pounding. "You know, this isn't quite what I had in mind thinking of you undressing me," she muttered in an irritated voice.

"You have something else in mind, do you?" Alicia grinned as she tugged Reed's pants down her long legs.

"Oh yeah—I can't stop thinking about you." Reed wasn't even aware of what she said she was in so much pain, but Alicia heard it clearly and her body went on full alert.

"We'll deal with that later. Now, I need to slide your shirt off you."

"Alicia, I'm not wearing a bra," Reed admitted, as Alicia's hands slid under her tee shirt.

"Good, then I won't have to take one off you. Come on, sweetheart, I know you feel horrible." Alicia gently slid the tee shirt up over Reed's generous chest and then carefully over her injured hand. Despite the fact that Reed was hurt, Alicia couldn't resist admiring her nearly nude body. She was wearing underwear that fit snugly, navy in color. Alicia had never seen anything quite as sexy in her life.

"Whoa, baby," Alicia muttered as she covered Reed up with her sheet and blankets, gently placing her injured hand on an extra pillow. "Reed, I'm going to get an ice bag."

"Okay." Reed struggled to open her eyes. "I'm sorry we can't go out on the boat tonight."

"Oh, honey, we have plenty of time to go out on the boat. Close your eyes, sweetheart." Alicia bent over and stroked Reed's pale face.

"Alicia, I can't thank you …"

"Shush." Alicia kissed Reed, effectively silencing her, her mouth gentle. Reed's lips met Alicia's in a kiss that made Alicia's knees weak.

"You're not just kissing me because I'm hurt?"

"No, I'm kissing you because I care about you."

"Define care," Reed whispered against Alicia's lips.

"Care as in *I want to get to know you better, and I want to jump your bones* care."

Reed's eyes flew open and found Alicia gazing down at her, grinning. "Oh, man why did I have to get hurt today of all days?"

"Reed, close your eyes. I'm not going anywhere."

"You promise?"

"I promise."

Reed's eyes slid closed. Alicia watched her for a moment and then quickly went into the garage to make up an ice bag. She entered Reed's room and placed the ice bag on a towel against her hand. Reed was barely able to talk to her.

"Go to sleep, honey."

"You'll stay?"

"I'll stay," Alicia promised, as she stroked Reed's face until she slipped back into restless sleep.

Alicia sat on the side of the bed staring at her sleeping countenance for quite awhile. There was no doubt in Alicia's mind that she had fallen in love with Reed. The minute she kissed her, she had experienced something she had never felt before—honest to goodness real passion, and it scared her to death.

Chapter Ten

"How is she?" Bet asked, as Alicia sat down next to her on the living room couch.

"Still out like a light. She's been sleeping since I put her to bed."

"Her hand is a mess." Bet leaned against Alicia and looked at her face. "And you look worried."

"I just hate it that she's hurt."

"You sure that's all it is?" Bet studied Alicia.

"I kissed her."

"Yeah, how was it?" Bet grinned up at her.

"Amazing!" Alicia smiled and poked Bet, then frowned. "Reed asked me if I kissed her because she was hurt."

"What did you say?"

"I told her I kissed her because I care about her and I want to jump her bones."

"Really!" Bet laughed heartily. "What did Reed say to that?"

"She complained about getting hurt today of all days. I told her I wasn't going away." Alicia's face glowed with emotion, her eyes glittering with humor.

"Alicia, Reed isn't going to believe you're really attracted to her."

"Why not?"

"Because she sees you as Maddy's straight sister. She'll be afraid of crossing a line."

"It didn't stop her from kissing me back," Alicia smirked.

"Kissing is one thing, and making love to you is another. You're going to have to convince her that you really want to be with her. Do you really want to be with Reed?"

"Bet, when we kissed, it was the first time I really felt something that power-ful. I feel totally alive when I'm around her."

"Alicia, I love you and I love Reed. You need to make sure that you under-stand what being with another woman means. People will look at you differently. Are you ready to have people at work know that you're with a woman? Because they *will* find out And Reed won't want anything less than a committed relationship with you. Are you ready for something like that?"

"I don't know anything other than that I want to be with Reed. She makes me laugh, she makes me feel safe, and she makes me want to touch her all the time." Alicia spoke softly but with conviction.

Bet grinned at Alicia and reached out hugging her. "Welcome to the fold, older sister."

Alicia chuckled and hugged Bet back. "So are you going to help me sweep Reed off her feet?"

"Absolutely."

Reed struggled to open her eyes, as she felt a warm washcloth soothing her skin. Her hand throbbed and her stomach ached. Her eyes opened, and she found Alicia bent over her washing her sweaty face.

"Hey."

"Hi, sweetheart, how are you feeling?"

"Not so hot. I'd like to take a shower."

"Honey, I don't think you should do that until you feel a little better."

"I'm all sweaty," Reed whined, as Alicia wiped her shoulders with the washcloth. "I must stink."

"You don't stink. Do you think you could eat some chicken noodle soup? I don't want to give you another pain pill without getting something on your stomach."

"That sounds good." Reed struggled to sit up without letting the sheet fall, exposing her naked body. She was embarrassed to have Alicia see her like this.

"Here, let me help." Alicia bent over, sliding her arm behind Reed's back and scooting her up against her headboard. She reached down and pulled the covers up and straightened them over Reed's bare breasts. She placed the palm of her hand against Reed's face. "I'll get you another ice bag and then I'll bring in a bowl of soup."

"Alicia thanks …"

"Reed, you don't need to keep thanking me." Alicia smiled and bent down until she was inches from Reed's face. She kissed her swiftly and then turned and left the bedroom.

Reed was overwhelmed by Alicia. She groaned as she reacted to the kiss and Alicia's attentions, unable to do anything more than follow her with her eyes as she left the room. She moved her legs restlessly under the covers.

"How are you feeling?" Maddy asked, as she slipped into the room.

"Like shit," Reed sighed, looking up at Maddy.

"Yeah, I bet."

"Maddy, I kissed Alicia."

Maddy laughed and sat down on the side of the bed. "That's not what I heard. Alicia told me she kissed you."

"Well, yeah, but I kissed her back."

"Good for you."

"You're not mad?" Reed's eyes watched Maddy fearfully.

"No, I'm certainly not mad. My sister cares about you, Reed, and not just as a friend."

"But …"

"But—what? You can't tell me you don't care about her. I can see it on your face."

Reed ducked her head down, her eyes filling with tears. "Yeah, but I'm not sure Alicia really wants to be with a woman."

"Honey, you aren't just any woman." Maddy reached over and hugged Reed. "Trust Alicia, she's an honest person."

"Hey, how goes our patient?" Bet entered the room and placed an ice bag on Reed's hand. "Alicia said to keep this on your hand. She's on her way with some soup."

"I look like shit," Reed admitted running her hand through her hair.

Maddy and Bet looked at her and laughed. "You do not. You look kind of sexy sleeping in your underwear. I'm sure Alicia appreciates it very much."

"Guys, cut it out." Reed blushed with embarrassment.

Maddy stood up and reached for her girlfriend. "Come on, she's way too cranky for me."

Bet grinned at her girlfriend as they left the room. They were finding Reed and Alicia's budding relationship very entertaining. They found Alicia in the garage heating up the soup. "Boy, I can't wait until you have your kitchen appliances installed. This cooking in the garage is for the birds."

"You could take her to your place," Maddy suggested, winking at Bet.

"She's more comfortable in her own room."

"She's cranky."

"She doesn't feel good." Alicia filled a bowl with chunky chicken noodle soup and surrounded it with soda crackers.

"You're staying here, aren't you?"

"I thought I would. I took tomorrow off. I can work from here and make sure she keeps ice on her hand."

"Good."

"There's enough soup for all of us. Help yourself. There's fresh bread and a Caesar salad, too. I picked everything up when I ran to my office."

"Thanks, sis."

"I'll be right back." Alicia headed back into the house with a tray of food for Reed.

"She's toast," Bet remarked, as she prepared plates of salad for them.

"So is Reed."

"I never expected this, but it feels right. They seem to fit together," Bet admitted to her lover.

"I know, and I never saw it until now."

"It's going to be hysterically funny watching them figure everything out." Bet grinned at her girlfriend.

"What are you doing out of bed?" Alicia inquired sharply as she stepped into Reed's bedroom.

"I thought I could put a shirt on," Reed responded hurriedly covering her nearly naked body with the sheet as she stood unsteadily by the bed.

"I suggest you get your butt back in bed. I'll get you a shirt to put on." Alicia's silver blue eyes pinned Reed.

"Okay," Reed acquiesced. She sat unsteadily down on the bed. She had to admit she still felt a little rocky.

"I need you to eat some soup and crackers before you take another pain pill, otherwise I'm afraid you'll be sick to your stomach. Where can I find a shirt?"

"Second drawer down on the left. There should be a tee shirt or a button shirt I can wear."

Alicia opened the drawer and pulled out a flannel shirt. It was worn and faded, very soft, and smelled just like Reed. "How about this one?"

"That'll work." Reed spoke softly. She was a bit overwhelmed at finding Alicia in her bedroom, taking care of her.

"Here, honey, let me help you put it on." Reed sat up and put her arm through the shirt sleeve and then leaned forward as Alicia tucked the shirt around her and gently pulled it up over her injured hand. She then calmly sat down next to Reed and slowly buttoned the shirt. Reed's eyes studied Alicia's beautiful face. She still couldn't believe that Alicia had kissed her. "There, honey. Now, will you eat something?"

Reed reached out and placed her good hand on Alicia's waist. Alicia looked up and saw Reed's face. She could see in her eyes how much Reed wanted her, and she smiled as she leaned into her. Reed pulled Alicia tightly against her body tucking her head into the crook of her neck. "Can I hold you for a moment?"

"Of course you can." Alicia slid her arms around Reed's waist and snuggled up against her, resting her head on Reed's shoulder. Reed's fingers stroked Alicia's hair. She felt an overwhelming sense of peace as Alicia relaxed against her body.

"I'm feeling better," Reed whispered against the fragrant blond hair.

"Good, you'll feel a whole lot better with some food and another pain pill."

"Are you staying?"

"Yes, I took tomorrow off. And I thought I would stay here and make sure you take care of yourself."

"What about work?"

"Work will be fine without me." Alicia breathed in Reed's scent and snuggled more tightly against her.

"I'm glad you're here."

"So am I." Alicia gently moved away from Reed. "Can you eat some soup?"

"Are you going to have some?"

"I thought I would."

"Why don't you eat in here with me?"

"I'll be right back." Reed was compelled to watch Alicia walk out of the room. She was about ready to crawl out of her skin she was so attracted to the woman. Never in her wildest dreams would she have thought someone like Alicia would be interested in her.

Alicia came back into the room moments later with her own soup and salad. She sat down on the left side of Reed's bed, and both began to eat their dinner. They talked about the accident and Reed's current remodeling jobs, then Alicia's job. Not once did either one of them look at the clock. More than an hour later, Alicia noticed the time.

"Reed, you need to take a pain pill."

"I will. I need to clean up a little bit."

"Are you sure you're up to it?"

"I'm sure. I feel a whole lot better after eating."

"Okay, I'll leave you to get cleaned up and then you're getting another pain pill and a fresh ice bag."

"Deal." Reed grinned, her dimples winking in her cheeks.

"I'm going to go tidy up the garage and change my clothes. Call if you need anything." Alicia carried the dirty dishes out of the bedroom.

No matter how badly Reed felt, she was going to wash up. She really wanted a shower. She slowly made it into the bathroom, hissing when she moved her hand.

It throbbed with pain. She started the shower and climbed out of her underwear and unbuttoned her shirt, removing it slowly. Holding her injured hand up in the air she stepped into the shower and sighed with relief when the hot water hit her body.

"What are you doing in the shower?" Alicia's voice echoed in the bathroom.

Reed stopped her one-handed face scrubbing and glanced through the shower door to see Alicia standing in the bathroom. "I needed a shower."

"Do you want me to come in there and help?" Alicia's voice held a tinge of humor.

"No," Reed responded, finding it difficult to ignore Alicia.

"Then I suggest you get your butt out of the shower immediately and get back into bed."

"You need to get out of the bathroom."

"Why?"

"Because I'm naked!"

"I should hope so." Alicia couldn't keep the laughter out of her voice. She didn't mean to tease Reed, but a glimpse of her naked body in the shower was enough to turn Alicia inside out. Reed was absolutely beautiful.

"Alicia, please …"

"I'll give you five minutes to get back into bed."

"Okay, out."

Alicia laughed as she exited the bedroom. Maddy met her in the hall. "What's going on?"

"I just threatened to get in the shower with Reed if she didn't get her butt back in bed."

"Did it work?" Maddy chuckled at her sister's comment.

"Oh yeah." Alicia grinned as she headed toward the stairs.

"Bet and I are going to watch a movie in our bedroom. Are you and Reed going to be okay?"

"We'll be fine. I'm going to convince her to stay in bed for the rest of the night."

"Okay, goodnight Le Le."

"Goodnight, Maddy. Give Bet a kiss."

Alicia went upstairs after her sister and changed into a tee shirt and a pair of shorts and then trotted back downstairs. She was just in time to catch Reed climbing back into bed, a pair of flannel boxers and a tee shirt on her still damp body.

"Here's your pain pill and some water. I'll go get an ice bag for your hand."

"Alicia, can we talk?"

Alicia's heart jumped right into her throat as she looked at Reed. She looked so damned cute sitting in bed with her legs crossed, her black hair snarled and still wet from the shower. Alicia came and sat down on the side of the bed waiting for Reed to speak.

"Earlier today you said you cared about me."

"I think I also said that I cared about you as more than just a friend and that I wanted to jump your bones." Alicia spoke quietly, her eyes sparkling as she looked directly at Reed.

"Yeah—that. Did you mean it?"

Alicia bent until she was within inches of Reed's face. "Yes, I meant it."

"Good because I feel the same way." Reed's smile was huge, her dimples deep in her cheeks.

"Then you have a good reason to stay in bed and get better quickly, don't you?" Alicia laughed as she pressed a kiss against Reed's cheek.

Reed wrapped her arm around Alicia and pulled her against her body until she lay tight up against Reed on the bed. Alicia rested her head on Reed's shoulder and placed her hand on Reed's flat muscular stomach. Reed relaxed against her pillow, closing her eyes. "Can we just stay like this for a little while?"

"I'd love that."

Maddy slipped back under the covers and curled up against Bet's warm back after returning from checking on Reed and her sister. Bet rolled over and looked at her lover. "How are they?"

"Sound asleep on Reed's bed. Alicia is nestled up against her, and they're both sound asleep. I put another ice bag on Reed's hand. It's fairly swollen."

"I think Alicia is just what Reed needs to recuperate."

"I've never seen Alicia like this," Maddy admitted. "She is so much softer around Reed. She seems so completely happy."

"Does it bother you?"

"Not at all, I'm happy for both of them. I couldn't have picked someone better for Alicia, and you know how much I respect Reed."

"Do you think they'll be sleeping together soon?"

"I'd say very soon."

"What do you say to a little lovemaking of our own?" Bet teased as she slid on top of her lover. Maddy's response was immediate, swallowed up by Bet's kiss as her lover overwhelmed her with her attentions. It had always been like this with

Bet. Their lovemaking was spontaneous and perfect from the very first time, and their relationship continued to grow stronger.

Chapter Eleven

Alicia slowly awakened to find herself stretched over Reed's body, her leg slung over her hips and her arm around her waist. Reed slept undisturbed next to her, her chest moving softly up and down with each breath. Her face was turned toward Alicia's and her hand was caught in Alicia's hair. Alicia lay quietly enjoying her view of Reed's sleeping form. Her lashes were long and as black as her hair, her mouth slightly pouty. Her face was flushed with a rosy glow of color unlike the pallor of the day before. Alicia felt her heart catch when she remembered seeing Reed in the emergency room, her hand covered with blood. That sight had scared her beyond anything she had dealt with in a very long time. She slowly reached up and brushed Reed's long bangs out of her eyes, leaving her hand resting against her cheek. She was such a gentle woman. Even in sleep she held Alicia softly, cradling her all night. Alicia hadn't meant to fall asleep, but she had been so very relaxed. Once Reed was comfortable, Alicia had nodded off, not moving all night. She hadn't had such a restful night's sleep in a long time.

Alicia sighed as she thought about her relationship with Reed. It was not the direction in which she had had expected her life to go, but it felt right. Nothing seemed hard when she was with Reed. Everything just seemed to fall into place. With Stephen, everything had been difficult, and it felt like all the pieces never quite fit together. She always felt like she didn't belong in her own life. Now she felt like she was living it. Some things scared her, though. She wasn't quite sure how to make love to Reed and she wanted to. Her body ached with attraction almost all the time. She had this overwhelming need to touch, to taste, and to see every bit of Reed's healthy body.

Reed felt Alicia stir next to her and slowly opened her eyes. Alicia lay quietly against her chest, her eyes open. "What are you thinking?"

Reed's deep voice with her slow, sexy delivery brought a smile to Alicia's face. "I was thinking I've never slept so well before. How does your hand feel?"

"Sore, but about what I expected." Reed pulled Alicia tighter against her body and rolled onto her side so they faced each other. Her left hand lay above Alicia's head flat on the pillow, her other hand was on Alicia's hip. "Good morning."

Alicia leaned into the kiss wanting that slow, perfect softness of Reed's mouth against her own. Their lips met and Reed's tongue traced her lower lip then entered her mouth, and Alicia was lost. She sucked on Reed's tongue as the kiss grew more urgent, and her body melted. Reed's mouth met hers again and again as Alicia moved closer to Reed, relishing the feel of her body against her own. Alicia grew ravenous as she met Reed's kisses with her own, feeling her skin tingle and her heart race. Her hands moved of their own volition to touch Reed's stomach and arms. She wanted, no, she needed to touch her.

A knock on the door interrupted them, and Alicia moaned against Reed's wonderful mouth. Reed growled and spoke in Alicia's ear. "I'm going to kill your sister or Bet."

Alicia giggled and rolled away from Reed, standing up and smoothing her clothes. "Come in."

"Hey, I'd thought I'd check on you two before I headed to the store. Do either of you need anything?" Bet almost laughed aloud. It was obvious from the look on both their faces that Bet had interrupted them. Neither woman looked at all pleased with the intrusion.

"We need some bags of frozen peas. They'll make better ice bags. Can you pick up two or three?" Alicia asked, blushing as Bet grinned at her.

"I can. What about food? I'm fixing dinner tonight, so if you have any choices make them now, or you're stuck with whatever I come up with." Bet was an experienced cook, having prepared meals for a very discerning crowd of firefighters for several years.

"Can't think of anything special, we're fine with whatever you decide to make," Alicia responded, heading for the door. "I'm going to get Reed an ice bag and then take a shower."

Bet waited until Alicia returned with the bag and went up the stairs before sitting down on her friend's bed. "Is everything okay, Reed?"

"Yes." Reed didn't look Bet in the eye.

"Look at me, honey. Are you okay?"

"I am more than okay." Reed's smile was huge. "She said she likes me."

"Likes you?"

"Jump my bones, likes me."

"Ah ha, and I interrupted," Bet laughed as Reed blushed.

"I'm not going to make love to her in her sister's home with a bum hand," Reed grumbled sitting up.

"From the looks you're getting from Alicia I don't think she cares about that. She wants you as much as you want her."

"What do you mean?"

"Honey, from what I can tell Alicia is as nuts over you as you are over her."

"Really?"

"Really. So what are you going to do about it?"

"Do about it?" Reed seemed to be flummoxed over Bet's statement.

"Well, aren't you going to sweep her off her feet?"

"How the hell do I do that, especially with this?" Reed held her bandaged hand up in the air, nervous frustration on her face.

"Court her."

"Court her—you sound like a damn romance novel," Reed snorted, as she pushed herself up in bed.

"Reed, that's what Alicia needs, romance. She's never been in a relationship where someone took the time to romance her. I believe you told me you were falling in love with her."

"Fallen is more like it," Reed admitted. "So I should romance her?"

"If she were anyone but Maddy's sister, what would you do?"

Reed thought about it a minute, then smiled. "I'd take her out to my house for a picnic, show her my dream home, and maybe even spend the night there."

"That's the spirit! But I think you might wait one more day and let your hand get a little better. I don't think Alicia's going to let you do much of anything today."

"Maybe you can pick up some nice romantic movies we can watch later today."

"You hate romantic movies, and Alicia likes scary ones."

"Okay, get a couple of really scary movies."

"Anything else?"

"My wallet is up on my dresser. Take some money out of it. Could you get a bouquet of spring flowers for her?"

"My, now we're really cooking—flowers, huh?" Bet teased her friend. She had never seen Reed so off her game before. Reed was normally so steady, so level, that this new view of her told Bet just one thing—her feelings for Alicia were the real deal. Bet didn't know whether to rejoice or worry.

"A nice big bunch." Reed smiled, thinking about other romantic gestures she could make.

"Will do, oh romantic one." Bet stood up chuckling.

"Thanks, Bet." Reed grinned up at her.

"No problem. Go get cleaned up. Your new girlfriend will be down in a minute."

Reed hastily climbed out of bed as Bet laughed at her and headed down the hall. It was so easy to tease Reed.

Alicia found Reed in the garage making coffee when she came back down the stairs. "What are you doing?"

"Making a fresh pot of coffee," Reed innocently responded, as she turned around to look at Alicia. The sight of her standing just inside the garage door was almost more than Reed could stand. Her blond hair was freshly washed and hung shining to her shoulders. Her face was without makeup but more beautiful than Reed could believe. But it was her silver blue eyes that caught at Reed's heart. They looked at her with such openness. "God, you are so incredibly beautiful."

Alicia was struck silent by Reed's declaration, as she stared back at her in surprise. "Thank you."

Reed reached out and tugged on her hand with a grin. "You were going to yell at me, weren't you?"

Alicia couldn't help but smile back at her as she let Reed tug her closer. "So you decided to tell me I'm beautiful so I won't yell at you?"

"No, you are beautiful, and you can yell at me now." Reed ducked her head and kissed Alicia softly, gently surrounding her with her good arm.

"Oh, yeah, I'm going to yell at you after you make my bones melt kissing me," Alicia teased, wrapping her arms around Reed's neck. "I think I've got you figured out. You are just too charming to get into trouble."

"You think you've figured me out, huh?"

"Yep, but your charms are not working right now. I want that hand up and an ice bag on it." Alicia played with the hair at the base of Reed's neck.

"My charms aren't working?" Reed pouted and then leaned over and nuzzled Alicia's neck with her lips, teasing her with her teeth and tongue. Alicia moaned as she reacted to Reed's playfulness.

"Honey, go sit in the living room and put your hand up. I'll bring you a cup of coffee and some breakfast," Alicia whispered, as Reed all but seduced her in the garage.

"I'd rather stay here with you," Reed admitted, as she began kissing Alicia's ear, her lips sucking lightly on her earlobe.

Alicia's libido struggled with her common sense until she pulled away from Reed and placed her hand on her chest, rubbing her breast bone. "I'd rather stay here too, but you just broke two fingers yesterday, and they need to be iced so they'll heal correctly. Please, go sit on the couch, honey."

Reed's grin was contagious as she let Alicia go and slowly sauntered away from her. Alicia almost chased her into the living room and jumped on her. She was way too sexy in her shorts and tee shirt, her feet bare.

Alicia brought Reed a cup of coffee and an ice bag before going back to the garage to fix something for breakfast. Within minutes, Reed had a plate of cut up cantaloupe and a toasted bagel on her lap. Alicia sat next to her with her own plate. Reed had turned the television on, and they tried to concentrate on cable news while sharing their breakfast.

By the time Bet got back, Reed was sound asleep on the couch, and Alicia was sitting at the living room table with her computer in front of her. She was getting a lot of work done considering how often her attention wandered to the woman slumbering on the couch.

"How's Reed doing?"

"She's out like a light. I think the pain meds knocked her out. Her hand is extremely swollen and black and blue. It must hurt like hell, but she's not complaining."

"I'm not asleep," Reed commented groggily, as she struggled to sit up.

"I see they make you cranky too," Bet teased, her eyes twinkling.

"I'm not cranky. Did you get the things I asked you to pick up?"

"Yes."

"Thanks, Bet."

"No problem. How's your hand feeling?"

"It aches a little and it's stiff, but the pain pills help."

"You need to keep it elevated and keep ice on it," Alicia reminded her.

"I know." Reed stood up and moved slowly down the hall. "I'll be right back."

Alicia's eyes followed Reed before she turned back to Bet. "Do you need some help with the groceries?"

"Nope, I brought them all into the garage. How're you doing?" Bet watched Alicia, seeing concern on her extraordinary face.

"Fine. They're doing well without me at work, and I'm able to get enough work done here to keep everyone happy. I was going to go to my place and get a change of clothes. Can you stay with Reed while I run over there?"

"Of course. I'm off today."

"Thanks, Bet."

"No problem."

"I'll just tell Reed and then get going." Alicia headed for Reed's bedroom and knocked softly. "Reed."

"Come in." Reed had just come out of her bathroom.

"I'm going over to my place to pick up some things. I won't be gone long." Alicia didn't miss the worried look Reed's face. She went up to her and slid her arms around her waist. "Honey, I'll be back in less than an hour. Even if you weren't injured, I'd want to spend the day with you."

"I know you probably have things to do."

"Reed, are you trying to get rid of me?" Alicia teased, her eyes sparkling with fun.

"No, I want you here," Reed interrupted, her eyes serious.

"Good because I plan on hanging around you a lot. I'll be back within the hour. If you need anything, call me on my cell phone."

"Okay." Reed wrapped her good arm around Alicia's waist and bent to kiss her. She met Alicia's lips with a soft gentle pressure. It felt like much more than an ordinary kiss. She felt Alicia slide against her, her lips meeting Reed's with a promise of more to come—sexy, full kisses that made both women tremble.

Alicia slowly stepped away from Reed, her hand trailing down Reed's right arm. She squeezed her hand gently before stepping out of Reed's bedroom. She sailed down the hall, grabbed her purse, and was out the front door before Reed left her room. Reed heard the growl of tires on gravel as she pulled away. Reed sighed loudly and returned to the living room. She sat down on the couch, putting her hand on a pillow.

"How're you feeling, buddy?"

Reed turned and looked at Bet before answering. "I'm doing okay."

"You and Alicia seemed to be doing okay?"

"Yes, more than okay. I feel like I should pinch myself to make sure it's real," Reed admitted.

"It's real, buddy. So are you going to marry her?"

"If she wants that, I'm all for it." Reed didn't have to consider her answer for even a moment. If Alicia wanted her heart, she could have it.

"Whoa, are you serious?" Bet sat down next to Reed on the couch.

"Completely, I fell in love with her the first night she looked at me with her gorgeous eyes," Reed admitted, gathering Bet's hand in hers. "I know falling in love with a straight woman is not very smart but there is something there between us."

"You really are serious?" Bet watched her friend's eyes. Reed could keep nothing hidden from her. They knew each other too well.

"Who was it who called me after spending one hour with Maddy at a softball game?" Reed teased her.

"Yeah, but that's me. You've never sounded this serious before."

"I've never met anyone like Alicia. I'm not sure if she really knows what it's like to be with a woman. She may decide she doesn't want to be with me after we sleep together."

"Trust your heart, Reed. What does it tell you?"

"I have to try and make it work." Reed had no choice. Her heart was already committed.

"Okay, buddy, I like the two of you together. Alicia's going to have my head if you don't lie down and put some ice on that hand. In case you haven't noticed, she's intent on making sure you take care of yourself."

"Okay, I'll put some ice on it."

"Peas—I picked up some bags of frozen peas. I'll go get a bag. Put your feet up and lay back, girl."

Reed did as Bet suggested and within minutes she'd fallen back to sleep. Bet covered her with a light blanket and headed for the backyard. She was going to get some weeding done. Bet was not someone who sat still for long. Maddy compared her to a Mexican jumping bean. She ran at full speed all day long and then dropped into a heavy sleep until the next day began when her frenetic activity started all over again.

Chapter Twelve

Alicia's cell phone rang just as she climbed back in her car with her overnight bag. "Hello."

"Alicia, Jake wants to have a meeting with you tomorrow at nine. Can you make it?"

"I'll be back to work tomorrow morning. I can meet with Jake at the time he suggested. Is there anything else going on?"

"No, actually it's pretty calm. How're you doing? Is everything okay?"

"Yes, things are settling back down. I'll tell you about it when I get back to work." Julie had been Alicia's secretary for almost five years, and they had developed a close friendship during the time they had worked together. It was so rare for Alicia to take time off that Julie knew it had to be something fairly serious.

"Take care then."

"Thanks, Julie. Call me if anything comes up."

"You're welcome, and I'm only going to call if it's urgent. Take some time for yourself, Alicia."

Alicia smiled as she disconnected from the call. She *was* taking time for herself. She was going to make sure Reed knew she was interested in a relationship. The more time she spent with Reed, the more she liked the person she was getting to know. And she was extremely attracted to her. It didn't feel the least bit odd to be attracted to a woman.

Alicia pulled into the driveway and parked behind Reed's truck. Slinging her overnight bag over her shoulder, she walked in the front door. No one was in the living room. Alicia went immediately to Reed's bedroom and quietly pushed the door open. Reed was sound asleep on her bed, her hand lying on a towel, a bag of peas resting on her hand. She slept soundly, covered with a sheet, her other hand tucked against her face on her pillow. Alicia placed her bag on the ground, went to stand next to her and watched her sleep. She smiled as she thought of how silly she must look. She turned and saw her name scrawled on an envelope leaning up against a vase of brilliantly colored spring flowers. She picked up the envelope and opened it. There was a plain note card inside. She pulled it out and smiled when she saw the signature on the card. It read *Thanks, Reed*. Alicia turned back to the bed and felt her heart tremble as she looked at Reed. She was such a sweet-heart, and she had a way of making Alicia feel valued for who she was. Alicia slipped out of the room and sat at the dining room table with her computer. She worked steadily for another hour until Reed snuck up behind her and kissed her on the neck.

"Hey, are you getting some work done?" Reed whispered against her neck as her lips laid soft kisses on her fragrant skin.

"I was! How's the hand feeling?" Alicia reached up and tugged Reed's face down and kissed her quickly.

"Better." Reed sighed as she reacted to Alicia's kiss.

"I'm about ready to take a break. Can I get you to put some ice on your hand?"

"Only if you'll sit on the couch with me, I had Bet pick up some movies earlier. She said you like really scary ones."

"I do. Hey, thank you for the beautiful flowers."

Reed blushed and nuzzled her face against Alicia's just wanting to touch her. "I'm glad you like them. Did you get everything you needed from your place?"

"Yes, I brought my overnight bag with clothes for tomorrow. I thought I might stay here another night." Alicia waited to see Reed's reaction.

Reed kissed Alicia on her neck and whispered in her ear. "Are you going to cuddle with me again tonight?"

"I'd like to."

"Good." Reed's heart settled in her chest.

"Go get comfortable on the couch. I'll get a fresh bag of peas for your hand and you can cuddle with me while we watch a movie." Alicia smiled up at the woman who could turn her inside out with just a smile.

"That sounds wonderful." Reed brushed a kiss on her lips, stood up and walked over to the couch, where she made herself comfortable.

Alicia shut her computer down, retrieved a bag of peas from the freezer and placed them on Reed's hand. She stuck her head out the back door and called to Bet. "Bet, we're going to watch a movie—want to join us?"

"I'll be right in."

Alicia went and sat next to Reed's right side in order to stay clear of her bad hand. Reed raised her arm and wrapped it around Alicia's shoulders tucking her tightly against her side. Alicia turned and pulled her feet up under her legs, slipping an arm around Reed's waist.

"Reed, I have to go in to work tomorrow. I'd like to stay home with you, but I can't."

Reed turned and she faced Alicia, her brown eyes sparkling as she bent closer to her. "It's okay, Alicia. I'll be fine. I have some paperwork to take care of for work."

"Can I come over after work?" Alicia was still unsure as to where their relationship was heading.

"I'd like that a lot."

"Good, so would I." Reed kissed Alicia, her tongue sliding against Alicia's as they melted together.

"Hey, I thought you were going to watch a movie," Bet teased as she entered the room, grinning at the two women.

"We were waiting for you."

"Sure you were." Bet slumped on the living room chair, and Alicia started the movie and tucked up against Reed's body, a feeling of contentment settling over her.

"So what movie did you pick?" Alicia asked.

"Alien II," Bet responded with a grin. "I've always had a crush on Ripley."

"Cool."

The three women enjoyed the movie immensely, even though they had all seen it before. Alicia remained curled up against Reed and didn't move from her cozy position. Reed thought that holding hands with Alicia was one of the most romantic things she had done in a long time. She felt like she and Alicia had been together forever, comfortable and safe. By four o'clock, Bet was ready to start cooking an early dinner, and Alicia was bound and determined to change the dressing on Reed's hand.

After some discussion, Reed acquiesced and let Alicia remove the bandages that covered her stitches and replace them with fresh dressings. Her hand was a mass of bruised black and blue tissue and not a pretty sight.

"Honey, you need to make an appointment with your regular doctor and have him check this out," Alicia reminded her, as she gently covered the swollen hand.

"I'll do that first thing in the morning," Reed promised and then snagged Alicia around the waist holding her between her long legs. "Alicia, would you go out with me Thursday night on a date?"

"A date?" Alicia smiled at Reed in surprise.

Reed felt just a little bit shy. "Yes, if you'd like to go out with me."

"I'd love to. What do you have in mind?"

"How about I surprise you? It won't be anything terribly fancy, but I think you'll like it."

"Reed, I enjoy spending time with you. I'm sure I'd like anything you choose to do."

Reed tugged Alicia closer and looked up at her and grinned, her dimples deep on her cheeks. "So if I take you off to a hidden rendezvous for a night, you wouldn't mind?"

"I'd love to sneak off with you," Alicia admitted with a smile.

Alicia leaned down and kissed Reed slowly, her mouth soft and sweet against Reed's. Reed's arm tightened around her waist, and Alicia wrapped her arms around Reed's neck as the kiss swept her away. She wanted to climb into Reed's lap and never leave.

Maddy burst through the front door startling them and making them pull apart, but Alicia kept her hands resting on Reed's shoulders as she smiled at her sister.

"Hi Maddy, how was work?"

"Good, long—I need a beer." She slumped on the couch.

"Here, I'll get you one. Why don't you put your feet up?" Alicia asked.

After Alicia left the room, Maddy turned to Reed with a questioning smile on her face. "So what are your intentions with my sister?"

Reed's face lit up with a smile of her own as she responded. "I'm going to marry her."

Maddy's look of amazement made Reed laugh. "For real?"

"For real, if I can convince Alicia. Maddy, I'm serious about Alicia."

"I think she's serious about you."

"God, I hope so," Reed sighed, rubbing her hand over her heart.

"Welcome to the family." Maddy poked her in the side.

"Don't jinx it. Alicia may not want to be with me. She's never been with a woman before."

"Oh, I think once you use your considerable charm to woo her she won't stand a chance."

Reed and Maddy cracked up when Alicia returned with a beer for her sister and sat down next to Maddy. 'What's so funny?"

"Maddy was giving me advice about taking you on a date."

Alicia looked at Maddy and snorted. "You! Your first real date with Bet was in a tow yard after parking your car in a no parking zone. I hope Reed isn't listening to you."

"Hey, there was nothing close to the restaurant. Man that was an expensive date." Maddy took a long sip of beer and reminisced.

'What about the time you took her to see the Christmas ship at Alki Beach and almost ran her over with your car?"

"That was an accident. I couldn't see her in the dark." Maddy shrugged and took another sip of her beer to hide her red face.

"Maddy, no offense, but I don't think I want any of your advice," Reed commented, her eyebrows rising in mock horror.

Maddy glared at her sister and Reed. "Hey, she married me, didn't she?"

"Yes I did, honey, but it wasn't because of your stellar dating techniques," Bet pointed out as she entered the living room.

"Why did you marry me?" Maddy was getting ready to pout.

Bet raised an eyebrow at her lover and gave her a sexy grin. "It was your stellar technique in bed that won me over."

Reed and Alicia burst out laughing as Maddy tumbled Bet into her lap, giggling as she kissed her lover.

"Okay, who wants vegetarian pizza for dinner?" Bet asked after Maddy released her from her clutches.

The evening flew by as the four women visited while eating dinner. There was never a lull in the conversation. Their long friendship allowed them to be comfortable with each other in the most ordinary situations.

Not long after dinner, Reed suggested she go take a shower and get ready for bed. Alicia helped Maddy with the dishes.

"Le Le, do you need any advice about sex?" Maddy asked as she put the last plate away. She grinned impishly up at her sister.

"No thank you, I think I have it figured out," Alicia commented, cuffing her sister lightly on the shoulder.

Maddy turned serious and faced her sister. "You're okay with making love with Reed?"

"God, Maddy, if we don't do it soon I'm going to implode," Alicia admitted, her eyes shining with emotion.

"That's a good thing."

"I know, but with Reed's injured hand I don't think it's the best time to be considering it," Alicia admitted.

"You do understand that Reed is assuming you want to date her as a lover."

"I should hope so! I've been dropping enough hints!" Alicia's face lit up as she spoke. "Maddy, it's like I've waited my whole life to meet her. She makes me feel sexy, safe, and she makes me laugh. I don't feel at all uncomfortable with her."

Maddy hugged her sister tightly, expressing her love for her. Whether Alicia fell in love with a man or a woman, all Maddy wanted was that he or she would love Alicia completely. She knew without a doubt that Reed would do that. She still had a few concerns about Alicia's first time with a woman. That was a very big step.

"Good, I'm glad. You better go get ready for bed. Reed's probably wondering where you are."

Alicia turned and headed for Reed's bedroom where she had left her overnight bag. She had effectively moved into Reed's room. Reed was just coming out of the bathroom, her body wrapped in a large towel.

"Whoops, sorry, I should have knocked." Alicia started to back out of the room, her face bright red with embarrassment.

"Alicia, where are you going?" Reed looked at her patiently.

"I thought I could give you some privacy." Alicia was finding it hard to look at Reed.

"I don't need any privacy from you, honey." Reed waited for Alicia to look at her. "I don't want to make you uncomfortable, though."

Alicia smiled at the stunning half-naked woman and moved up to within inches of her scantily clad body. "You certainly don't make me feel uncomfortable. I think you're incredibly sexy."

"Yeah?" Reed blushed and moved closer to Alicia.

"Oh yeah." Alicia slipped her arms around Reed's waist and kissed her gently. "Now, if you don't mind, I'm going to pop into the bathroom and take a quick shower."

"Not at all." But Reed did mind. She wanted her hands and mouth on Alicia, and it was all she could do to stand still. Her hand wasn't going to allow her much mobility, and she mentally cursed her unfortunate timing.

Alicia kissed her once more and then reached down and grabbed her overnight bag and headed for the bathroom. Reed sighed loudly after the door closed and slumped to a seat on her bed. She struggled one handed into a clean pair of underwear and a tee shirt. Pulling the covers back on the bed, she arranged the sheets and pillows the best that she could and then slipped under the covers. She laid back and tried to relax.

Alicia stepped into the shower and rapidly scrubbed her body. She still tingled from their earlier kisses. She couldn't control her unruly body whenever she was around Reed. Fifteen minutes later she came out of the bathroom wearing a silk sleep shirt that hit her mid-thigh. Her blue eyes met Reed's dark eyes across the room.

"You are so beautiful it takes my breath away," Reed volunteered as she drank in the long slender legs and the remarkable face staring back at her.

"I feel the same way when I look at you," Alicia admitted as she dropped her overnight bag next to the dresser.

"Can I ask you a question?"

"Of course, honey." Alicia sat down on the bed and turned to face Reed. Reaching a hand out, she clasped Reed's.

"Do you really want to have a relationship with me?"

Alicia saw the vulnerability in Reed's eyes, and she reached up and placed a hand on Reed's cheek, knowing her answer was critical. "Reed, more than anything I want to have a relationship with you. I know you find that hard to believe because I've never been with another woman. I've never wanted to touch someone like I do you. If you aren't looking for a commitment or a serious relationship, you should tell me now."

"I want you now and years from now." Reed slipped an arm around Alicia and tugged her into her lap. She leaned her forehead against Alicia's as she spoke from her heart. "I'm not someone who's comfortable with casual sex, so when we sleep together it's a commitment from me to you. I know this is all completely new to you, and I promise I won't rush you about anything."

Alicia kissed Reed softly and then whispered in her ear. "I want to be rushed."

Reed pulled back and looked at Alicia's face then wrapped an arm around her waist and pulled her tightly against her as she kissed her. These weren't the soft gentle kisses that Alicia was used to, this was hunger and need. Reed heard the moan of pleasure from Alicia and gently rolled Alicia onto her back and bent over her kissing her again and again.

Reed's tongue swept through Alicia's mouth, creating a firestorm. Alicia's hands stroked down Reed's shoulders and back feeling the strength of her body as she traced her fingertips over solid muscle. Reed's mouth traveled to her neck, her lips slid under her chin, her tongue tasting the tender skin between her breasts. Reed's strong thigh rolled over Alicia's hips pinning her tightly against her long body, while her right hand touched her stomach and stroked in slow circles.

Alicia's hands couldn't stop touching and she slid them under Reed's tee shirt to experience her skin. Reed hissed as Alicia's hands reached up and molded her upper arms and shoulders. God, she wanted Alicia's hands on her body. She trembled as her right hand moved under Alicia's silk shirt and finally was able to stroke her soft skin. Reed nuzzled, with her lips and tongue, the tops of Alicia's breasts, and her fingertips memorized each rib as she moved her hand up Alicia's body.

Alicia was on fire and she became restless, unaware that her hips pushed against Reed's hard thigh trying to appease the need between her legs. She was unbelievably wet reacting to Reed's lovemaking. In her whole life she had never felt this way before. She was trembling with hunger for Reed's touch.

"God, Alicia, I want you so much and I feel like I'm not able to love you very well because of my hand," Reed muttered, her head dropping onto Alicia's chest as she lay panting.

"Reed, just touch me, please." Alicia was willing to beg to get some relief.

"Are you sure baby?"

"Reed, love me." Alicia reached up and turned Reed's face so she was looking into her eyes. "I need you to love me."

"Jesus, I don't want to scare you, but I don't think I can wait a minute longer to touch you." In one move Reed stripped the shirt off Alicia's body and struggled with her own tee shirt. "Goddamn it, I need to feel you."

"Reed, let me help you." Alicia saw the raw need on Reed's face, and a rush of heat and painful pleasure moved through her. "Let me."

Alicia gently lifted the tee shirt off Reed's torso as Reed's hot eyes all but devoured her. Alicia's pupils were dilated, and her hands trembled as she reached up and slid her fingertips under the waistband of Reed's underwear. Slowly Alicia pushed them down Reed's hips and all but gasped when she saw her body in all its naked glory.

"Reed, you have a perfect body," Alicia whispered, her eyes sweeping from her feet to her face.

"I think yours is perfect." Reed reached out and pulled Alicia gently on top of her, using her knees to spread Alicia's thighs around her hips.

"Oh, my God!" Alicia cried out as she came in contact with Reed's skin, their breasts pressed tightly together.

Reed clenched her teeth as Alicia's body settled against hers. Reed and Alicia's mouths met in a full kiss, Alicia tasting Reed's mouth with her tongue while Reed's hand stroked over her hips and buttocks. Alicia ran her tongue along Reed's collarbone and tasted the hot skin above her full breast wanting more than anything to kiss her nipples that stood stiff and darkly red. Her mouth moved insistently over Reed's full breast and sucked her nipple into her mouth.

"Jesus, God." Reed arched into Alicia's mouth as her body reacted to her hot tongue.

Alicia's fingertips teased her other nipple until Reed was straining to find relief. But she wanted Alicia's first time to be special, and she swiftly rolled over until her body completely covered Alicia's.

"Wrap your legs around my hips," Reed ordered, as she captured Alicia's nipple between her teeth and teased her. First one breast and then the other were painstakingly loved until Alicia's head fell back, her body crying for release.

"Reed …"

"I know baby, I know." Reed heard the want in Alicia's voice, and she ran her right hand down Alicia's stomach into the pale blond hair that covered Alicia's throbbing lips. Her long fingers gently covered Alicia.

Alicia's hips jumped at the first touch of Reed's seeking fingers, and her body released more welcoming fluid. Reed's fingertips stroked lightly spreading the moisture as she slipped her fingers into Alicia until her fingers were fully encased.

Alicia cried out and spread her legs wider as Reed touched her deeply. Slowly Reed moved in, then almost out as she stroked Alicia. Again she filled her as Alicia wrapped her hands around Reed's hips. Using her hips she pushed deeper into Alicia and then pulled out increasing the speed until Alicia's hips began to move against her hand picking up their own rhythm. Reed kissed Alicia's neck and shoulders. Alicia began to pant, her body writhing with pleasure so acute she wanted to scream.

Reed felt the rippling of her body that told Reed she was close to an orgasm, and she renewed her efforts filling her tightly as her own body began to shake.

"Alicia, look at me," Reed called to her, wanting to see her eyes as she went over. Alicia struggled as her body began to tumble. Her silvery eyes opened to find Reed's dark eyes locked onto her face. She cried out loudly and tightened her hold on Reed's strong hips as she began to shudder.

"I'm coming," she cried out, as Reed's fingertips found her clitoris and flicked it back and forth. Reed covered Alicia's mouth with a kiss, and she felt her own body start to tumble.

"God … I'm …" Alicia reached up and squeezed Reed's nipples as her head snapped back, her eyes slamming shut. The orgasm tore through Reed's body, and she pounded her hips into Alicia's.

Alicia muffled a scream against Reed's shoulder, her teeth biting sharply into Reed's muscle. Reed reacted with another orgasm that shot straight up her legs and hit the center of her body. Gasping for air, Reed slumped onto Alicia, her fingers still deeply inside her.

Alicia lay limp beneath her trying to calm her wildly beating heart. She had never experienced anything remotely close to what had just transpired. Before she could do anything more, Reed stirred and slid down her body. She began to run her tongue around her embedded fingers, lapping at Alicia's soaked center.

"I have to taste you," Reed muttered, as she slowly removed her fingers and began to suck on Alicia's clitoris. Her tongue slid into Alicia, and she felt another orgasm starting to build. Reed's hunger for her brought her quickly back to begging for release, and Alicia could do nothing but react to Reed's talented mouth. "You are so sweet."

Alicia's fingers threaded into Reed's dark hair and held her tightly against her center until she began to dissolve. Reed felt her clitoris stiffen, and she sucked harder shoving two fingers deeply into Alicia. Alicia's scream of pleasure made Reed bolder, and she all but devoured her with her mouth until Alicia grew limp on the bed.

Reed wiped her face on the sheet and rolled up to lie quietly next to Alicia who had an arm stretched over her eyes as she tried to catch her breath. Reed's hand covered her breast and cradled it as she waited for Alicia's reaction to her lovemaking.

Alicia slowly opened her eyes and found dark brown ones watching her closely. She smiled slowly, and then her smile grew wider as she leaned over and spoke softly to her new lover. "I've never had a lover who made love to me the way you do. I don't know what to say to you other than, can we do that again?"

Reed released the breath she had been holding and leaned up to kiss Alicia. "Does that mean you liked it?"

"Honey, you know I liked it." Alicia placed her hand on Reed's chest and slowly stroked her breast. "I think Bet and Maddy know how much I liked it."

"Yeah, you did scream a little," Reed teased, tugging Alicia over until she lay on top of Reed. "I wasn't exactly quiet either."

Alicia fingers reached up and stroked Reed's face as she leaned on her elbow and looked down on Reed's face. "You're an amazing lover. I want to love you now, and I'm not really sure what to do."

"Alicia, do whatever pleases you. I just want to be close to you." Reed kissed her slowly, gently loving her with her lips.

Alicia covered Reed's face with light, feathery kisses and then moved down her impressive body. Her lips and tongue tasted and teased Reed's shoulders and arms and then kissed her full breasts. Alicia found Reed's breasts fascinating, and she sucked on her nipples and licked the tender skin around them. Reed's breathing grew erratic as Alicia moved down her body, her tongue playing with Reed's navel. She was long and lean, the muscles of her stomach solid and well-defined.

"You have such an incredible body, I just want to taste and feel every inch of it." Alicia's fingertips slid across her hips and down her thighs, as Reed trembled from her touch. Alicia didn't hesitate. Her fingertips trailed up the inside of Reed's thigh and touched her very center. Reed was wet and swollen.

"Oh God," Reed choked out, arching her back as Alicia's fingers slid inside her.

Alicia had never felt anything so sexy in her life. She slid her fingers deeply into Reed, stroking slowly as Reed's body rippled around her fingers. She watched her fingers enter Reed, and she felt the connection all the way through her own body. She bent over and touched Reed with her tongue, slowly tasting her.

Reed's hips jerked against Alicia's mouth, and she kissed Reed again before sucking lightly on her clitoris while her fingers continued to stroke deeply inside her body. She felt Reed's legs tense against her, and then her body froze and shuddered, her face a study in passion.

Reed's deep cry and her hips moving hard against Alicia's mouth and fingers grew frantic. Alicia's tongue tasted her over and over until Reed jerked once, and then went slack on the bed.

Alicia kissed her softly once more and slid up Reed's body and kissed her chin and then her lips. Reed opened her eyes. They were glassy with emotion as she stared up into silver blue eyes. "That was wonderful."

"I like touching you, loving you."

"Good, because I like it, too. Are you okay, Alicia?"

"Reed, I'm wonderful. I can't believe how perfect that was. I have been waiting all my life for you to find me." Alicia's eyes flooded with tears as she spoke from her heart. "I've never had an orgasm before."

"Never?" Reed was shocked and a little pleased that she was the one to provide Alicia with such pleasure.

"Never."

"Then I'm glad it was with me."

"So am I, honey. Reed, I know it might be hard for you to trust me, especially since I've never been with a woman before. Maddy always told me it didn't matter whether you fell in love with a man or a woman because it depended more on the person you needed to make yourself whole. I'd been living a half life until I met you, without passion or color. It's you that makes me whole. You make me able to believe that my life can be more, so much more."

Reed responded to Alicia's vulnerability, tightening her arm around her waist. "Alicia, from the moment I met you I wanted to know everything about you—what makes you laugh, what makes you sad, and what dreams you have. I knew the moment I saw you that if I had the opportunity I'd want to help make those dreams come true. All I ask is that you talk to me about what you're feeling. If being with a woman gets too hard for you, tell me. I'm a gay woman who doesn't try to hide it. I would never want to make you uncomfortable."

"Reed, you couldn't do that. You are beautiful, talented, and sexy. It makes me feel lucky that you want to be with me. I'd be proud to be seen with you in any environment. If you and I are to be together, I don't want to hide it."

"What about your job? Wouldn't it affect your career?"

"Reed, I'm where I am because of my brain not because of who I choose to be with."

"People will judge you differently now."

"I don't care. If you're my lover and partner, you're more important to me than anything else."

"I am your lover, and I'd like to be your partner."

"I'd like that too." Alicia stroked Reed's cheek.

"So does that mean we're monogamous?"

"Reed, as far as I'm concerned, you're it. I want to make this work."

"Good because Maddy wants to know my intentions toward you." Reed kissed Alicia softly.

"What did you tell her?" Alicia bent and rubbed her cheek against Reed's, breathing in her scent. "God, you smell so good."

Reed ran her tongue along Alicia's ear and then whispered her answer. "I told her I wanted to marry you."

Alicia had no time to respond because Reed covered her mouth with a kiss, stroking her hand down Alicia's naked back and across her buttocks. Rolling her hips, she quickly moved Alicia onto her back. Her hips spread Alicia's thighs wide until she was solidly pressed against Reed's stomach. Reed growled at the feel of Alicia's wet center sealed against her stomach. Reed's earlier lovemaking had been slow and gentle. This was fast and hot as Reed's mouth streaked over both breasts while her fingers slid into Alicia's wetness.

"I need to be inside you!" Reed declared, as she pushed into Alicia and rocked her hips against her. Reed moved harder and faster, and Alicia tightened her thighs around Reed's, her arms locking around Reed's neck. Reed's body was one long lean line of toned muscle as she arched into Alicia, her neck corded and her head thrown back. Alicia had never seen anything quite as sensuous as Reed's dark eyes watching her.

"Reed, God, I ..." Her eyes slid shut as she trembled.

"Wait for me!" Reed gasped, as she bent down and sucked on Alicia's lower lip. Alicia opened her eyes to find dark brown ones watching her with an intensity that made Alicia want to weep. "God, I can't believe how incredibly beautiful you are right now."

It was her words as much as her passionate lovemaking that carried Alicia even higher. She cried out as she came in a violent rush, and Reed moaned as she shuddered and then collapsed next to Alicia on the bed. Alicia reached over and lovingly stroked Reed's bangs out of her face just drinking in her striking looks. There was no way she'd back away from this relationship.

"Reed ..."

"Yes?" Reed opened her eyes and smiled at Alicia.

"I told Maddy two days ago that I was falling in love with you."

Reed's face lit up with delight and then she laughed. "Maddy didn't tell me that. It would have saved me a lot of worrying if she'd mentioned it."

"You were worried?"

"Hell, I was scared to death. I was falling in love with a straight woman who's my best friend's sister."

"Are you scared now?"

"No. I'm happy, overwhelmed, and ecstatic, but not scared." Reed punctuated her words with kisses.

"I guess then you might have to ask me to marry you some day." Alicia snuggled up to Reed's side and stroked her back.

"That sounds absolutely perfect."

"Now that we have the rest of our lives settled, maybe we ought to get some sleep."

"You're going to be tired at work tomorrow," Reed commented, as she rolled onto her back and pulled Alicia closer to her. "It's after one in the morning. What time do you need to get up?"

"I need to be up by six. I'll have to go home and change before work."

"Are you coming over after work?"

"I'd like to, if you're sure you won't get tired of me."

"Not a chance."

Alicia reached up and kissed Reed slowly, then laid her head on Reed's shoulder. She reached down and pulled the covers up over them and laid her hand on Reed's stomach. "Goodnight, honey."

"Goodnight, baby."

Chapter Thirteen

The buzz of her telephone startled Alicia out of her daydreams. Despite getting less than five hours of sleep, Alicia felt energized. She'd barreled through her work day catching up on everything and getting necessary work done on a couple of accounts.

The meeting earlier with her boss had gone very well. He was pleased with her work and was still talking about moving her up in the ranks again.

"Alicia, I've decided to promote you to Senior Vice-President, and all I need to do is get our lawyer to write up the offer. The job requires a lot more work, and you'll need to give me some suggestions for your replacement. You'll also need to delegate more. I don't want you putting in any more hours."

"I can handle it." Alicia smiled at her boss.

"I know you can, but you need a life too."

Alicia smiled as she responded. "I'm working on that, too."

"Good, I'm glad."

Alicia left Jack's office with a big smile on her face. After her night of lovemaking with Reed and her meeting with Jack, Alicia was on cloud nine.

"Alicia Towers speaking."

"Hello, how's your day going?"

Reed's sexy voice was all it took. Alicia vibrated with need as she smiled and responded, "Better, now that you called. How're you doing?"

"Good. I ran out to check on a couple of jobs, iced my hand for an hour this morning, and I'm icing it again right now."

"Good. How's it feeling?"

"Better, it doesn't ache so much."

"I'm glad."

"So, I wondered what time you might get over here."

"Some time around six, why?"

"I'm fixing dinner, and I want to make sure I have everything ready by the time you arrive."

"Should you be cooking with your hand?"

"Honey, you should know I can do anything I need to, even with a bum hand," Reed teased, chuckling.

"Oh, I do know. I miss you, Reed."

"I miss you too, baby. I'll see you soon."

Alicia grinned as she replaced the receiver and thought back to that morning. Reed had awakened early to make love to her—gentle, passionate love—and Alicia had floated to work in a rosy haze. Her dreaminess hadn't gone unnoticed by Julie, her secretary. Alicia had been dodging her questions most of the day.

"Okay, it's break time, and I know something is going on," Julie declared, as she burst into Alicia's office.

"What do you mean?" Alicia tried to look innocent, but she couldn't keep the smirk off of her face.

"Alright, who is it?"

"Who is what?"

"Who is making you grin like a Cheshire cat? Don't tell me it's Alex!"

"No, it's not Alex." Alex had ceased to exist since she found Reed.

"Oh ho, it is *someone*."

"All right, I am seeing someone, and it's going very well."

"Who is it? Is it someone here at work? How long has this been going on?"

"Julie, slow down," Alicia laughed. "It's not someone at work and it's been a couple of weeks."

"So, are you having hot, sweaty, wild sex?"

"Julie …"

"Well, you must be, the way you're grinning all the time."

"I am not!"

"Who is it?"

"It's a friend of my sister's." Julie knew Maddy. She had met her several times.

"Your sister introduced you to a hottie? Who is he?"

There was the question. Alicia hesitated a moment, remembering her conversation with Reed the night before. She would not duck the hard questions. "Julie, it's not a he, it's a she."

To say Julie was shocked was an understatement. Her mouth dropped opened and her eyes widened. "It's … it's a woman?"

"Yes, a gorgeous, sexy woman."

"Wow!"

"Wow is right." Alicia watched Julie for any sign of discomfort or disapproval. "It wasn't something I planned on."

"You really care about this woman?"

"I'm in love with her," Alicia admitted.

"Double wow. So what's she like? What's she do? When can I meet her? Can she support you?"

Alicia was tickled to death over Julie's questions. "Let me see if I can answer all of those questions in order. She's taller than I am, and her body is spectacular—muscles from head to toe. She has dark brown eyes and black hair to her shoulders. She has her own contracting firm, and she's a master carpenter. She has a very good job and is building a home out in East Lake Sammamish. She's romantic, sexy, and head-to-toe gorgeous. You can meet her some day if she comes to work."

"Does she love you?"

"She wants to marry me," Alicia sighed.

"Wow, if I wasn't married, I'd take her." Julie grinned at her friend.

"It doesn't bother you that I'm with a woman?"

"Why would it? Are you happy?"

"Extremely."

"That's all I care about. You might want to tell Stephen before he hears it from someone else. I don't think he's going to be that happy, not that I care one little bit," Julie said, wrinkling her nose in disgust.

"He's getting married and having a child. Why would he care?"

"He's not the kind of man to understand this at all."

Alicia had to agree with her. Stephen wouldn't take the news very well, but she couldn't care less. "Do you think others in the firm will have a problem with it?"

"There might be a few, especially a couple of the more macho men, but I think most people won't care. You probably need to tell Jack so that he doesn't hear it through our gossip chain."

"It's so new I haven't shared it with anyone other than Maddy, her partner, and now you."

"I'm glad you told me, Alicia. You seem really happy lately—settled you know?"

"I know what you mean. It's like my life just finally came together."

"That's so cool. I can't think of anyone who deserves it more. Can you bring a picture in so I can see this sexy thing?"

"I'll see what I can do," Alicia agreed with a happy grin.

"So, are you having hot, passionate sex all the time?" Julie teased as she stood up to leave.

"Absolutely!"

"Oh, you rock, girl!"

Alicia had to agree with her as she put her head down and concentrated on the work in front of her. She had to think of how to approach Stephen and her boss. She hadn't really thought that through. She wanted to discuss it with Reed before she did anything.

An hour later, Jack interrupted her and she had her chance. "Alicia, the contracting firm that was going to remodel our front office has bagged out on us. Julie said you might know a good one we could call."

"I do know an excellent contractor, but it might be a conflict of interest," Alicia volunteered, as Jack sat down across from her.

"What do you mean a conflict of interest? Do you own the company?" Jack asked settling into the leather chair across from Alicia.

"No, but I am involved with the owner."

"You're seeing someone? That's nice, Alicia. I'm really glad you're finally over that putz you married."

"You don't like Stephen?" Alicia was shocked. Jack had never given her any indication of his dislike for her ex-husband.

"Can't stand the jerk. Don't get me wrong. He's excellent at business, but when it comes to personal relationships, he's clueless. I could never understand what you saw in the guy."

"Well, that's water under the bridge now," Alicia admitted, relieved to realize she wasn't the only one who had difficulties with Stephen. She had actually believed that the downfall of their relationship and marriage was all her fault.

"So tell me about this new guy." Jack grinned at Alicia.

Alicia took a big deep breath. "Jack, it's not a guy."

"What do you mean it's not a … oh."

"Her name is Reed Thomas, and she owns a contracting firm and is a master carpenter. She does exceptional work. I'm telling you about this now because of your need for a new contractor." Alicia watched Jack's face as he absorbed the information. "Does it bother you that I'm seeing a woman?"

Jack could read the uncertainty in Alicia's voice. "Alicia, all I care about is that you're happy and well loved."

"I am."

"Then I think it's wonderful."

"Does it make a difference at work?"

"Not with me it doesn't, and since I own the company that should be the end of it. I can't predict how others will act or feel. We have a non-discrimination policy, but that won't stop people from seeing you differently. All I would ask is that you don't bring your personal life into your client relationships."

"I wouldn't do that, Jack."

"I know you wouldn't, but some of our clients are red-necked white males, and they would have a problem with it." Jack took the sting out of his words with a grin. "Have you told Stephen?"

"Not yet."

"Boy would I like to see his reaction. He's going to explode."

"Why do you say that?"

"Alicia, how could you have been married to the guy and not see what a jerk he is? His idea of how to treat women is to keep them barefoot and pregnant. He hated that you were promoted to Vice-President."

"He did?" Alicia was shocked at that. Stephen had even taken her out for a celebration dinner.

"Yes, he lobbied against your promotion saying you weren't ready for the responsibility."

Alicia went cold inside as she stared back at Jack. "He never said a word to me."

"Stephen is one of the sneakiest bastards I know. Be careful with him. He's not above doing something nasty to you. If he becomes a problem, you let me know. If he wasn't so damn good at his job, I'd get rid of him."

Alicia couldn't believe what she was hearing. "I don't think it's going to be a big issue. He's getting married and becoming a father."

"Just promise me you'll let me know if he does anything to bother you."

"I will, Jack. Thanks for being so understanding."

"Alicia, I really am happy for you."

"Thanks, I am too."

"Now, let's talk about your girlfriend and see if she wants to take on the front office remodel."

"You don't think it's a problem?"

"No, and if she's as good as you say she is, the whole job will probably end up being even better than we had originally planned. Can you find out if she's interested in looking at the job?"

"I'll call her right now and talk to her about it."

"Good." Jack rose up out of his chair, his lanky body unfolding as he stood to his six-foot-two-inch height. "Let me know. I'm off to watch a soccer game."

"Which son?"

"Lee. That kid is something else on the soccer field. I think he's good enough to get a college scholarship." The pride in his voice was evident.

"Have fun."

Jack waved his hand as he left her office. He had a brilliant financial mind, was a direct and fair boss, and more importantly was a very good husband and father. Alicia had enormous respect for him. The fact that he had voiced his acceptance of her relationship with Reed pleased her no end. Her life just couldn't get any better. She quickly dialed Reed's cell phone number.

"Reed."

"Hi, honey."

"Hey, baby, how's your day going?"

"Wonderful." Alicia could hear the sound of hammering and sawing in the background. "Reed, where are you?"

"At one of my jobs. We had a minor problem, and I'm checking on it."

"You aren't working with that hand are you?"

Reed grinned at the tone of disapproval in Alicia's voice. "No, honey, I'm not working. I'm just watching and talking."

"Good because I'd hate to have to yell at you."

"You don't have to. I'm taking good care of my hand. I want it to get better too. It's hampering my ability to make love to you."

"Reed …" Alicia laughed and felt her face flush with embarrassment. "I did call to tell you something and ask you a favor."

"Shoot."

"I told my boss about you."

Reed was absolutely stunned and didn't know how to respond.

"Reed, did you hear me?"

"I heard you, baby." Reed's heart filled with emotion. "God, I wish I could touch you right now. That is so wonderful."

"It's okay that I told him?"

"It's outstanding. I want everyone to know." Reed laughed, her body filled with happiness. "Was he okay with everything?"

"He said he was glad I found someone that could make me happy."

"Did you?"

"Reed, you make me very happy."

"I hope so, because I feel the same way."

"He also wanted to know if you'd be interested in a contracting job for him. We had an architect redesign our front office, but the contractor Jack hired has backed out due to a conflict with another job. He wanted to know if you might be interested in it."

Reed hesitated for a minute. It was one thing to come out to your boss. It was another to have your new girlfriend working in your office. "Would it bother you if I came into your office?"

Alicia was surprised at Reed's question. "Of course it wouldn't, honey. I think you're an amazing carpenter. I believe you'd be perfect for the job. But you don't have to do it for me. I'd be fine if you said no."

"I'll tell you what. I'll meet with your boss and go over the plans. If I don't feel comfortable doing it, I can at least recommend a couple of other good contractors I know so he's not left without someone to complete the job."

"That's great. When would you be able to come in and talk to Jack?"

"Any time tomorrow or Friday would be fine, since I can't really do much on the job."

"Let me check with him and talk to you about it tonight."

"Great. I'll see you at six."

"Yes, you will. And despite your injury, I think you're a fabulous lover."

"You should see what I can do with two good hands," Reed teased.

"I can't wait." And Alicia meant it.

"See you later, baby."

Alicia quickly buzzed Jack in his office hoping to catch him before he left.

"Hello."

"Jack, Reed said she would look over your plans and see if she could do the job. She also said if she felt she wasn't right for the work, she would recommend a couple of good contractors who might be."

"Excellent. When can she take a look at the job?"

"Any time tomorrow or Friday."

"How about if I send the plans home with you so she can take a look and then she can come in tomorrow at two?"

"That'll work."

"I'll drop them off on my way out. By the way, Stephen's in the office."

"Maybe I should talk to him."

"Do you want me to hang around?"

"No, I can handle it, thanks." Alicia hung up and then buzzed Julie's extension.

"Julie, can you see if you can locate Stephen and ask if he has a few minutes for me?"

"Will do. He's in the main conference room working."

"Thanks, Julie."

Alicia took a few breaths to calm her nerves. She braced herself thinking of how to broach the subject with Stephen. She didn't really believe that he would make it an issue. Jack, on the other hand, expected Stephen to go ballistic. He had about thirty minutes before he needed to leave, and he was going to stick around just in case. Stephen was the most sexist man Jack knew. He kept it fairly quiet, but spending any time with him brought one to the realization that he really treated women as second class citizens. Jack would have fired him if he had done anything remotely wrong at work. The problem was that he was a brilliant investor. There had been rumors about infidelity in the office, but Jack had not been able to confirm the gossip. If the rumors had been true, Stephen would be gone.

"Alicia, Julie said you needed to speak with me?" Stephen entered her office, his impeccable suit perfectly creased, his silk tie knotted and centered. For some reason, he looked slightly off center, though he was perfectly dressed and his hair was carefully styled. Alicia couldn't quite put a finger on it, but something was always a little off with Stephen. She could no longer figure out why she had even dated him, let alone married him.

"Yes, I just need a few moments. Could you close the door?"

Stephen looked at her inquiringly as he shut her office door and stood waiting for her to speak.

"First of all, I really do want to congratulate you on your upcoming wedding and your baby's birth." Alicia smiled as she spoke.

"Thank you."

"I needed to tell you something before someone else told you. I'm seeing someone and it's serious." Alicia watched Stephen's face for an indication of his reaction.

"Okay." Stephen waited silently.

"I didn't want you to find out from anyone else. It's a woman."

Stephen froze, and his eyes widened with shock. "Excuse me—I thought you said a woman?"

"I did." Alicia stared at him, watching the information sink in.

"You're a dyke?" The words came out in a snarl. His face flushed with anger. "You're a fucking dyke!"

"Stephen, watch your mouth!" Alicia rose up from her chair, furious at his words and his tone of voice.

"I'll say what I goddamn please! It's that slut of a sister you have. I knew it!"

"Don't talk about Maddy that way!" Alicia was white hot as she reacted to his attack on her sister.

"So, you're fucking women now? No wonder you were no good in bed! I'm so glad I got rid of you!" Stephen's words came out with vicious intensity.

"Get out!" Alicia wouldn't put up with his abuse.

"Glad to—a fucking dyke! Wait until I broadcast this news!" Stephen's face was distorted with hatred, his eyes dark with abhorrence.

Alicia froze as she stared into the glaring eyes of her ex-husband. "You tell anyone and I will let them know what I found on the computer at our house."

"You wouldn't dare!" Stephen moved up to Alicia's desk, menace in every step.

"Just try me!" Alicia had never told anyone that her husband had been collecting porn on their home computer. Some of it contained very young girls. The content had turned Alicia's stomach when she had found it, making her sick with revulsion. The last time she had let Stephen touch her was just before her discovery. Her stomach had revolted at the thought of him coming near her.

"No one would believe you." Stephen raised his hand as if to hit her.

"I wouldn't touch her if I were you." Jack's voice was soft but it carried across the room. "I suggest Stephen that you go to the restroom and compose yourself. When you calm down, I'm sure that you will understand that I will not tolerate any abusive words or actions toward any of my employees. That will get you terminated."

Stephen remained silent, his eyes blazing with anger. He turned and, without another word, stormed out of Alicia's office.

Alicia sat down, shaking, in total shock over the events of the last few minutes. "Alicia, are you okay?" Jack asked, his eyes kind.

"I'll be fine in a minute. Thanks, Jack."

"I'm sorry."

"You have nothing to be sorry for. I'm the one who should apologize. I should have spoken to him outside of work hours." Alicia was appalled and embarrassed at the scene between her and Stephen. The fact that her boss had come upon it was devastating to her. How could she have lived with Stephen for almost two years and not know him at all?

"Alicia, you did nothing wrong. Put the blame where it belongs, with Stephen," Jack responded. He was glad that Alicia's secretary had called him. She had heard Stephen's vicious attack on his ex-wife.

Alicia's hurt eyes met Jack's. "I can't believe what came out of his mouth."

Jack wisely didn't remind her that he had warned her. "Alicia, promise me. If Stephen says **or does** anything else inappropriate to you, you let me know."

"I think **the worst** is over, Jack."

Jack knew better. He was going to have his own talk with Stephen. "Promise me."

"I promise. Now, go on and get out of here. You have a soccer game to get to." Alicia didn't want to talk about the ugliness any more.

"I dropped the plans off with Julie."

"Thanks. I'll have Reed look them over before tomorrow."

"Alicia, let it go," Jack requested softly. "It's Stephen's problem, not yours."

"I know." Alicia managed a shaky smile as her boss left her office.

Chapter Fourteen

Alicia tried to let it go, she really did. But the more she thought about it, the more upset she got. By the time she arrived at Maddy's, she was completely furious, hurt, and overwhelmed. She entered the front door, and Reed smiled at her as she came to meet her. Reed didn't have to be told something was wrong. Alicia's pale blue eyes were cloudy with hurt, and Reed could see into her soul.

Reed reached out and gathered Alicia to her with her good arm and hugged her tightly. Alicia pressed into the embrace, locking her arms around Reed's waist and let the warmth of her new lover comfort her.

"Hi baby," Reed whispered as she placed a kiss on her cheek. "What's wrong?"

Alicia looked into deep brown eyes and sighed. She needed to tell Reed and Maddy what had happened, but the hurt was so fresh and raw. "I told Stephen about us."

"And ..." Reed placed her hand on Alicia's pale cheek and watched her carefully.

Alicia tilted her head against Reed's hand as she answered, needing the touch of her to make her feel safe. "He didn't respond too well."

Reed felt Alicia start to tremble, and her heart splintered. "Come here, baby."

Reed led Alicia into the bedroom and then she gently sat her down on the bed. She knelt in front of her, her hand clasping Alicia's as she looked up at her. "Tell me what happened."

"Oh, Reed, it was awful! He was so angry and he called me a fucking dyke, then he threatened to tell everyone."

Reed felt her temper blaze as she listened. Now was not the time to show her anger. "What did you do?"

Alicia placed both her arms around Reed's neck as she spoke. "I never told Maddy why I stopped sleeping with Stephen within months of marrying him. I found out he collected pornography on our home computer. He had pictures of little girls having sex with older men. I threatened Stephen that I would tell everyone about his collection if he said anything more. I didn't leave him then and I should have, but he threatened that if I divorced him, he would make me pay. It wasn't until everyone knew he was screwing around that I felt safe enough to divorce him."

Reed saw the horror on Alicia's face and she tightened her hold on her hand. She was so angry she could have killed Alicia's ex-husband on the spot. "It's going to be okay, Alicia."

Alicia heard the cold anger in Reed's voice and worried that it was her fault. "Reed, I don't care about people knowing about us. It was what he said that was so degrading to us and Maddy. I never knew he felt that way. When I threatened to tell others about his pornography, I was afraid he was going to hit me."

Reed stood swiftly, her eyes shooting daggers as she looked around for her wallet and keys. "I'm going to kill the bastard!"

Alicia rose and grabbed Reed by the waist. "Honey, wait, he didn't touch me. Jack came in and suggested that Stephen leave and get himself under control. Jack told him he wouldn't tolerate any abusive language or behavior. Stephen left."

"I could kill him with my bare hands," Reed hissed. Her anger toward the man was almost unmanageable, her body taut with strength and rage.

Alicia reached up and placed both hands on Reed's face tugging her closer until they were inches apart. "But you won't because I love you and I don't want you involved."

Alicia's profession of love knocked every bit of anger out of Reed's mind. "God, I love you," Reed choked out as she pulled Alicia close and kissed her.

Alicia was overwhelmed by Reed's statement. Her kisses covered her face and neck, finally meeting her lips again in a way that told Alicia more than any words how much Reed cared about her. Alicia stroked Reed's back and hips, loving the strength and shape of her as they kindled the passion that lay just below the surface.

"I need to touch you," Reed confessed, reaching down and tugging Alicia's silk shirt from her pants.

"I need you, honey." Alicia trembled as Reed stepped away and stared at Alicia.

"You said you love me. Do you mean it?"

"With every part of me." Alicia smiled as she slowly unbuttoned her blouse and slid it down her arms. Reed's eyes dropped to her snowy white lace bra and then back to her face.

"God, you are so incredible. I just can't believe that you want to be with me," Reed said, reaching out with her hand, placing it on Alicia's stomach, and slowly caressing her perfect skin.

"Believe it," Alicia whispered, as she unbuttoned Reed's work shirt and pushed it carefully off her injured hand. Seeing Reed's unfettered breasts, so full and accessible, made Alicia groan. She bent her head, and her tongue slid flat against Reed's nipple.

"Jesus!" Reed cried, as Alicia backed her up to the bed and then pushed her flat on her back. Alicia straddled Reed's hips, as her lips worked first on one nipple and then the other, and her hands rapidly unbuttoned Reed's pants. Before Reed could do anything other than lie back and enjoy the sensations flooding through her body, Alicia had her completely naked.

"I love your body. I don't think I'll ever get enough of it," Alicia admitted, as she knelt between Reed's legs, her eyes drinking in the view in front of her. Alicia slid her hands up Reed's thighs to where they met in the center, her fingers trailing in the wetness glistening in the dark triangle of hair. "I need to taste you, honey."

Reed thought she would explode when Alicia's hot mouth met her body, and she sucked heavily on Reed's clitoris. Alicia's fingers played at the entrance to Reed's body, teasing her while her lips and tongue wreaked havoc.

"Baby, I need you inside, God, please," Reed begged, and Alicia snarled with pleasure pushing two fingers deeply into Reed's body. "Yes, that's it."

Alicia stroked and plundered until Reed was weak and trembling on the bed, too overwhelmed even to speak. Alicia kissed her way slowly up Reed's now slack body until she met her mouth gently, softly. She laid her head on her chest.

"Reed, I love you." Alicia turned to look into Reed's eyes as she spoke, her heart full of passion for the woman that had awakened her heart.

Reed reached up and stroked the hair away from Alicia's face and cupped her fingers around her neck, pulling her closer. "I will always love you, Alicia. There is nothing you can't talk to me about. I will always be there, making sure your dreams come true."

"You are my dream."

"Then I guess we better talk about when you want to have children." Alicia's eyes overflowed with tears as she looked at the smiling face of her lover. "I'd better finish our house and put in a nursery."

"You would do that?"

"In a heartbeat," Reed promised, as she gently rolled Alicia onto her back. "But promise me you will keep your boat. We can teach our kids to swim. I fell in love with you on the boat."

"We'll keep it," Alicia promised, as Reed's fingers began to tease her nipples.

"Don't move, baby. I need to touch you in the worst way." And touch her she did. Reed covered every inch of Alicia's body with her mouth and her fingertips until Alicia was begging for release. And then Reed's mouth covered her swollen, wet center and brought her to orgasm so many times Alicia lost count. She fell asleep after screaming in pleasure against Reed's chest, drifting quietly into a light slumber.

Reed enjoyed watching Alicia sleep, knowing it was due in part to her emotional day and partly to their incredible lovemaking. She loved how she looked so relaxed and happy, her face tucked against Reed's shoulder, her arm around Reed's waist. Reed gently slipped away from her and lovingly covered her with a sheet before cleaning up and dressing. She left her to finish preparing dinner.

Reed was in the newly finished kitchen pulling lasagna from the oven when Maddy came bursting through the front door.

"Hey, Reed."

"Hi, Maddy."

"Where's Alicia?" Maddy had seen her car parked behind Reed's truck.

"She's sleeping." Reed placed the casserole dish on the stove.

"Sleeping! It's six-thirty, what's she sleeping for? You wear her out?" Maddy grinned at Reed, opened the refrigerator, and pulled out a bottle of water.

"She's had a rough day, Maddy." Reed began to set the table for three people.

"What happened?" Maddy was instantly concerned.

"She told that bastard of an ex-husband about me today. He threatened her."

"He what? I'll kill him, goddamn him, I'll rip his prick off and stuff it down his throat!" Maddy raged and turned to leave the kitchen. She was going to kill him!

"Maddy, I'm okay." Alicia's calm voice cut through Maddy's tirade. She entered the kitchen wearing a button shirt of Reed's and a pair of jeans. Her face showed signs of sleep, but her eyes were clear. She went up to Reed and kissed her softly.

"Alicia, tell her what happened," Reed requested, her hand gentle on Alicia's face.

Alicia sighed and turned to face her sister. "Maddy, promise you'll let me handle this?"

"But, I ..." Maddy was white hot furious.

"Promise me," Alicia insisted.

"Okay, Le Le, but if he hurts you, I won't be able to keep my promise."

"If he hurts her, you'll let me handle it," Reed demanded, wrapping an arm around Alicia's waist. Reed's was no longer the out-of-control anger that Maddy displayed. Reed's was fury that would wait until she could exact restitution for her lover. It was deadly. Maddy recognized and respected Reed's feelings.

Alicia turned to Reed and slipped her arms around her holding her tightly. "Reed, promise me you won't do anything without talking to me first. I can't let you do anything that will put you in the middle, please."

"Alicia ..." Reed pleaded.

"Promise me." Alicia's beautiful face stopped Reed in her tracks.

Sighing, Reed bent and touched her forehead to Alicia's. "I promise I won't do anything without talking to you first."

"I love you."

"I love you."

"Goddamn it, tell me what happened!" Maddy was still unappeased. "Le Le, what happened?"

Alicia went to her sister and hugged her before speaking. "Maddy it wasn't that bad. Sit down and I'll tell you."

Maddy reluctantly took a seat at the counter, and Alicia calmly repeated what had happened with Stephen. The story only made Maddy angrier. "Le Le, why didn't you tell me about this before? I would have demanded you leave that prick months before you did. He's sick."

Before Alicia could respond, Reed interrupted Maddy. "It's over with, Maddy. Stephen will never ever bother Alicia again. None of us will allow it."

"But ..."

"Maddy, let it go." Reed knew Alicia needed to move on and let go of the past. It was time.

"Le Le, I love you. I think you are the most amazing person." Maddy hugged her sister tightly.

"I love you, Maddy. I've learned so much from you. You've been there for me through everything."

"Now I get to see you be happy with my best friend. I think that's pretty cool."

"So do I." Alicia's eyes caught and held Reed's and she smiled. Reed loved her, and that was all that mattered.

After dinner, Reed sat at the dining room table reviewing the plans for Alicia's office remodel. Alicia sat next to her going over a spreadsheet on her computer. Maddy had gone to her room to curl up with a good book. The house was silent and peaceful. Alicia turned and studied Reed as she worked. She would look at the plans and then scrawl something on a tablet and then go back to the plans. Her focus was total while she worked, and Alicia couldn't help noticing how sexy she was in her jeans and tee shirt, her dark hair tousled. Alicia bent over and ran a hand up her back in a slow caress.

"Hey, how are you doing?" Reed turned her head and looked at Alicia, her eyes warm with feeling.

"I'm fine. I just needed to tell you how much you mean to me."

"I love you, Alicia. Everything is different now that you're in my life."

Alicia's fingertips touched Reed's chin and she smiled. "You've made my life whole. Everything has changed for me. I think I can handle anything as long as you're with me."

"Then we should be fine because you're stuck with me, baby." Reed smiled and bent over to kiss her.

"I know. Isn't that perfect?" Alicia kissed Reed and then turned back to her computer.

Reed grinned and watched Alicia for a moment, then went back to the plans in front of her. A little over an hour later, Reed sat back and turned to find Alicia watching her with a beautiful smile.

"You ready to go to bed?"

"Yes." Alicia continued to stare at her with pleasure.

"What?" Reed chuckled as she stood up, reached down and tugged on Alicia's hand.

"I think you are so sexy. I just love looking at you."

Reed pulled Alicia against her and nuzzled her neck with her lips. "How about we go to bed and you can do more than look at me?"

"I'd love to." Alicia followed Reed into the bedroom. After sharing the sink to wash up and brush their teeth, they both crawled into bed and met in the middle, facing each other.

"Alicia, I know this is happening very fast and if you're finding any of this uncomfortable, please tell me."

Alicia moved closer to Reed until she was touching her naked body from head to toe. She loved how Reed's eyes grew darker when she was aroused. "I'm not uncomfortable. I was thinking all night long of how to ask you to move in with me while you finish building your house."

"Our house—and all you have to do is ask."

"Reed, will you live with me?"

"Yes." Reed covered Alicia's mouth in a kiss, a promise, a—commitment—one they both wanted to make.

Reed was gentle with her lovemaking bringing Alicia slowly to an orgasm and, as Alicia peaked, Reed tumbled with her. This was the most perfect culmination to their commitment.

"Oh, God," Reed gasped, as Alicia cried out her pleasure. Alicia wrapped her arms around Reed's trembling body, their faces touching, their eyes staring into each other's.

"It's always so perfect," Alicia whispered as Reed rolled to the side of her, still holding her tightly.

"It is incredible," Reed admitted as she stroked Alicia's face. "You need to go to sleep, baby. It's getting late.

"I will. I just need to hold you for a little longer."

"I'll hold you all night."

They drifted into perfect sleep, still in each other's arms, protected and secure.

The cell phone vibrated softly where it lay in Alicia briefcase. No one heard it in the silent house. It kicked over into voice mail, and the vicious message would remain unheard until the next morning.

Chapter Fifteen

Alicia listened to the message on her way to work and it scared her to death.

"Hello bitch! You think Jack is going to keep me away from you? You will pay for making a fool out of me, you fucking dyke! I am going to punish you, you bitch. You and your fucking sister are going to pay! When I'm through with the two of you, you will wish you were dead!"

Alicia thought long and hard about telling Reed or Maddy about the call and then decided against it. As long as Stephen just left threatening messages she could deal with it. If she told Reed or Maddy, they would go after him. She couldn't let that happen. She wouldn't let either one of them get hurt. She would protect them with her last breath.

Alicia's day was so busy she'd put everything to the back of her mind until one-thirty. Reed was scheduled to arrive in thirty minutes, and Alicia was extremely nervous. They'd spoken briefly before lunch but that had been three hours earlier. Reed had been at her Capital Hill job checking on the crew that was due to arrive to install the wallboard. She also had a walk-through with the owner of the house who wanted a status report. She hadn't been able to talk long.

Alicia fidgeted at her desk as she thought of how much her life had changed in such a short time. She couldn't imagine her life without Reed in it. It hadn't been two weeks since she met Reed, and already she was completely and irrevocably committed to her and their life together. Her intercom beeped as she sat in thought.

"Alicia, your hottie is here," Julie whispered.

"I'll be right out." Alicia smiled as she rose from behind her desk and walked out to meet Reed. She was completely amazed at the sight of her lover. Reed was wearing a dark blue silk suit and a pale blue tee shirt. Gone was the jean-clad carpenter, replaced with the fashionable owner of a successful company. Reed's dark eyes met Alicia's, and then there was a subtle wink that made Alicia grin. "Hello."

"Hi." So much could be said without words. Reed conveyed with a lift of her eyebrow and the dimples in her cheeks just how much she loved Alicia.

Alicia walked to within a foot of Reed and placed her hand on Reed's arm. "Reed, this is Julie. Julie, this is Reed Thomas."

"Hello, I've heard a lot about you, Ms. Thomas."

"Only believe half of it," Reed responded, her voice deep and musical. "I believe I have a two o'clock appointment with Mr. Turner?"

Alicia snorted with humor as Julie grinned at the charming woman. "Julie, I'll take her to Jack's office."

"It was nice to meet you, Julie." Reed smiled and followed Alicia down the hall.

Julie stared at the receding figures and then let out a breath. "Oh, wow, no wonder Alicia bit the dust!"

"Stop it," Alicia whispered, as Reed glanced her way.

"Stop what?" Reed asked, innocently.

"Charming the pants off Julie," Alicia whispered, her eyes locked onto her lover.

"The only woman I'm interested in charming the pants off is you. I only want you," Reed whispered, her eyes hot with emotion.

"I love you."

"Good, because I adore you."

Alicia rapped her knuckles on Jack's door. "Come in."

"Jack, this is Reed Thomas. Reed, this is my boss and the owner of the company, Jack Turner."

"Hello, Mr. Turner." Reed reached out and shook his hand.

"Jack. Please have seat Ms. Thomas." Jack took stock of the woman that had captured Alicia's affections.

"Call me Reed." Reed took a seat, making herself comfortable in the leather chair across from Jack's desk.

"I'll leave you two to talk." Alicia turned to leave the office.

"Alicia, stay," Jack requested, smiling at her. "You know as much about this remodel as anyone."

"Certainly." Alicia sat down next to Reed in the matching chair. She was looking forward to watching Reed at work.

"What happened to your hand?"

"I put it in the wrong place at the wrong time and a beam landed on it," Reed responded. "It looks worse than it is."

"I hope there's no lasting problem."

"The prognosis is that everything will work just as well as it always has, though the healing will take some time."

"You must be happy about that! So, Reed, I assume you've had a chance to review the plans?"

"Yes, I did and I have some questions." Reed pulled a folded piece of paper from her jacket pocket. "Your previous contractor provided you with an estimate of time and materials that, in my review, is not accurate. The materials are way under priced, and the time and labor was padded by about thirty percent. You wanted a mahogany wood front desk that curved around with no straight edges. The estimate is not for solid wood. The quote is for a laminated wood product. You won't be happy with it after six months. It won't look like real mahogany, and it won't stand up to the normal use of a reception desk."

"I see. Have you prepared a new estimate?" Jack looked thoughtfully back at Reed. His experience in business had taught him to keep his thoughts to himself until he had all the information at his disposal.

"Yes, the materials will easily be twice as much as the original bid, but we can get the job done in a little more than three weeks if we work during the evening and at night so as not to disrupt your business. If we can also work during the day, we could finish the job from start to finish in less than ten days." Reed handed the typed bid to him.

"Starting when?" Jack asked as he reviewed the detailed, itemized bid.

"We could start Monday of next week."

"Did you bring a contract for me to sign?" Jack found Reed's direct delivery very appealing. There was no nonsense, just complete professionalism in her manner. He also respected the fact that she wasn't afraid to point out the issues she had uncovered in the previous bid. His brief contact with Reed told him a lot about her character.

"I did. I also took the opportunity to add an incentive clause to the effect that if we complete the job to your satisfaction in seven days, you'll pay my crew ten percent over the contract."

Jack's grin was wide, his expression one of appreciation. "I like your business style, Reed."

Reed's face broke into a smile, her dimples winking in her cheeks. "Thanks—honesty usually works well in business."

"Yes, it does. Hand me the contract. I'll sign it right now."

"Don't you want your legal team to review it?"

"Nope, your word is good enough. Let me sign it."

Reed pulled the completed contract out of her pocket, unfolded it and handed it to Jack. She glanced over at Alicia and met her eyes, hot with emotion. She winked and then turned back to Jack.

"Jack, is there any problem with my taking this job given the fact that Alicia and I have a relationship?"

Alicia's eyes widened at the question. She hadn't been expecting Reed to be so open with him. She watched as Jack looked up from signing the contract. He studied the two women in front of him before responding.

"Reed, there is nothing remotely wrong with your relationship with Alicia. I for one am extremely pleased that Alicia has found someone worthy of her. There will be talk in this office from some, if and when they find out about the two of you. I'm sure you both can handle a little gossip. I am worried about Alicia's ex-husband. I'm watching him very carefully and I don't want to overreact, but Stephen may be a problem."

"I will …" Alicia started to speak, but Reed placed a hand gently on her arm and interrupted her.

"He will not hurt Alicia in any way. I will not allow it. He is only powerful if he thinks he can control someone. He has no control over Alicia or me. I want you to assure me that Alicia's job is not in jeopardy because of our relationship."

Jack's respect for Alicia's choice in partners went up by several notches. He gazed back at Reed's face and her serious dark eyes. "I assure you Reed Alicia's job is not now nor ever will be in jeopardy due to her relationship with you. I will also assure both of you that if Stephen does anything else inappropriate or unacceptable, he will be terminated. You have my word."

"Thank you." Reed looked directly into Jack's eyes and saw his resolve. She could trust him.

"You don't need to thank me. I care about Alicia." Jack smiled at the couple and then chuckled. "Now, let me sign your contract."

Reed knew Alicia was probably not too happy about her bringing their relationship into the meeting. She fully expected Alicia to react negatively. She took the signed contract from Jack and signed it herself. "Can I get a copy of this? Then I'll leave the original with you."

"Certainly. Alicia, can you have Julie make a copy for Reed?"

"I will." Alicia's eyes were veiled, her thoughts hidden. Reed stood up and shook Jack's hand.

"It's been a pleasure, Reed."

"Same here. We'll be on site as soon as you give the go ahead."

"Let's start on Monday and I have no issues with your crew working during the day. I'm sure you know how to work around a functioning office."

"My workers are very competent."

"Excellent. I look forward to paying the incentive fee." Jack grinned at her. He fully expected Reed and her company to complete the job early and perfectly.

"Then Monday it is. I'll be here at six a.m. to get them started. Is there a security guard or someone else that we can contact to let us in?"

"Alicia, can you provide Reed and her team with a security card for entry? The guard office is down in the front lobby."

"I can."

"Good. Reed, let me or Alicia know if you run into any unforeseen problems."

"I will. Thank you." Reed and Alicia stepped out of his office.

Jack watched the two stunning women walk down the hall side by side. *Alicia, you made a very good choice*, he thought. Two smart, professional, thoroughly sexy women and they were a couple. You only had to look at them to know that they were together. They were an excellent match.

Chapter Sixteen

R eed remained silent as she followed Alicia down the hall to Julie's desk.

"Julie, can you make a copy of this contract for Reed? The original should go back to Jack for his files. Also, we need to prepare an access card for Reed and her team. They're starting the remodel of the front office next Monday."

"Cool! Yes, I can take care of that. Can you wait a couple of minutes for me to get the card done?"

"Yes, we'll wait in my office."

"Julie, if we move your desk over to the far right of this room while we work, would you be too inconvenienced?" Reed had been studying the space, her mind working out how to set up the work.

"Nope. I don't care if I have to work in a closet during the remodel."

Reed grinned down at her. "I promise you we won't put you in a closet. And I will make sure everyone understands it's a working office."

"I can't wait for everything to get under way."

Alicia stepped through the door to her office and Reed followed her inside, closing the door behind her. She fully expected to be chastised. Alicia turned and her eyes studied Reed's face. She closed the space between them until she was inches from her. Alicia placed her hand on Reed's chest and spoke.

"I need to talk to you about your trying to protect me."

"Alicia, I ..."

"I love you, Reed, so much that I can't imagine life without you. The fact that you talked to Jack about our relationship is so important to me. I know you feel the need to protect me and I love that about you. But I need to remind you of something—we are a couple. I need to protect you as much as you feel the need to keep me safe."

Alicia's lips met Reed's softly, and then she stepped away from Reed before she was overwhelmed with her feelings.

"I'm sorry, but I go crazy inside thinking about your ex-husband," Reed admitted, her eyes hot with feeling.

"That's okay—I go crazy thinking about your last girlfriend," Alicia admitted with a frown. "I don't want to think of anyone else touching you."

"No one ever touched me the way you do," Reed whispered, reaching out and trailing her fingers down Alicia's cheek.

"Reed, Stephen called my cell phone last night at two-thirty in the morning. I listened to the message this morning on the way to work. It was pretty awful." Alicia had to tell Reed about the call. They were lovers, and she wanted Reed to be able to trust her. Being honest about the call was the only way.

Reed froze at Alicia's words. "Why didn't you call me after you listened to it?"

"I didn't want you to go after him." Alicia could feel Reed pulling away from her and her heart froze. "I don't want anything to happen to you."

"Don't you think I feel the same way? We're a couple. He's threatening you. I want to kill him!" Reed lashed out, her eyes wild.

Alicia reached out and locked her arms around Reed's neck. "But you won't because you love me, and I want to be with you for the rest of my life. Stephen doesn't count."

Reed's arms tightened around Alicia, and she pressed her forehead against Alicia's. "You will tell me if he calls you again or does anything else?"

"Immediately, I promise. I love you." Alicia felt Reed's body relax against her. "Reed, how soon can you move in with me?"

"How's this weekend sound?"

"Perfect, absolutely perfect."

"Alicia, I'm not a pauper. I expect to pay my way."

"Honey, we'll talk about it tonight. Would you stay at our place tonight?"

"You're not getting out of my sight."

"Good. I'll write down the address, and I'll be home by six."

"I'll be there." Reed took the address from Alicia and moved to the door, then turned and grinned at Alicia. "I liked your boss."

"He liked you."

"Good thing since you're going to marry me," Reed responded, stepping through the door. "Julie, can I get the copy of my contract and the security card?"

"It's all right here."

"Thanks see you on Monday."

Julie watched the dynamic woman stride down the hall. It was then she noticed the bandaged left hand. She burst into Alicia's office and found her standing, looking out her window.

"Alicia, what happened to Reed's hand?"

"A beam was dropped on it. She has two broken fingers and a large cut. That was the emergency I left work for."

"Is she going to be okay?"

"Yes, she's going to be fine."

"Alicia, she's gorgeous," Julie responded with a big grin, "smart, charming, and beautiful."

Alicia smiled and nodded. "Yes, she is. She's special."

"And she's yours."

Alicia laughed with happiness. "Yes, she is."

"You both got very lucky."

Alicia had to agree with Julie. Her life was perfect. She had almost forgotten all about Stephen.

Reed would have agreed to Alicia's assessment if she'd heard it and if she'd had a free moment to think about it. She needed to get all the supplies ordered and delivered to meet the weekly deadline to complete the job. She had not a moment to spare. She was also still worried about Stephen. She didn't want him to hurt Alicia any more. She headed for Maddy's home to change and make some telephone calls. Reed loved a challenge, and she needed to form a plan about how to protect Alicia.

"So you can give me a week?" Reed was making her last call.

"I can. The faxed plans don't look so hard. I can get the mahogany here by Friday afternoon, and I'll make a jig Saturday and steam the wood. It'll be shaped by Monday morning. Then I'll work on the molding and top. It should be ready for staining by Tuesday morning and installation by Wednesday."

"Good, I'll be there on Wednesday to help with the install."

"With your bum hand, I don't think so."

"I'm just glad you're available." If Reed couldn't do the woodworking, her best carpenter was her second choice. Tim had worked for her father and now Reed for years. He knew more about woodworking than anyone, including Reed.

"Always, for you. Besides, this is your new girlfriend's company. We have to make a good impression." Tim's voice was full of humor. He loved to tease Reed.

Reed knew she was being teased and took it graciously. "Thanks, Tim."

"Don't thank me. Your dad and now you have kept me in paychecks for many years."

"You do great work."

"Well then, let me get to it."

"See you Tuesday and call me if you run into any problems."

"Will do."

Reed reviewed her list and checked off another item. She was actually surprised that she had accomplished so much in the last few hours. She would finish up early tomorrow and be ready to stage the job at Alicia's office by late afternoon. Checking her watch, she stood up and collected all of her papers. She shoved them inside her battered briefcase and headed for her bedroom.

"Hey, roomie, what are you up to?"

"I'm heading over to Alicia's place for the night," Reed met Bet at the foot of the stairs.

"Things are going good between the two of you?"

"Things are going perfectly."

"I'm glad, Reed."

"Gotta go. By the way, I'm moving in with Alicia this weekend, so I'll be out of your hair by Sunday." Reed had decided to keep the knowledge of Stephen's telephone call to herself. If she told Bet, Maddy would find out and she would want to go after Stephen.

"You're what?"

"You heard me. I'll explain it all this weekend." Reed grinned and entered her bedroom. Grabbing her overnight bag, she turned and headed back down the hall. Bet was still standing at the foot of the stairs.

"You're moving in with Alicia? Does Maddy know?"

"No, why? Will she have a problem with it?" Bet's question stopped her in her tracks.

"No, she won't have a problem with it. She and I were hoping that you two would hit it off. She's worried about Stephen bothering Alicia, though."

"He won't." Bet had no doubt Reed would protect Alicia. She knew her friend well.

"Good, she'll be relieved." Bet hugged Reed affectionately. "Let us know if you two need help moving you."

"Tell her not to worry. I've got to go."

"See you."

Bet was just finishing preparing a salad when Maddy burst through the front door. Bet smiled at her lover's entrance. Maddy was exuberant about everything. It was one of her most endearing qualities. "Hey, honey, I'm working in our newly remodeled kitchen!"

"Reed did a great job, didn't she?"

"Yes, she did. By the way, she's moving in with Alicia this weekend."

There wasn't much that surprised Maddy, but that news set her back. "For real?"

"Yep, and Reed told me to tell you not to worry about Stephen."

"Yeah, and that isn't going to happen," Maddy snorted. "I always knew he was a sicko."

"Yes he is, and I don't think he is going to leave Alicia alone. I think he's going to try and punish her in some way for being with Reed."

Maddy listened to Bet carefully. She trusted Bet's perspective on everything. "So what do we do?"

"Let Reed do what she does best—love Alicia completely. She won't allow Stephen to harm Alicia. She'll protect her with her life. She loves Alicia."

"Isn't that amazing?"

"It is, isn't it?" Bet hugged her girlfriend tightly.

Chapter Seventeen

Reed pushed on the buzzer to the front door of the high-end building. She had her overnight bag and briefcase with her, along with one perfectly formed sterling silver rose. "Come in."

"Don't you think you ought to ask who it is?" Reed spoke loudly into the speaker.

"Look up in the corner of the entry. There's a security camera. I know exactly who you are, my stunning lover." Alicia's voice was full of humor. "The rose is beautiful. Are you coming in?"

Reed just snorted as the door clicked open. She stepped through the doorway and headed to the elevator. She knew Alicia's place was on the third floor. By the time the elevator door opened, Alicia was standing just outside her door. She was wearing silk pajamas the color of peaches, and she looked stunning.

"Hello." Alicia's smile was full and welcoming.

"Hi. Since you already saw the rose, here you go." Reed handed the rosebud to Alicia.

"Thank you. It's beautiful and so are you." Reed was wearing a pair of faded 501s that hung on her slender hips. A bright red tee shirt fit snugly on her upper body, and she wore leather moccasins. Her coal black hair was shiny and tied back by a leather cord. Alicia thought she looked incredibly sexy.

"Can we take this inside so I can kiss you?" Reed surrounded Alicia with her good arm, walking her backwards into the loft. "I really need to touch you."

"That's good to know because I have a craving to be touched by you."

Reed met Alicia's mouth with a hungry kiss. It was a few minutes before either woman could catch her breath. "Well, that was a warm welcome."

Alicia laughed. "Come on, I'll show you around."

Reed liked the open feel of the loft with the high ceilings and the natural lighting that flooded the space. The kitchen was open to the dining area and the living space, with a small office, laundry room, and bathroom nestled behind the kitchen area. A free-standing wood staircase rose up majestically to the second story which contained two large bedrooms and an equally spacious bathroom. Reed was fine until they entered what was clearly Alicia's bedroom. Her scent permeated the room. Reed couldn't help but wonder if Alicia had slept with Stephen in the king-sized bed.

Alicia sighed as she watched the flood of emotions play across Reed's face. She didn't have to be told what was going through Reed's mind. "Honey, Stephen and I never slept in any bed in this place, and he never slept with me in this room."

Reed sighed and leaned into Alicia, as Alicia slid her arms around Reed's waist. "Glad to know."

"You are the only one to sleep with me here, and you will always be the only one. I love you."

"I love you, baby." Reed held her tightly against her, breathing in her citrus scent.

"Come on, let's feed you. Then you and I are going to talk about your need to protect me from Stephen."

Reed knew she hadn't dodged Alicia's irritation over her heavy handedness in Jack's office, and she understood. What Alicia didn't understand was that Reed would literally die if anything happened to Alicia. Her heart wouldn't take it. She couldn't stop from protecting her any more than she could stop breathing.

They shared a large crab salad and sipped on a crisp Pinot Blanc, sitting at the dining room table. It took Alicia quite a few moments to gather her thoughts before speaking to Reed. Alicia turned to face her, took a deep breath, and opened her mouth to speak. Reed beat her to the punch.

"I know I should apologize to you for bringing our relationship into your boss's office, Alicia. I know it wasn't appropriate, but you need to know that it would destroy me if anything happened to you."

"Honey, I'm not mad at you. I just need you to know that I can and I will take care of myself. I know you and Maddy think I'm a wimp, but I really can handle this."

"We don't think you're a wimp, but Maddy loves you so much. She would do anything for you and so would Bet. You're family."

"It's *our* family. You're as much a part of it as I am."

"Then you have to understand that when it comes to you, all of us want to protect you. Stephen is out of control." Alicia had walked directly into that one and she knew it.

"I agree, and so did Jack. I told him about the call. He called Stephen into his office this afternoon and wrote him up. He has a permanent record on file and a written warning. If he does anything else inappropriate to me, Jack will fire him."

"Good." That news didn't make Reed's uneasiness go away. She was afraid the humiliation of being chastised by his boss was going to incite Stephen to more drastic and dangerous behavior. "Could we talk about something else? I don't want to think about that creep any more than we have to tonight."

"Absolutely. Do you think you could handle living here until you finish our home?"

"It's an amazing space. I think we can handle this place, but don't you want to see what kind of house I'm building before you agree to live in it?"

"Reed, I know the type of work you do. It could be a one room cottage and I would want to live there with you."

"Then you'll really appreciate the fact that it's a one-story, three thousand square foot cottage. It has three fireplaces and a wraparound deck, so there's a perfect view of the lake. It has one hundred feet of lakefront property and a boat dock."

"It sounds unbelievable. How did you get such a large piece of property?"

"Years ago my dad decided investing in real estate was a smart thing to do. Every time he found a piece of land he liked and could afford, he bought it. By the time he passed away, he owned about fourteen separate parcels of land all over King County. I'm in the process of selling all but the one on the lake. In fact, do you know anyone who could guide me on some investment strategies?" Reed nuzzled Alicia's neck affectionately.

"I think I might know someone who could help you with that." Alicia smiled and rubbed her cheek against Reed's face. "Your parents must have been very proud of you."

"My dad was, he told me often enough. I think my mother would have been happier if I had been a little more feminine."

"You are feminine, and strong, smart, and beautiful."

"What about your parents? Would they have understood your relationship with me?"

"Reed, my parents loved Maddy and me unconditionally. My mother always said that when you loved someone and were true to your heart, no one had any reason to judge you. She would have liked you very much."

"What about your dad?"

"Dad and I were a lot alike. Maddy and my mom were the free spirits in the family. He taught me everything I know about finance. He was an accountant. His one love was my mother. He would like you very much because of your commitment to me."

"He sounds like a very nice man."

"You remind me a lot of him. He would have appreciated your dedication and talent. He would also have understood your need to protect me. He would have done anything to protect his family."

"As I will." Reed placed a soft, gentle kiss on Alicia's mouth. "Now, I have some work to do if I'm going to get your office remodel done in a week. Do you mind if I take an hour or so to study the plans?"

"Not at all. I have some of my own work to catch up on. I seem to have had a hard time concentrating this afternoon after you left." Alicia brushed her hand across Reed's broad shoulders. "But first I want to change the dressing on your hand and clean the wound. Did you make an appointment with your doctor?"

"I did. I have an appointment in the morning. He's going to take another set of x-rays and check the stitches."

"Do you need me to go with you?" Alicia knew her question would irritate Reed, and she wasn't mistaken.

"Honey, I can make it to the doctor by myself," Reed responded, her voice holding a trace of irritation.

"I know you're a big girl. I'm allowed to worry, too, aren't I?"

Reed grinned at Alicia. "I'm a very big girl, as you well know. I'll call you after the appointment. I'll need to set up some equipment and store some supplies at your office. Can I get in Saturday morning to do that?"

"Sure. I can let you in, and while you're working I can get some stuff done in my office."

"Excellent. Then I'm going to sweep you away for a night of romance at our new house."

"That sounds perfect."

"Okay, where can I work?"

"How about on the dining room table? It should be large enough for you to spread out your plans."

"Where will you work?"

"I can either work in my office or at the table right next to you."

"Right next to me, where I can look at you frequently and touch you as often as possible."

By ten o'clock Reed felt she was familiar with every inch of the plans. She had four pages of notes and three major changes she was going to suggest to Jack. They would save him some money and make the design even more impressive. She stretched in her chair and turned to look at Alicia who moments earlier had been hunched over her computer typing madly. Reed had to smile as she caught sight of her sleeping lover. Alicia had dozed off, her computer propped on her lap. Alicia's head leaned back against the couch, and her feet rested casually on the coffee table. Reed stood up and walked quietly over to her, gently removing the computer and closing it before glancing back down at her lover. Alicia had had an emotional day, and Reed wasn't surprised that she was exhausted. Normally Reed would pick Alicia up and carry her to bed but with her injured hand she was unable to do that. She hated having to wake her up.

"Come on, baby, time for bed." Reed bent over and nuzzled Alicia's neck.

"I'm sorry, honey. I must have drifted off." Alicia sleepily stood up, sliding her arms around Reed's neck.

"That's okay, let's go crawl in bed so we can both get some sleep. It's been a busy couple of days." Reed tugged Alicia by the hand and almost before she knew it, Alicia was comfortably ensconced in her warm bed, Reed's naked body curled next to hers.

"I would love to make love with you but I am exhausted. Do you mind?" Alicia whispered as she kissed Reed.

"Oh honey, not at all. I love holding you as much as making love with you. Close your eyes, baby. We have the rest of our lives to make love. Go to sleep."

"I adore you, Reed."

"Isn't it amazing how that works? I love you."

"Goodnight."

They had been sleeping for almost two hours when the telephone rang, jangling loudly in the darkened bedroom. Alicia fumbled around and then picked up the receiver as Reed stirred beside her.

"Hello." Alicia's first thought was that something had happened to Bet or Maddy.

"You bitch! You think you and your dyke girlfriend are going to best me! I'm going to make you pay for turning Jack against me! You think you're safe from me? I'll destroy you and that half-man half-woman you are fucking!"

Alicia was so shocked at the foul, evil mutterings she was unable to respond. Her face had turned pale as she listened to the monster that was her ex-husband. Reed snatched the telephone from her hand.

"Listen you bastard! Don't call or speak to Alicia again or I will hunt you down and destroy you with my bare hands! You don't frighten us. We aren't going to play your game. Starting right this minute, we're calling the police and filing a report. We'll have a restraining order by midday. See if you can keep your job with something like that on your record."

"You fucking dyke, don't you love to play your dirty games with my ex-wife? Well, I had her first and she wasn't that good, so you're welcome to her!" Stephen slammed the telephone down.

Reed didn't hesitate. She dialed 911. "Hello, police, we just had an irate ex-husband make threats against his ex-wife. Could you have an officer come and see if he's outside her home? Reed Thomas, I'm her partner, and he just called. Yes, we'll both be here. Thank you."

Reed turned to Alicia and her heart almost broke. Alicia was weeping quietly. "Honey, I'm so sorry."

"It's not your fault. I brought Stephen into your life. He could hurt you."

"We won't let him hurt anyone. Come on, sweetheart. The police are on their way here and we'll file a report. He won't get away with this." Reed climbed out of bed and gathered up some clothes to put on.

By the time the police arrived, Alicia had been able to get a handle on her emotions and was thinking rationally. She was now royally pissed. Reed let the two officers into the loft, and Alicia calmly recited her story. The officers asked several questions as they recorded information.

"Ma'am, we didn't see anyone outside the building but that doesn't mean he isn't out there somewhere. We strongly suggest you file a restraining order against him. It will give you a little legal recourse. To be honest with you, unless he does something other than call you on the telephone, there's little we can do."

"I appreciate your coming out here at this time of night."

"No problem. Here's the number of our unit and our names. We'll file a police report, and you can use it to get a restraining order. I'm not sure they'll grant one with so little activity."

Reed swore under her breath. She felt totally ineffectual. She walked the officers to the door and then turned to look at Alicia. She hated not being able to fix everything. Alicia looked absolutely devastated once again.

Alicia watched the turbulence in Reed's eyes and knew exactly what her lover was thinking. "You can't make this go away, Reed."

Reed stepped up to Alicia and caught her as Alicia threw herself into Reed's arms. "I'm so sorry this is happening."

"Alicia, look at me, honey." Reed lifted Alicia's chin until she was looking directly at her. "This is not your fault, none of it. We'll deal with Stephen. He won't get away with intimidating us. I love you and nothing is going to change that."

"I love you, Reed, and I wish I could make this go away."

"Baby, I would do anything to make this end for you. Stephen has power only if we allow him to scare us. We won't let him get away with this."

"But he could hurt you." Her eyes were full of fear, and tears slid slowly down Alicia's face.

"He can't hurt me."

"We need to call Maddy and Bet and tell them what's going on. He might go after them." Alicia began to panic, and she struggled in Reed's arms.

"Alicia, wait honey. We'll call them first thing in the morning. Let them sleep. Morning will be soon enough. Come on, baby. Come back to bed and let me hold you for a little while."

"But ..."

"Come on, baby." Reed led Alicia back upstairs to bed. It took her a little over an hour to get Alicia to fall asleep. Reed lay awake long afterwards, worried about Alicia and what she could do to protect her. She would not let Stephen hurt Alicia, no matter what.

Chapter Eighteen

Both Alicia and Reed were quiet as they got ready for work. But it was the telephone call to Maddy and Bet that broke Alicia's control. She began to cry, and Reed held her and took the receiver from her hand.

"Bet, it's Reed."

"Reed, what did that bastard do?"

"He called and threatened Alicia last night. We called the police and filed a police report. They don't think we have enough for a restraining order, but we're going to contact my lawyer this morning and see what he thinks."

"We can help."

"You and Maddy need to be careful. He threatened all of us, and Alicia is worried he'll try to hurt you in some way."

"Oh, Reed!" Bet's heart broke for Alicia.

"Let me talk to Alicia," Maddy demanded, her heart pounding in her chest.

"Honey, Maddy wants to talk to you." Alicia's tearstained face made Reed ache. She handed the telephone to her.

"Maddy, I'm sorry."

"Honey, it's not your fault." Maddy began to cry. "Don't you worry about us, we'll be fine. You take care of Reed."

"I will. I'm so sorry."

"It's okay, sweetheart. It's going to be okay. Let me talk to Reed again." Alicia handed the telephone back to Reed, her pale blue eyes red with exhaustion.

"Maddy, it's Reed."

"Don't let him hurt her," Maddy cried, her heart aching for her sister.

"I won't. I promise you."

"Good."

"We'll call you later after I get Alicia to work. I'm going to drive her in and pick her up. She'll be fine at work. Her boss knows about Stephen, and he won't let anything happen."

"Call us."

"I will." Reed put the telephone down and wrapped her arms around Alicia, holding her tightly. She rubbed her hand up and down Alicia's back trying to help her relax.

"I love you, Reed."

"Alicia, I love you."

"Let's go to work. I'm through letting Stephen control my life. If he thinks I'm going to cower because of his threats, he's crazier than I think he is." Alicia's pale eyes snapped with temper.

Reed sighed with relief. At least if Alicia was mad she would be able to deal with Stephen. "Come on, baby. I'll drop you off at work and get to the doctor's. Then I'll start staging everything this afternoon at your office. You and I can get away from all this and have a nice quiet weekend."

"That sounds delightful."

"We'll stay at Bet and Maddy's tonight and go to the house in the morning. You can help me grout tile."

Alicia's grin lifted Reed's spirits. She clasped her hand and declared, "I'd love to help. Come on, carpenter girl, let's go to work."

Reed chuckled as she picked up her bag and briefcase and followed Alicia into the elevator. Alicia would be fine. She was getting back on her feet.

In the truck, Reed kissed Alicia softly and then insisted on walking her into the building over Alicia's objections. Reed calmly and rationally ignored her as she explained that she needed to look at the work space. Both women knew that was just an excuse, but it made them both feel a little better to remain in each other's company for a little bit longer.

"Good morning, Julie."

"Hi, Alicia, Ms. Thomas."

"Call me Reed."

"Reed then. Jack has been waiting for you, Alicia. He wanted to speak to you the minute you arrived."

"Reed, I need to go talk to Jack." Alicia's eyes spoke volumes as she looked at Reed.

"I'll wait in your office for you."

"Reed ..."

"I'll wait."

"Okay, I'll be right back. Julie, could you get Reed a cup of coffee?"

"Of course."

Reed entered Alicia's office and sat down on a chair in front of her desk. She was worried that something else might have happened.

"Here's a cup of coffee and sugar and cream if you want some." Julie smiled and handed the cup to Reed. She could tell Reed was worried about Alicia. Her face was drawn, her eyes troubled.

"Thank you, Julie."

"You're welcome. If you need anything else, let me know."

Not two minutes later Alicia walked slowly into the room and sat behind her desk. Reed waited for her to speak. "Jack wanted to tell me that he had terminated Stephen as of last night. According to Jack, Stephen started talking to quite a few people in the office about my relationship with you. He was very disgusting about it, and several people went to Jack with their complaints. Stephen was fired for cause last night after I left."

Reed saw the devastation on Alicia face. She was mortified that people in the office had been involved. Reed reached out and gently clasped Alicia's hand. "I'm sorry, honey."

"I'm so embarrassed," Alicia confessed, her eyes brimming with tears.

"None of this is your fault, baby. Place all of this on Stephen's head. What else did your boss say?"

"He told me not to worry about my job or what Stephen said. He said the same thing—that this was all Stephen's doing. He not only fired him, he threatened to call the police if he ever bothered anyone who works for the company."

"No wonder he called you. He blames you for getting fired."

"He's not going to go away any time soon."

"He may just go back to Paris and leave you alone."

"He doesn't have any reason to go to Paris. His pregnant girlfriend also gave him the boot." Alicia's hand shook in Reed's grasp.

Reed looked at Alicia patiently and then responded. "We'll make sure he doesn't hurt anyone."

"Reed, I'm a little scared."

"So am I, Alicia," Reed admitted. "You'll be fine here at work. I'll be back at lunch time with my crew. I don't want you to leave this office, okay?"

"I won't. Please be careful, honey."

"I will, baby. I love you. Call me anytime."

Alicia watched Reed stride out of the office and then turned on her computer. She would focus her attention on her work. She had more than enough to keep her busy.

Alicia managed to stay occupied for most of her morning, dealing with one client file after another until she was caught up. Then she started identifying a list of potential new customers based on her latest research. By eleven, Alicia had all but forgotten about Stephen. Her brilliant mind had kicked in, and she did what she was best at. Julie interrupted her concentration.

"Alicia, Reed is on her way in and she's bringing lunch. She said she'd be here by noon. You were on the telephone when she called."

"Thanks, Julie."

"No problem. Alicia, are you okay?"

"I'm fine, why?"

Julie sat down on one of Alicia's chairs and spoke softly to her. "There are a lot of rumors going around today and one of them is that Stephen threatened you after he got fired last night."

Alicia sighed as she looked at Julie. "It's not a rumor."

Julie's compassionate heart overflowed. "God, I'm sorry, Alicia."

"It's okay, Julie. Jack is dealing with all this. And the police are watching out for Stephen."

"Is there anything I can do for you?"

"No thanks, Julie, I'm fine. I just need to concentrate on work."

"Okay, I'll get out of here unless you need me."

"Julie thanks." Alicia smiled up at her assistant.

"You're welcome. By the way, I sure like your Reed. She gave me her cell phone number and told me to call her if I thought you needed her here. She's a sweetie."

Her Reed, she was hers. Alicia smiled at Julie and shook her head in agreement. "She is a sweetheart."

Alicia's sweetheart arrived thirty minutes later bearing multiple gifts and accompanied by her team of workers. Alicia was surprised when she was introduced to her crew. They were polite and friendly, teasing Reed when they thought Alicia couldn't hear them.

"She's gorgeous! What's she see in you?" one guy whispered.

"Boy, are you one lucky stiff."

"Thanks, Pat." Reed glared at him. "Now, can we all concentrate on the job and not my girlfriend? Here's the space. We can stage everything in the parking garage that we don't need up here. I already spoke to security and the building super. He's given us a generous area. He also gave us a key to the freight elevator. Let's start by moving Julie's desk over to that far corner. There's power there and a network jack. Remember, this is a working office."

"Will do, Reed." Jason, her job foreman, was one of the best workers in Reed's employ.

"Okay, Jason, you're in charge."

"Come on guys, let's get to work. If we get this job done in a week, we all get bonuses."

While her team worked to move Julie's desk and office supplies, Reed carried her two bags of goodies into Alicia's quiet space. Alicia had a big smile on her face as she watched her come in. "Hi."

"Hello."

"You don't have a bandage on your hand."

"The doctor removed it and put a splint on my two fingers and a small bandage on my hand. He was pleased with the x-ray. He said my fingers are already starting to show signs of healing."

"I'm glad. How's it feeling?"

"Good. I brought lunch. Can you take a little bit of time to eat?" Reed saw the signs of exhaustion in her lover's eyes.

"Yep, I can take a full hour if I want." Alicia rose to her feet and went to stand next to Reed. "I wish I could kiss you right now."

"Hold that thought until later tonight and then you can have as many kisses as you want." Reed's eyes twinkled at her as she started rummaging through her bags. She pulled out some paper plates and put them on Alicia's desk, then napkins and plastic utensils. "Why don't you make yourself comfortable while I get this ready?"

Alicia sat back down and allowed herself to stare at her beautiful girlfriend, drinking in her features as Reed concentrated on lunch. She was such a loving woman. Dressed in faded jeans and a work shirt, she was one of the sexiest people Alicia had ever met. She moved with self assuredness that revealed to Alicia that Reed would and could tackle anything. Reed finished her table setting, put an unwrapped sandwich on Alicia's plate and one on her own, and then she put a handful of chips and a dill pickle on each plate. She set a cold bottle of iced tea next to each plate.

"There—lunch is served." Reed sat down and looked at Alicia with a grin. "Oh wait, I forgot one thing."

Reed reached down and rummaged through another bag. She pulled out a black flannel bag and handed it to Alicia. Alicia took the heavy bag from Reed wondering what it could be.

"Open it," Reed suggested, as she picked up a chip and munched on it.

Alicia slid the knotted top of the bag open and found a velvet jeweler's box in the bag. She glanced up to find Reed watching her intently, her dark eyes serious. Alicia flipped the lid open and saw two gleaming wide platinum bands sitting side by side. Her eyes filled with tears as she looked up to find the gentle eyes of her lover smiling back at her.

"I thought until we could really get married that we could wear these and know that no matter what's going on, you and I will be okay as long as we stick together."

Alicia saw the love on her girlfriend's face. She stood up and walked around her desk kneeling next to Reed's chair. "Give me your hand."

"Honey, I can't wear mine on my left hand until the swelling goes down." Reed placed her right hand on Alicia's left one.

"You can wear it on your right one until then." Alicia's voice broke with emotion as she took the larger ring from the box and slid it on Reed's right ring finger. Reed removed the other ring and slowly placed it on Alicia's left hand, then brought it to her lips and kissed it.

"There, we'll be fine for the rest of our lives."

Alicia's eyes overflowed with tears, but she managed to say, "Yes, we will."

"Honey, eat your lunch."

Alicia squeezed Reed's hand once more and returned to her chair. Her heart felt light as she looked at the glistening ring that fit perfectly on her finger. "I love you, Reed."

"I love you."

Alicia picked up her sandwich and took a bite. She was suddenly very hungry, her heart full of love.

"Reed, can we see you a minute?" Reed rolled her eyes as Jason poked his head in Alicia's open office door. "We have a minor problem."

"I'll be right there." Reed turned back to Alicia, her eyes sparkling. "Don't go anywhere."

Alicia chuckled as Reed left her office already focusing on what her foreman was telling her. Alicia glanced down and sighed as she looked at her ring again. Nothing could have filled her heart as completely as Reed's making a commitment to her in the middle of such a horrendous couple of days. She felt very, very lucky.

Reed was never able to return and finish her sandwich. She sent Julie in to eat with Alicia, while Reed took care of a few details. Reed had brought lunch for Julie, too, and Julie couldn't stop raving about how charming Reed was. Then she noticed the ring on Alicia's hand.

"Give me that hand," Julie demanded as she pointed to the ring. Alicia reached out and held it up for Julie to look at. "Wow, that's platinum isn't it? My

God, it's beautiful. Does Reed have a matching band? When did she give it to you?"

Alicia started laughing as Julie peppered her with questions. "She gave it to me before lunch. Yes, she has a matching one."

"Are you guys like a committed couple?"

"Yes, we are."

"So, are you going to get married?"

"Julie, it's not legal in Washington for two women to marry."

"I know that, but I've heard that some gay couples have a commitment ceremony."

"Right now we're going to concentrate on getting the office remodel finished and then work on our house. After that we're going to enjoy the rest of our lives together."

"I'm glad. I really like her. She just fits you, you know?"

"Yes, I know." Alicia had to agree with Julie. Reed was a perfect fit.

"Hey, Alicia, I need to head out and pick up some more supplies. I'll be back in a couple of hours. If you need anything, call me on my cell phone. If you can't reach me, ask Jason for help." Reed poked her head in the door and grinned at the two women. "Save my sandwich."

"Reed?"

"Yes?"

"Thanks for lunch and everything." Alicia's eyes spoke volumes to her lover.

"You're welcome, and I should be thanking you." Reed lifted her hand up and kissed the ring, then turned and left.

Alicia turned back to find Julie grinning at her. "Is she always like that?"

"Like what?"

"So romantic?"

Alicia laughed as she responded. "You haven't seen anything yet."

"Boy, are you lucky."

"Yes, I am." Alicia knew that Reed was her soul mate. She felt it deep in her heart and soul. She felt very, very lucky.

Chapter Nineteen

By seven o'clock that evening, both Reed and Alicia were exhausted. They climbed out of Reed's truck and dragged themselves into Maddy's house. They had stopped at a deli next to Alicia's work to grab a bite to eat before heading home. Neither woman had much of an appetite. Maddy and Bet were on the couch wearing their version of pajamas. Bet was in a long tee shirt, and Maddy wore a pair of boxer shorts and a tank top. Maddy was stretched out on top of her lover, and they were absorbed in an episode of *CSI*.

Maddy leaped up at the sight of her sister and rushed to her, flinging her arms around her. Alicia's arms locked around her sister in a rejuvenating hug. "I'm sorry, Le Le."

"So am I, Maddy. I just want all this over with so I can get on with my life with Reed." Alicia clung to her sister tightly, her eyes closed as she fought to control her emotions. She was tired of dealing with her ex-husband. All afternoon rumors were flying about the building, and she felt curious eyes upon her whenever she came out of her office. Alicia had always been a private person, and this situation was severely testing her fortitude, although she tried to keep herself focused on work. It was terribly difficult to ignore the looks and the whispered conversations.

"Come on, Le Le, you and Reed get cleaned up for an early bedtime, and Bet and I will fix some hot chocolate."

"You can tell us about everything later. Go now, honey, and get ready for bed." Bet accurately read the emotional exhaustion on both women's faces. Reed and Alicia walked the short distance to Reed's bedroom. Within ten minutes they were ready for bed, Reed in sweats and a tee shirt and Alicia in a shirt of Reed's. Not a word had been spoken, and the silence was uncomfortable for both women.

"Reed, can I get a hug?" Reed looked at Alicia's pale face and wrapped her tightly in her arms holding her securely.

"You're exhausted, baby." Reed held her protectively. She wanted to take Stephen out and thrash him for what he was putting Alicia through.

"No more than you. Are we okay?"

Reed gently lifted Alicia's chin until she was looking at her. "We're just fine. Everything will be okay, honey. We'll deal with everything together. Let's go have some hot chocolate and then crawl into bed. We have all weekend to ourselves." Reed kissed her softly before they walked out of the bedroom.

They held hands as they walked back to the living room. Reed pulled Alicia onto her lap as she sat down in an arm chair and cradled her girlfriend in her arms. Bet came out of the kitchen with two steaming mugs of chocolate. Maddy followed her with two more cups, and they sat on the couch side by side.

"What's the latest word on the bastard?"

"Nothing you don't already know about," Alicia answered, settling back against Reed. "He was fired last night and his girlfriend dumped him. No one knows where he is or what he's up to."

"I'm sorry, Alicia." Bet spoke softly.

"So am I Bet."

The sound of something hitting the front window followed by the explosion of breaking glass caught the four women off guard. A large brick landed heavily on the carpet. It had the word *DYKE* scrawled across it in white on the red brick. Reed pushed Alicia to her feet, jumped out of the chair, and ran to the front door just as a car squealed away from the house. Reed swore loudly as she watched the dark car without lights pull swiftly away. There was no way to identify it. She couldn't make out the license plate, but she knew who it was. She was furious. She wanted to track Stephen down and beat him to a bloody pulp!

"Reed, did you see anything?" Maddy asked, pulling on a pair of jeans as she came out the front door.

"No, how are Alicia and Bet?"

"Alicia is scared to death, and Bet is trying to calm her down."

"Should we call the police?"

"Yes, they need to have a record of that ass's behavior. God, Reed, I want to kill the fucker!" Maddy lashed out. She stood in her front yard looking at her shattered living room window.

"Not before I beat him senseless!" Reed responded, her face white with fury. "It kills me to have Alicia treated this way."

"Hey, guys, is everything okay?" Bet called.

"Yeah, he was gone before we got outside. I'm going to call the police. Don't touch the brick or the window until after they get here," Maddy responded. She and Reed turned and headed back into the house.

"Reed, are you okay?" Alicia was pale and unnaturally quiet.

"I'm fine. Everything is okay." Reed hugged her tightly and felt Alicia begin to tremble in her arms.

"He's not going to leave us alone. He'll find me everywhere I go. He'll never stop." Alicia began to cry. Her tears broke Reed's heart.

Reed picked her up and sat down on the couch, holding her closely and whispering words of consolation to the brokenhearted woman while Maddy dialed the police.

"Reed, the police are on their way." Maddy spoke softly, her eyes on her devastated sister. "Alicia, we'll get him. He can't get away with this."

"I'm so sorry Maddy. I shouldn't have come over here. He could have hurt any of you. I couldn't survive if he hurt one of you."

"He won't hurt us, honey." Maddy knelt down in front of her. "He wants to hurt you. He's after you and we'll protect you. He won't hurt you. I won't let him."

"Alicia, we're family here, and we'll make sure he gets punished for everything he's been pulling. This is not your fault." Bet spoke softly but with authority.

Alicia looked up at her sister and Bet and smiled. "I love you both so much. Despite this mess, I'm so happy with my life. I can't tell you how much both of you mean to me. You brought Reed into my life and I'm so thankful. I love you, Reed."

Reed smiled at Alicia as she responded, "I love you, Alicia, and I will for the rest of our lives. We'll get through this."

"I know." Alicia wrapped her arms around Reed's neck and held on, drawing emotional nourishment from her partner.

The blue lights of a police car lit up the front curtains, and all four women stood up together to go meet the officers. Alicia tucked her hand in Reed's, she drew a deep breath, and followed Maddy and Bet out the front door.

"Is one of you Madeline Towers?"

"I am, officer."

"You called nine-one-one to report a brick being thrown through your window?" The two young officers, one a swarthy man and the other a blond haired woman, stood on Maddy's front porch.

"I did. We saw a dark sedan race away after the brick came through the front living room window, but we didn't see anyone throw it. As you can see, it took out my front window."

"Was anyone hurt?" Both officers recorded Maddy's responses in their notebooks.

"No sir, the brick is still where it landed. We didn't clean anything up."

"Do you all live here?"

"It's my home with my partner, and Reed Thomas lives with us. This is my sister, Alicia. She's staying here for a while." Maddy pointed to each woman as she spoke.

The police officer and his partner walked up to the front window and while his partner snapped some photographs of the destroyed glass, the first officer looked around the area. "Can you show me the room where the brick landed?"

The two officers inspected the brick and, after taking several pictures of it where it lay on the floor, they bagged it to take back with them.

"Ma'am, we're going to try to get some fingerprints from the brick. Can you tell us why you think it's your sister's ex-husband that did this?"

Maddy glanced at Alicia who looked shell-shocked sitting quietly on the couch next to Reed. Reed held tightly to her hand, a worried look on her face.

"Alicia, do you want to explain to the officer what is going on?" Maddy kept her voice soft.

Alicia took a big deep breath and gazed up at Reed before she turned to the officers. "I told my ex-husband this week that I'm in a committed relationship with a woman. He didn't want to hear that and got very nasty. We worked for the same firm, and he threatened me at work. He also spread some nasty rumors that caused others in the office to complain to our owner. My boss had several conversations with my ex-husband before the situation got totally out of control. Stephen was fired from his job. He also has a pregnant girlfriend in Paris, where his job was located. She broke up with him. He's been calling my home and my cell phone and threatening me. He seems to think that I'm the cause of all of his problems."

"What's he been saying?"

"He says I'm going to pay for getting him fired. He threatened to harm my sister and her partner and Reed, my lover. He wants to hurt Reed." Alicia was fine until she realized that Stephen wanted to hurt Reed because Alicia was in love with her. She began to cry.

Reed wrapped her arms around Alicia and held her tightly. She began to feel tears of her own sliding down her face. She looked up at the two officers and was surprised to see compassion on both their faces. "He's called in the middle of the night several times and left vicious messages and now this."

"Did anyone see him do this?"

"No, all we saw was a newer black sedan as it raced away without any lights on. I couldn't see a license plate, but I think the car might have been an Acura."

"Do you know what kind of car Stephen drives?"

Alicia spoke softly, still held tightly in Reed's protective embrace. "He would be driving a rental, probably from our corporate provider, Hertz. He probably picked one up at the airport when he flew in to Seattle last week."

While one officer finished writing in his notebook, the other one stepped closer to Alicia and Reed. "May I call you Alicia?"

"Yes." Alicia sat up still holding tightly to Reed.

"Do you think your ex-husband is capable of harming you or your family?"

Alicia turned and looked at Reed for a long moment before responding. "Stephen is capable of just about anything. His entertainment of choice is pornography with very young girls. He would do anything to keep his image intact, but his reputation is crumbling around him. I think he will lash out at everyone he blames for his failures."

"We can't prove he did this without more evidence and even if we were able to bring him in, this would not be a felony. You need to be able to prove that he's harassing you and get a restraining order. I suggest you change your telephone number to an unlisted one. I also suggest that you continue to stay at your sister's for a while. There is safety in numbers. I really wish I could offer you a better solution." The woman officer had seen more than her share of scared women being harassed by a boyfriend or ex-husband. It broke her heart to be unable to offer them anything in the way of protection. She was painfully aware that this type of criminal behavior happened more often then most people were realized. Despite strong stalking laws, this type of harassment was extremely difficult to prevent.

"We appreciate your getting here so quickly." Maddy stood up and shook both officers' hands. "Are you going to file a police report?"

"Yes. I'll leave you the number, and you can go online or call and request a copy. We'll get going now."

Maddy walked the two officers to the door. Bet went up to Alicia and squatted down in front of her so they were eye to eye. "This is not your fault. It is Stephen's. He is the only one to blame for this."

"But I …"

"But nothing honey. You are one of the most generous and loving persons I know. Do not take any of this on yourself."

"He could hurt any of you."

Reed placed her hand on Alicia's cheek and made sure she was looking at her. "He won't hurt any of us. I promise you, he will not hurt you." Reed bent and touched her forehead to Alicia's.

"I love you," Alicia whispered, wrapping her arms around Reed's neck.

Reed picked Alicia up and placed her on her lap so she was tucked up against her. "I love you and no one will ever get between us, not Stephen, not anyone."

Maddy had come to stand next to Bet, and they both smiled as Reed cradled her girlfriend in her arms.

"Hey, what is that on your hand? And if I'm not mistaken, there's a matching one on Reed's hand!" Maddy squealed and knelt next to her sister. "Are those matching bands?"

Reed hugged Alicia to her and responded. "Yes, we needed to remind ourselves of what was important today. We'll make it through anything if we have each other."

"I think that is just about perfect." Maddy laughed happily. She picked up her sister's hand and admired the ring.

"So do we." Alicia smiled back. "Now, let's clean up this living room and get some wood to block that window. I'll call for a window replacement in the morning."

"I'll call and get the window replaced," Maddy responded. "You're going to let me deal with this."

"Why should you have to pay for it?"

"Because you're my family and I love you."

"I'll get a replacement window and have a couple of my guys put it in on Monday morning. And before either of you say a word I can get a window wholesale." Reed grinned, helping Alicia to her feet and standing up.

Alicia hugged Maddy and then Bet while Reed watched with a smile on her face. "Bet, can you help me attach a piece of plywood to the window while Maddy and Alicia vacuum this glass up?"

"You betcha." Bet and Reed headed out to the garage. Thankfully, there were a couple of sheets of plywood left over from the kitchen remodel. Reed retrieved her carpenter's belt from her truck and fastened it onto her waist. It held her hammer and a pocketful of nails. They carried the plywood outside and leaned it up against the front of the house covering the fractured glass well enough to get through the night. Reed hammered a few nails in both sides avoiding doing any damage to the window frame or siding.

She and Bet walked back into the house to find Maddy admiring Alicia's ring, her arm slung around Alicia's waist. Alicia turned to Reed, and her eyes were hot. There was no mistaking the look on Alicia's face, and Reed's body reacted. "God, I think you are so sexy, especially when you're working."

Reed leaned down and kissed Alicia. Alicia tightened her arms around Reed's neck and returned the kiss until her knees were weak. Bet and Maddy looked on in amusement until they separated, both women breathing heavily.

"Well, I guess I'm going have to get a carpenter's belt," Bet remarked with a grin.

"Honey, you just need to put on your uniform and you make me hot!" Maddy grinned and grabbed her girlfriend for a quick kiss.

The rest of the night, the four friends studiously avoided any topics that reminded them of the seriousness of Stephen's act. They talked about Reed's remodeling job at Alicia's office, Maddy's latest new product, Alicia's work, and Bet's pending new position. She'd been asked to be on the mayor's domestic terrorism task force team. The appointment was a big promotion and an even bigger honor. She and Maddy were considering what it might mean to their lives. It was after eleven before Alicia fell asleep in Reed's lap.

"She's had a busy week," Bet remarked, watching Reed brush the hair out of Alicia's face.

"It's been very rough on her," Maddy commented.

"If things weren't so crazy right now, I'd book us tickets for a week in Hawaii and get her away from here," said Reed.

"I just want her safe," Maddy whispered.

"She is, Maddy. I've made arrangements to keep her safe."

"What do you mean?"

"She'll have a private security guard watching her at all times." Reed delivered her news with quiet deliberation. "I will also have a private detective watching Stephen."

Bet and Maddy's eyes grew wide in surprise. "When did you arrange this?"

"I spoke to my lawyer this evening after the police left, and he's making arrangements to take care of everything. The security guards will be in place Monday morning when I drop her off at work."

"Have you told Alicia?"

"Not yet. There just hasn't been a good time to talk about everything."

"Reed, you need to tell her."

"I will, after she's had a good night's sleep. She's exhausted. I'm going to take her out to the house tomorrow so she can see the place. She's already agreed to live there with me without even seeing it. I thought walking through the house might keep her mind off things for a while."

"Tell her in the morning." Maddy didn't make it a request.

Reed met Maddy's eyes, and she saw the deep concern for her sister. "I will, first thing."

"Good. Do you need help getting her to bed?"

"No, I'll wake her up in a little bit and take her to bed."

"Good night."

"Goodnight, you two. Thanks for everything tonight." Bet and Maddy climbed the stairs as Reed settled back, wrapped her arms around Alicia's slender body, and cradled it against her. Alicia's head rested against Reed's chest, her hands wrapped around her neck sleeping heavily. Reed didn't sleep. She sat quietly enjoying the solitude and her slumbering girlfriend. It was over an hour before Alicia stirred against Reed, and her eyes fluttered open.

"Honey, what time is it?" Alicia asked, putting her hand on Reed's face.

"It's almost one."

"Why didn't you wake me so we could go to bed?"

"You were too comfortable, and I was enjoying holding you." Reed bent and met Alicia's mouth with a soft, generous kiss.

Alicia melted against Reed and returned the kiss. Several long moments passed before Alicia silently rose to her feet and tugged Reed up behind her. Without a word she led them to Reed's bedroom and shut the door. She then turned to face Reed and reached over and pulled her tee shirt over her head. Reed's naked upper body rippled with muscles. Alicia untied Reed's sweats and slid them down over her hips and dropped them to the floor. Reed stepped out of them and stood completely naked.

"I love looking at you. Your body is amazing." Alicia ran her hands down Reed's chest and stomach, enjoying the effect her touch had on her lover.

"I think you are overdressed." Reed grinned and reached out to unbutton her shirt that hung on Alicia's slender frame.

"You think so?"

"Oh yeah," Reed removed the shirt button by button and dropped it to the floor. She slid the loose shorts down over Alicia's hips until they too, fell to the floor. Her fingertips slid down the center of Alicia's body to her waist and then moved around to rub her buttocks. Alicia pressed her body against Reed's. She gasped as Reed turned her around and bent to nibble on her shoulder while her hand teased her breasts.

Alicia moaned as Reed pulled her tightly against her and put her hand between her legs. "Oh, God, you are so wet!"

Reed's fingers entered Alicia, and she kissed her neck and back. Alicia reached back and locked her arm around Reed's neck, tilting her head back. Alicia's other hand grasped Reed's wrist. She brought Alicia quickly to a thunderous orgasm that buckled her knees and left her gasping for air. Alicia turned in Reed's arms and slid her tongue into Reed's mouth while she teased Reed's nipples. Alicia was hungry for Reed, and she couldn't stop touching her. Reed was overwhelmed by Alicia's attentions, and when Alicia knelt between her legs and covered the very center of her with her mouth, she was completely lost.

"Oh God, Jesus, I ..." Reed cried out as Alicia's mouth sucked hotly on her clitoris and her fingers filled Reed completely.

"That's it, honey, come for me," Alicia whispered, feeling Reed begin to descend into a body-shaking orgasm.

Reed trembled and reached down and lifted Alicia to her feet, her mouth hungrily kissing her until they were both breathing hard. Alicia wrapped her arms around Reed and held her tightly while Reed's emotions calmed.

"Come on, sweetheart." Alicia gently moved Reed over to the bed and held the covers open so Reed could climb under them. Alicia followed her, and she tucked her body against Reed's, stroking her hand against the silky skin of Reed's stomach. Reed reached down and lifted Alicia's left hand up and kissed her ring before settling it back down on her stomach. She slid almost immediately into sleep, and Alicia followed a few moments later.

Chapter Twenty

"So what do you think?" Reed asked. She wanted so badly for Alicia to like the house she was building.

Alicia spun around the center of the cavernous great room and was amazed at how much work had been done on the large house. The structure was well on its way to completion. The one-story house sitting squarely on the wooded lot was shingled with cedar shakes stained a natural color. The roof was low and gently sloped. The wide front entryway had a natural stone walkway and stairwell that led to a big wraparound deck. The back of the house was floor-to-ceiling windows that provided a spectacular view of the lake.

"Oh, Reed, it's marvelous. I can envision the house completely furnished and livable. You've done a beautiful job. I love the interior wood beams and pillars. Are they going to remain exposed?"

"Yes, I'm putting in wall dividers that can be used to divide the space up or leave it open. I'm using Japanese paper wall screens as the dividers so that heat and light can spread throughout the space. The bedrooms will have solid walls except on the wall facing the hall, which will have sliding screens." Reed's face lit up with excitement as she gestured with her hands. The project was obviously being done with a lot of love.

"I love the natural stone fireplace."

"It's Arizona sandstone, and there's a natural gas insert in the fireplace. There are so many burning bans during the year that the house has been piped for natural gas fireplaces instead of wood burning ones. There's one in the main living room and one in the family room, also one in the master bedroom. There's also a built-in gas barbeque down by the dock."

Alicia walked up to Reed and slipped her arms around her neck. "You are so talented. I love what you're creating here."

Reed laced her fingers into Alicia's hair and held her head as she kissed her softly. "Alicia, will you live here with me?"

"Reed, I would live in a tent with you. Yes, I will live in your house with you."

"Our house! Come see the master bedroom." Reed grasped Alicia's hand and dragged her across the large front area to a framed-in space that was twice as large as Alicia's bedroom at her loft. She could see the walk-in closet framing and the walls to the already piped bathroom, and the fireplace was centered on one wall.

"Honey, this is a huge room."

"Yeah, I have a king sized bed frame that I made out of mahogany. It's a sleigh bed. It should fit nicely in here. I have a matching wardrobe and chest of drawers. Dad helped me finish and stain the set."

"I can't wait to see it. It must be very special."

"Alicia, I need to tell you something. Have a seat here on this coil of wire." Reed's face was serious, her eyes dark with worry.

"Reed, is everything okay?"

Reed stopped and put her hands on Alicia's.

"Everything is fine. I just did something yesterday evening that I need to share with you."

"Okay."

"I was nuts yesterday morning thinking about your ex-husband threatening you. When I talked to my lawyer yesterday morning, he offered me some advice and after the events of last night, I followed it." Alicia's eyes were locked on Reed's face. "I hired a private detective to follow Stephen and make sure he doesn't bother you. I also hired security guards to watch over you."

Alicia looked at Reed, her eyes crystal clear. She gazed into her lover's eyes and saw uncertainty reflected there. "I know."

"You know?" Reed stood up and paced back and forth.

"Maddy told me this morning while you were in the shower."

"Goddamn it!"

Alicia stood up and placed a hand on Reed's back, stopping her pacing. Reed's body was tight with anger. "Reed, stop."

Alicia's voice was soft, but it penetrated Reed's anger. Reed turned and faced Alicia. "Baby, I was going to talk to you about it last night, but there was just no great time. I wasn't trying to keep anything from you. I just had to do something to protect you."

The tears that rolled down Reed's face were Alicia's undoing, and she hugged Reed to her. "It's okay, honey. Everything is fine. I understand. Besides, Maddy made me promise not to get mad at you."

"She should have let me tell you." Reed tried to wipe her face free of tears. Alicia reached up and slowly wiped the tears from Reed's face.

"She told me that your protecting me was the strongest form of love she had ever seen. She was proud of you, Reed, and so am I. I understand why you did what you did. I would have done the same thing if you were in danger."

Reed tightened her arms around Alicia. "I would lose my mind if something happened to you."

"I feel the same way."

"So you're not mad at me?" Reed asked

"I'm not mad at you. I love you, Reed."

"I'm sorry I didn't ask you first." Reed touched her forehead to Alicia's.

"It's okay, everything is okay."

"At least I can give you some good news. Stephen got on a plane for Paris early this morning. He's no longer in the United States."

"I am so glad. I don't want him to come between us." Alicia voiced her innermost thoughts.

"No one will ever come between us," Reed promised as she kissed Alicia, holding her gently in her arms.

After lunch, Alicia knelt on the living room floor dressed in a pair of Reed's overalls. They hung off her slender frame, the pant legs and sleeves rolled up so she could move around comfortably. She was intently laying large stone tiles in the pattern that Reed had drawn on a piece of paper. The whole house was going to have tiled rather than linoleum or wood flooring. Reed had explained to Alicia how the heating system under the floor would work, keeping the floor warm in the winter. Alicia thought it was great idea, and she happily worked the afternoon away. Reed was expertly framing the windows with natural stained cedar. Alicia loved to watch Reed work, her carpenter's belt low on her slim hips. She found herself falling in love with Reed over and over again. She hummed as she worked, happier than she had ever been.

Alicia finished placing tiles until all that was left were pieces that needed to be cut. Reed was going to cut those tiles to fit. "Honey, I've run out of whole tiles."

"Okay, baby, I'll be right there." Reed finished the window frame and joined Alicia who sat on her tiled floor. "Nice job."

"You need to start cutting, honey."

"Okay, boss." Reed helped Alicia to her feet.

Alicia grinned up at her lover and slid her arms around her neck. "I love you."

"Good thing, because I adore you, now let's finish this floor. Then I suggest I barbeque something for dinner."

"That sounds perfect. What do you want me to do?"

Two hours later Reed finished laying the last of the floor. Alicia picked up the leftover cut tiles and placed them in a box. They would wait several days before doing the grouting. She stood on the front porch gazing at the finished floor. The design was intricate, made up of sandstone in two shades, one pale tan and the other a darker brown tone.

"The floor looks incredible, honey."

Reed looked up and grinned at her girlfriend. Both of them were covered from head to toe with dust. "It turned out very well. Have you looked in a mirror lately?"

Alicia looked down at her filthy overalls and laughed. "I can't seem to do anything without getting covered with dirt." Alicia waited for Reed to walk up to her. "And I'm not the only one who's covered with grime."

Reed just chuckled and grabbed Alicia in her arms and squeezed her tightly against her, picking her up off her feet. "We need a shower."

"Honey your hand!"

"My hand is fine. Come on, let's go get cleaned up."

"I hope you aren't planning on dumping me in the lake." Alicia warned Reed.

"Nope, I have an outdoor shower unit. We can shower with hot water. I use it all the time."

"I need some clean clothes."

"I already put towels down there and I'll get our bags in just a minute." Reed stopped and kissed Alicia softly. The two women embraced and exchanged a passionate kiss as the sun slowly set over the lake. It was a perfect moment.

Reed carried Alicia down to the patio and set her on her feet before reaching into the outdoor shower enclosure and turning on the water. "Here—you start showering and I'll go get our stuff."

Alicia looked around the property and made sure no one was around to catch her stripping, and then she rapidly shed her clothes and stepped into the shower. Sighing loudly, she relaxed as the hot water splashed over her tired body. The shower enclosure was huge, and three sides were made up of the same matching stonework as the patio. It was actually large enough for four people. She smiled when she saw the same shower soap that Reed used at the house. Alicia breathed in deeply as the fragrance surrounded her.

"Is there room for me?" Reed poked her head into the shower.

"Always." Alicia tugged Reed into the shower and slid her wet naked body against Reed's.

Reed's hands slid down her back and cupped her buttocks pulling Alicia tightly to her. Their mouths met in a kiss that tumbled them both quickly into passion. Reed gasped trying to catch her breath and lifted Alicia up. "Honey, hold on to my shoulders."

Alicia tightened her hold. Reed held her captive against her body, and her fingers entered her deeply. She rocked her hips against Alicia's, filling her over and over. Alicia spiraled quickly out of control, and her head dropped back. She cried out in pleasure.

"Reed, oh my God, Reed …"

"That's it baby, come for me. I've got you."

Alicia trembled and then gasped. She was inundated with an orgasm that took her breath away. She went limp against Reed and tried to catch her breath. Reed's lips covered Alicia's face and shoulders as she held her gently. "I love you, baby, so very much."

Alicia slowly opened her eyes and stared up into the sexy eyes of her lover, recovering her balance. She reached up and slid her hand against Reed's cheek and then down over her strong shoulder. Reaching up with her other hand, she cradled Reed's full breast and then leaned down and licked her nipple. Teasing Reed, Alicia sucked and tasted her breasts as her fingertips traced over her slender stomach and thighs. She worshiped the body that she craved and then knelt between her lover's legs and breathed in the scent of her. Her mouth covered Reed's quivering center and sucked heavily on her clitoris. Reed choked as her body clenched in reaction to the electricity of the orgasm shooting up her legs. Placing her hands on the shower wall, she trembled as her body was inundated with pleasure so acute her legs threatened to collapse.

"Jesus, Ali …"

Alicia shoved her fingers deeply into Reed and wrapped her other arm around Reed's strong thighs. She slumped against Alicia, her body buffeted with another wave of pleasure.

Alicia stood up and held Reed tightly in her arms her face tucked against Reed's feeling the trembling subside. "Alicia?"

"Yes, honey." Alicia looked up into Reed's face and saw the love in her eyes.

"Marry me, please?" Reed leaned down and looked into Alicia's eyes.

"Yes." Alicia's heart settled in her chest, and she relaxed in Reed's arms.

"Yes?"

"Yes."

"I will love you for the rest of your life."

"I will love you forever, Reed. I never knew how lonely I was until I met you. You fill my heart and mind. I found my dream, my soul mate."

"So what do you say to a romantic dinner and a night under the stars with me?"

"That sounds perfect."

The evening passed in a rosy glow. The two women again walked through their new, partially built home, dreaming about the day when it would be finished and they would live in it together. They ate dinner and talked about their future, naming the two children they both wanted. It was a night of dreams and passion. They lay comfortably on an air mattress in the master bedroom, giggling and slowly making love.

"Our first time in our bedroom, this will be an occasion we'll never forget." Reed spoke softly.

"One of many important dates I'm recording in my diary."

"You keep a diary?"

"Yes, I have for years."

"That's nice."

"The last few weeks it's been full of you." Alicia snuggled up against Reed.

"It has been a full couple of weeks." Reed yawned.

"Yes it has. Go to sleep, honey."

"Goodnight baby." Reed slipped quickly into sleep. Alicia watched over her until her eyes also closed.

She would write everything about the day in her diary and re-read it for many years to come. She and Reed were making memories that they could share for the rest of their lives. "God, I am so happy you brought Reed into my life. I promise I will watch over her and love her completely."

Chapter Twenty-One

"Jason, this is looking good." Reed glanced around the nearly finished front office. The curved front desk was majestic, shiny and beautifully stained teak to match the trim around the windows and the walls and coved ceiling. The wall sconces were set to up—light the pearl silk wallpaper and showcase the elegant paintings that would be hung on the walls. It had been a jam-packed week of activity.

"Yeah, it's turning out freakin' gorgeous!" Jason had reason to be proud. His team had the punch-out list to complete, and they still had a full day before their seven day deadline was up.

"Let's go over the list one more time. I'm walking through the room with our client tomorrow at nine."

"Okay. We should be finished around ten tonight. I have a few touchups on the nail holes, and I need to put plates on all the outlets. We need to shorten the doors and re-hang them. Then we just need to lay the carpet."

"Good, I'll be here to help. I'm proud of you guys. You deserve your bonus."

"Yeah, we kicked some as …"

"Hello, Jason."

"Hi, Alicia," Jason colored deeply red as he realized she'd overheard his comment. Reed was used to the swearing, but no way was he going to swear around Alicia. She was special, and everyone on the crew was half in love with her. She knew every one of their names and had brought coffee and pop to the team several times during the week. She never failed to tell them what a good job they were doing, but most of all she just glowed with feeling for their boss. No one on the team had any concerns that Reed and Alicia were together. They made a great couple.

"Reed, can I talk to you a minute?" Alicia asked quietly.

"Sure. Jason, I'll be back in a little bit to go over the list. You go ahead and start delegating the jobs. Don't forget to put me on something, too."

"Will do, boss."

Reed followed Alicia to her office.

"Hey, Julie, what do you think of your new space?" Julie had been working at her new desk for the past two days.

"It's gorgeous, I love it." Julie was impressed with the transformation.

"Good. We'll install the carpet tonight after all the cleanup. It'll be done by tomorrow morning when you come in."

"Cool."

Reed stepped into Alicia's office and shut her door. Alicia sat quietly behind her desk, her sharp ice blue eyes on Reed. Reed couldn't tell what she was thinking, her face was serious, her eyes large. Reed sat in the chair and waited for Alicia to speak, her heart speeding up in her chest.

"Reed, I received a telephone call from the police department a little while ago. Stephen has been arrested in Paris for assaulting his pregnant girlfriend. She's in the hospital under observation to make sure the baby is okay."

Reed leaned over Alicia's desk and gathered her hands in her own. "I'm sorry, Alicia."

Alicia felt the tears start. "I am too. I'm sorry for his ex-girlfriend. He deserves to be jailed for what he did."

Reed stood up and walked behind the desk. Kneeling next to Alicia, she reached out and gathered her into her arms, holding her tenderly. Alicia wept softly on her shoulder. Reed didn't have to say a word. It was several long minutes before Alicia could get control of her emotions, and then she sighed and sat back in her chair. "Thank you."

"For what?"

"For loving me." Alicia cupped Reed's cheek with her hand.

"Always." Reed's dimples deepened in her cheeks.

"You are so beautiful."

"Thank you, I think you are the beautiful one, inside and out. I'm sorry that Stephen hurt his girlfriend. She's as much a victim as you are." Reed looked at her girlfriend as she spoke. "Honey, I'm going to have to stay late with the crew and finish the office. We have some details to get done before we lay the carpet."

Alicia's eyes grew sharp. "You're not laying carpet with your hand."

"I ..." Reed started to grin until she saw the steel in Alicia's eyes. "I'll supervise."

"Good idea." Alicia hugged her girlfriend tightly.

Reed stood up and chuckled. "I ought to make you crew boss, you're tough."

"Yes, I am." Alicia giggled waving her fingers at Reed. "I'm going to stay here and work until you get done. I'll order pizza for everyone."

"Sounds good, I'll tell Jason."

"Reed?"

"Yes?" Reed turned in the open doorway.

"The front office looks fantastic."

"It did turn out very well."

"Your team did a fabulous job."

"Yes, they did." Reed winked at her and strode out into the hallway.

Alicia kept smiling long after Reed had gone. She knew her boss was very pleased with the job. He told her every day how impressed he was with the caliber of the work.

It was after six before Alicia's office door opened and Alex Barstow stepped in, his smile wide. Alicia had been engrossed in a new investment program she was going to discuss with Jack. She thought it might spark interest with some young startup companies. "Hey, Alicia, I'm going out for a late dinner tonight, want to join me?"

"No thanks, Alex," Alicia responded, her mind still focused on her work.

"Ah, come on, you're always here late. You need a break." Alex closed the office door and sauntered over to lean on Alicia's desk.

"No thanks, Alex. Really, I already have plans. I'm also seeing someone, and I'm really not interested in going out with anyone else." Alicia smiled up at him as she laid her papers down.

"So, it's really true then?" Alex sat on the corner of her desk.

"Is what true?" Alicia felt herself tense.

"You're a lesbian." The words were spit out, and the look on his face registered disbelief and disgust. "What a waste."

"Excuse me, Alex, but I don't remember asking your opinion." Alicia stood up, her silver blue eyes flashing with anger. "Now, would you leave my office?"

"Come on, Alicia, it's not as if you haven't been flirting with me." Alex moved around and wrapped his arms around Alicia bending his head as if to kiss her.

"Alicia, I think it's time to …"

Reed burst through the office door to find Alicia in the arms of Alex. "I'm sorry, I …"

Reed felt like her heart was being ripped from her chest at the sight of Alicia in the arms of a man. Her legs threatened to give out as she stood staring, completely in shock. *This can't be happening. I know Alicia—she wouldn't do this to me.* Reed had no idea what to do. She felt sick to her stomach and froze in Alicia's doorway.

"Reed, don't leave," Alicia called out to her devastated girlfriend. "Alex was just leaving. He wouldn't take no for an answer."

Reed's shock turned quickly to anger, as she saw the fear and discomfort on Alicia's face. Alicia was shoving Alex away from her. Alex turned to Reed and snarled, "You can leave. Alicia is busy."

Reed's eyes darkened with rage and she closed to within a few feet of Alicia and Alex. "I think I'll stay."

"Who the hell do you think you are?" Alex stood up straight and got close to Reed's face.

"She's my partner and the person I have plans with. I suggest *you* leave." Alicia's voice was direct and sharp, her eyes flashing with anger.

"Jesus, a construction worker, Alicia what is wrong with you? That is just so crude, and here I thought you had so much class." Alex shook his head in disgust as he turned to look at Alicia. The slap against his face caught him completely off guard.

"What is so disgusting is that you can't see that someone honorable and supportive has more class than you ever will. Reed is the most real and loving person I've ever met. You'd be lucky to meet someone of her caliber. Get the hell out of my office! I never want to speak to you about this again!" Alicia shoved Alex away from her.

He reached out and grabbed Alicia's arm. "What the hell!"

Reed's rage turned white hot. She quickly stepped in and grabbed Alex's hand, removing it from Alicia's arm. "I suggest you leave, now."

"What are you going to do about it?" Alex responded, looking down at Reed.

Reed's fingers tightened around Alex's hand, and she saw the grimace of pain flash on his face as he stared back at her. He might be slightly taller than Reed, but his strength was no match for hers. She squeezed a little more and watched Alex's face go pale. He was shrinking before Alicia's eyes.

"She isn't going to do anything without our help." Jason and Julie stood in the office doorway, and the rest of the crew stood right behind them. Their eyes were on Alex, and they were not going to let him bully either Alicia or Reed.

Alex wisely backed away from Reed and walked rapidly out of the office. The crowd separated to allow him to leave. The looks he received were mixtures of anger and disgust.

"Asshole," Jason muttered, as Alex shouldered his way through the group.

Reed looked at Alicia expecting to see embarrassment on her face, but she was mistaken. Alicia was grinning at the loyal people standing in her office doorway. "Thanks everyone."

"No problem, Alicia," Jason responded with a grin. "We won't let anyone bother our boss's girl."

Julie burst into laughter as did Alicia. Reed blushed with embarrassment, her eyes on her amused girlfriend. She was somewhat taken aback at what Alicia had said to Alex. She felt twenty feet tall.

"How about I order pizza?" Alicia suggested with a grin to the crowd.

"Great! We're going to clear the floor and get ready to lay the carpet. Everything else is done. We should be out of here no later than ten." Jason grinned broadly and then turned and headed back out of the office. Julie winked at Alicia and then shut the office door, leaving Reed and Alicia alone.

"Alicia, are you okay?"

Alicia moved up to Reed and slipped her arms around her waist. "I'm fine. It felt very empowering to slap Alex."

Reed pulled Alicia close to her and whispered again. "Are you really okay? I can't believe what you said to him."

"Which part—the part where you're honorable and supportive or loving and honest? I love you Reed, and I'm proud to be your partner in every way. I'll count myself lucky for the rest of my life that I found you."

"God, I don't know how I ended up with you, but whatever the reason I'm so damn glad." Reed's eyes filled with tears, her whole body trembling with emotion.

"I love it that your whole crew and Julie were willing to defend my honor. It speaks to the respect they have for their boss. I love their boss with all my heart." Alicia hugged her emotional girlfriend.

"I love you, baby. I'm sorry you had to deal with that. Is he going to be a problem?"

"No, I can deal with Alex. He's just a jerk." Alicia kissed Reed softly. "So, boss, how many pizzas should I order?"

The carpet was completely laid and the trim put in place by ten-fifteen. Then the crew, along with Julie and Alicia, stopped to admire the front entrance. It was perfect. Jason and his team began to pack up the last of their tools and equipment, while Alicia and Julie cleaned up the leftover dinner in her office. She and Reed were the last two to leave. They walked together out of the elevator into the parking lot to Reed's truck and Alicia's car.

"Meet you at home." Reed bent and kissed Alicia before climbing into her truck. "I'll wait for you to get in your car."

Alicia climbed into her sports car and with a squeal of her tires she headed for her loft, Reed following closely behind her. They were home and ready for bed by eleven. Reed lay quietly in bed as she waited for Alicia to join her. She yawned and stretched out to get comfortable.

Alicia couldn't help but notice the circles under Reed's eyes and the yawn. Reed had been working late every night to finish the job. Alicia knew she was exhausted and still recuperating from her hand injury. "Honey, you look completely done in."

"I'm okay."

"You're exhausted." Alicia slid under the covers and cuddled up to Reed. "Come on, let's go to sleep."

"I love you, baby."

"I love you. Goodnight sweetheart." Alicia kissed Reed slowly and then slid her arms around her waist, her leg over Reed's slender hips.

Reed was fast asleep in minutes, and Alicia held her tenderly while her lover slept. She was so proud of Reed and the work her company did. She was also gratified at how loyal her crew was. It verified what she knew in her heart about Reed. She was honorable, honest, and fair, qualities that Alicia valued very much. She smiled in the dark as she tightened her hold on Reed's body.

Chapter Twenty-Two

"Reed, you and your company deserve your bonus. The desk is especially handsome. I'm glad you convinced me to go with the solid wood. Everyone is pleased with the job. I'll sign off on the job this morning and write the final check right now. I'm more than satisfied with the whole remodel and equally impressed with you and your work crew. They were professional, thorough, and very personable. I hope we get the chance to work together again. I've written a glowing letter of recommendation, and you can feel free to use me as a reference any time." Jack was generous with his praise.

"Thank you. We appreciate the recommendation."

"Let me go sign off on the final review and get your check. Again, I'm very pleased with the work." Jack reached out and shook Reed's hand.

"Thanks."

"I'll be right back."

"I'll wait here." Reed took a seat in the waiting room. She didn't want to disturb Alicia at her work.

"Reed, Alicia asked that you stop by her office after you and Jack were finished."

"Thanks, Julie."

"You're welcome. Reed, it's a beautiful job." Julie smiled.

"Thanks, Julie."

"Julie, can you make a copy of this contract for Reed and a copy of the check for my files?" Jack inquired as he returned with the signed paperwork.

"I'll be right back."

"So, Reed, where are you off to next?"

"I've got four other jobs going on that I need to check on. I also have a few bids that I need to prepare."

"Business is good?"

"Business is booming."

"Good, after I tell all my friends about your fine work, you should be inundated with calls."

"Thanks, I can always use more work." Reed grinned back at Jack.

"Here's the copy of the signed contract and your check. Jack, I'll put your copies in your office file with the original contract." Julie handed the documents to Jack.

"Thanks, Julie. Reed, it's been a definite pleasure, thank you." Jack handed the check and the contract to Reed.

"Jack, this check isn't right!" Reed looked at it with puzzlement.

"Yes, it is. I included an incentive of my own."

"Jack, that was very generous of you." Reed was surprised at the added bonus.

"It was well worth it."

"Thank you."

"You're very welcome. I've got a conference call to make, so I'll leave you in Alicia's capable care." Jack grinned as he headed for his office.

Reed turned and headed for Alicia's office, shoving the check in her jacket pocket. Her crew would be very pleased with their bonuses when she paid them later that day. She knocked on the open door. "Hi."

"Hi, come on in. How did the walk-through go?"

"Very well, I have a check and a signed contract in my pocket."

"Good for you. I also have something for you."

"Something for me?"

"Yes, I hope you like it." Alicia wanted to thank Reed for everything she had done to support her the last few weeks. Alicia handed a jeweler's box to Reed and waited for her to open it.

Reed slid the black velvet box open to find a gold chain with a tiny gold hammer hanging from it. "Oh, wow, this is so cool!"

"You like it? I wanted to give you something to tell you how much I love you."

"I love it, thank you." More than anything, the gift told Reed how proud Alicia was of her and how much she approved of what she did for a living. Those feelings were more important than any gift

"You're welcome." Alicia touched Reed's cheek with her fingers. "You better go deposit your check. See you at home later?"

"Yep, I'm fixing a nice romantic dinner for two," Reed grinned, her brown eyes full of fun.

"I'll be there by six."

"I'll thank you later for the necklace."

"Yes, you will." Alicia saw the glint of mischief on Reed's face as she winked at her, turning, and striding out of Alicia's office. Alicia had a hard time not following her out the door. Having Reed around at work was seriously distracting. She put her head down and tried to concentrate on the paperwork on her desk.

"Alicia, can I talk to you a minute?"

Alex stood in her office doorway. Alicia stiffened with displeasure. She didn't want to have anything to do with him, but he was a colleague and there would be times when she would have to work with him. "Certainly, please leave the door open."

Alex came into her office, his face serious and a little sheepish. "Alicia, I need to apologize for my behavior last night. It was totally inappropriate and I'm really sorry."

"You're right. You were completely out of line. Alex, we have to work together, and I'd like to have a civil relationship with you. I'm not going to discuss my private life in the office, and I'm asking you to keep your opinions to yourself."

"I'm really sorry, Alicia." Alex spoke softly, his eyes full of regret. "I really respect and like you, and I should never have said anything at all."

"I like you, Alex. I'll accept your apology and let's just let it go."

"I apologized to your partner just a minute ago. She said it was you I needed to apologize to. She said that it would be up to you to forgive me."

"Reed knows this is my office and she respects that I'll be able to deal with anything that happens."

"She and her company did a nice job on the remodel. It looks very elegant."

"They're a talented group."

"Well, I'll let you get back to work." Alex hesitated before turning to leave.

"Alex, let's pretend that this whole thing never happened."

Alex smiled and shook his head. "Thanks, Alicia. As always, you're a class act."

"Alicia, oh, hi Alex—can I speak with Alicia for a few minutes?"

"Sure, Jack. The front office turned out beautifully."

"Yes, it did. Reed and her company are going to get a lot of business after this remodel. I plan on telling everyone I know about them."

"Talk to you later, Alicia."

"What's up Jack?"

"I just got a call from JetStream Wireless, the new voiceover IP company you have been wooing. They want us to manage their 401K plans and their retirement portfolio."

"That's great! That should be a nice big contract."

"And all because of your work. The CFO mentioned you by name as being instrumental in convincing them to go with us. Nice job!" Jack was beaming. JSW was an important customer to add to their growing clientele.

"Thanks, it was a team effort."

"I also wanted to ask you something personal."

"Sure." Alicia went slightly on guard.

"I'd like to invite you and Reed over to the house on Saturday. My wife and I are planning a barbeque with the kids and we wondered if the two of you would join us?"

"Sure, Jack. I'll call and check with Reed, but we would love to come over. What can we bring and what time should we arrive?" Alicia was absolutely stunned by the invitation.

"Bring some good beer. My wife has me on a low carb diet, and I'm seriously in need of a good brew. How's two o'clock sound?" Jack smiled.

"We'll be there, and I promise to bring some really good beer."

"Excellent. I've got to run and sign the contracts for JetStream and courier them back to their office."

Alicia smiled as Jack left her office. She had been invited two other times to Jack's home, but both had been parties having to do with work. She was surprised that they had invited both her and Reed. She laughed quietly and turned her attention back to her computer. Reed didn't know what she was getting into when she met Alicia.

Chapter Twenty-Three

"Hello there." Reed felt Alicia's arms slide around her waist as she stood at the counter making a salad.

"Hi. Can I help with dinner?"

"Nope, you can sit down with a nice glass of wine and just watch."

"I love watching you."

"The feeling is mutual." Reed turned and kissed Alicia softly on the mouth, then pushed her toward the dining room table where a vase of pale pink roses sat.

"The roses are beautiful. What's the occasion?" Alicia leaned over and breathed in the flowers' wonderfully fragrant perfume before taking a seat at the table.

"Well, I got myself a nice big bonus today, and I thought we could celebrate our sixteenth day together with a special dinner and some flowers."

"Sixteen days and counting! I have some news of my own to share. We were invited to Jack's home this Saturday for a barbeque," Alicia remarked, sitting down and taking of sip of her wine.

"The both of us?" Reed turned around and stared at her in surprise.

"Yes." Alicia grinned over her glass. "Are you up for a work barbeque?"

"I'd go anywhere with you," Reed responded with a grin of her own. "I'm going to have to do some shopping. I don't think a pair of cutoffs and a tee shirt will work."

"They work for me." Alicia's gaze traveled up Reed's body. Reed was wearing a pair of loose shorts and a tank top, looking healthy and sexy.

"I'll pick something up tomorrow so you won't be embarrassed by me."

Alicia stood up and went toward Reed, slipping her arms around Reed's waist and looking up at her. "Nothing you do would ever embarrass me. I love you, and I'm very proud of you."

"And I love you so very much."

"Alex told me he apologized to you today."

Reed reached up and placed her hands on Alicia's face. "Yes, he did, and I told him he needed to speak with you."

"He did, and I accepted his apology."

"He seemed genuinely remorseful."

"I hope so. How's your hand feeling?"

"Good. I have an appointment next week to have the doctor take another look at it."

"I'm glad it's healing. Honey, what's for dinner?"

"We're having baked pork chops, some oven-roasted potatoes, and a nice big salad."

"You have been busy."

"Go sit down. Everything is almost ready."

Alicia hugged Reed once more and then sat back down and let her eyes feast on Reed as she finished tossing the salad.

Dinner was delicious, and they ate slowly, relishing the quiet moments together. The leisurely, sit-down meal was enough to make the evening special. They had been running like mad for the last couple of weeks. They took their time cleaning up the kitchen, and then Reed took a shower and got into bed. Alicia was lounging there with a stack of papers on her lap.

"I heard from Julie that you clinched a new contract today," Reed commented, picking up her book from the nightstand.

"When did Julie tell you?" Alicia responded, surprised that Reed had heard the news.

"This afternoon when I dropped off a thank you basket at her desk."

"You were in the office this afternoon?"

"Yes, you were in a meeting so I didn't hang around."

"We did get a new contract today. It's one I'd been working on for several weeks."

"Good for you. Julie thinks you're going to be promoted to Senior VP," Reed volunteered, as she made herself comfortable on the bed.

"Boy, she was full of all kinds of news," Alicia laughed.

"Yep, she was a fountain of information." Reed stretched out next to Alicia and opened her book.

"Jack did talk to me about the possibility of a promotion, but that was before all of the mess with Stephen."

"Do you think that this stuff with Stephen will affect your getting promoted?" Reed sat up straight and looked at Alicia with concern.

"I don't know."

"Alicia, you deserve the title. Nothing that happened was in any way your fault!" Reed grew hot at the thought that Alicia would be treated differently because of Stephen's behavior.

"You know, Jack told me Stephen was dead set against my getting promoted to VP in the first place," Alicia admitted, hurt feelings in her voice.

"That's because he's a weak imitation of a man."

"So you wouldn't mind my getting a promotion?"

"Hell no!" Reed turned and looked at Alicia. "I would never ever be against anything you wanted to do with your career."

Alicia felt the warmth spread through her body as Reed's words sunk in. All she had ever wanted was someone who respected who she was and loved her without restriction. And she had found all that and more in Reed. "Thank you. That means so much to me."

"Alicia, I'm very proud of who you are." Reed reached up and placed her hand against Alicia's face.

"As I am of you."

"That makes us pretty damn perfect." Reed reached down and grasped Alicia's hand and kissed her ring.

Chapter Twenty-Four

"Reed, this is my wife, Jen. Jen, this is Alicia's partner, Reed Thomas." Jack introduced Reed to the petite dark-haired woman as he ushered them into the house. Jen and Jack were dressed casually in shorts and tee shirts, and greeted Alicia and Reed with friendly smiles. Jack towered over his tiny wife, as did Reed.

"Hello, Reed. Jack has been praising your talents all week. I saw the finished lobby. You did a remarkable job. It's stunning." Jen reached out and shook Reed's hand. The two women followed them into their striking home. The front entry way was large and inviting, full of oversized pots of greenery that contrasted attractively with the copper colored walls. It was a spacious home with an open living and dining room. The kitchen had long granite countertops stretching end to end. A commercial glass front refrigerator filled one side of the kitchen.

"Thanks, my team was pleased with the results." Reed smiled at the vivacious, friendly woman.

"Come on in and we'll get a drink and sit out on the patio. It's too nice a day to be inside. I want to talk more about the remodeling your company does. I'm fascinated with how you figure out what you can do with a remodel."

"Here, we brought some drinks to share." Alicia had picked out a couple of bottles of wine, and Reed had brought a selection of excellent microbrews. "Thanks for inviting us to your home."

"We're glad to have you, and I know Jack is going to want to try one of these beers," Jen hooked her arm in Alicia's. Jack just grinned and followed Reed into the kitchen. After they had admired the handsome room, Jack opened the massive sliding glass door and led the women outside Reed and Alicia were surprised to find that they were the only people invited to what appeared to be a family barbeque. Two teenaged boys were happily splashing in the pool, and the four adults took chairs on the used brick patio.

Reed was glad she had gone shopping. Her khaki shorts and short-sleeved camp shirt were perfect for the backyard function. Alicia looked cool and comfortable in a lightweight, pale blue sundress and sandals.

"Alicia, how long has it been since we've seen each other?" Jen asked with a generous smile.

"Since the Christmas party, I think."

"Right! You look fantastic. I hope Jack isn't working you too hard." She kissed her husband on the cheek and she stood up. "What can I get you to drink—beer, wine, or pop?"

"Wine would be fine."

"Reed?"

"A beer would be nice."

"I'll get them, Jen. You guys sit down and Reed, don't let Jen convince you to remodel the house again," Jack teased.

Jen just snorted and rolled her eyes at her husband. "Reed, Jack says you're building your own house. That must be fun."

"It is. It's the only time I can do exactly what I want and no one will change their mind, except maybe for Alicia." Reed grinned at Alicia.

"What's it like?"

Alicia responded before Reed could continue. "It's an incredible one-story, three thousand square foot work of art."

Reed flushed at Alicia's comment.

"I'd really like to see it."

"We'll have you over as soon as it's presentable. Right now it's a construction zone."

Alicia was surprised at how quickly the afternoon went by. The barbequed ribs were Jack's specialty and succulent. With a macaroni salad and some cut-up vegetables and dip, the meal was delicious. It was after nine before she and Reed got ready to leave. They talked all afternoon and evening, covering topics from politics to high finance. The two boys peppered Alicia with questions about her sailboat. After she promised to take them sailing, they happily went inside to watch a movie.

"Thank you both for inviting us to your home. We enjoyed the afternoon very much. We'll invite you over once we get the house ready for company." And Reed meant it. She had been extremely nervous about going to Alicia's boss's home. Jack and Jen had been gracious hosts, going out of their way to make both her and Alicia comfortable. She liked them both very much.

"It was our pleasure. Alicia, Jack and I are very happy that you've found someone who appreciates how special you are. Reed, it has been a sincere pleasure to meet you. I was serious when I said I would help you if you need any interior decorating as you remodel. It's rare that I get to put my rusty skills to work." Jen hugged Alicia affectionately.

"I'll take you up on your offer. We're always in need of interior decorating talent. Your home is a showcase."

"Thank you again, Jen. Reed and I would like to return the favor and take you and the boys out on our boat." Alicia was filled with happiness that they seemed to accept her and Reed.

"That sounds like fun."

"Thank you again for inviting us." Reed was startled by Jen's warm hug.

Alicia and Reed didn't say a word until they were halfway home.

"They're very nice people," Reed commented quietly.

"Yes, they are, and they had us over to show us that they both accept our relationship." Alicia's voice was full of emotion.

"I know." Reed reached over and clasped Alicia's hand. "Their two boys have a huge crush on you."

"They do not!" Alicia turned, her eyebrows raised in surprise.

"Oh, yeah, they do. I can't blame them. You have to be the sexiest woman I know." Reed grinned.

"I think the younger one thought you were pretty darn cute," Alicia chuckled. "He must have asked you three times if you lifted weights or wrestled in the WWF."

Reed blushed and shook her head. "It's nice to be invited out as a couple."

"It's very nice. I love you, Reed."

"Isn't it amazing how that works? I love you."

"You look pretty darn sexy in those shorts." Alicia hand slid along Reed's muscular thigh.

"Yeah, I bet I get your dress off before you can get my shorts off."

"Is that a bet?" Alicia's eyes sparkled with mischief.

"Absolutely."

"So when I win what do I get?"

"Two hours of uninterrupted lovemaking."

"And if you win?"

"Three hours of mind blowing sex!"

Alicia snorted with laughter. "This must be what they call a win-win situation."

"Yes it is." Reed grinned. "Hurry up! Our evening is just beginning."

Chapter Twenty-Five

Alicia was busy working at her desk, her head bent down studying the documents in front of her. As the new Senior Vice-President of New Accounts she was up to her ears in work, not that she minded. She loved her new job and the responsibilities it entailed. The work challenged her in ways that she had never envisioned. Her personal life was even better. Four months had gone by since she and Reed had become a couple, and her life was pretty close to perfect. Their lives had meshed together seamlessly, and both women were thriving in the relationship. Reed's hand was completely healed, and her company was swamped with work. Their house was on schedule to be completed in a couple more months, and both women spent every extra minute they had working on it.

The telephone interrupted her, the shrill ring echoing in the quiet office.

"Alicia Towers speaking."

"Ms. Towers, you don't know me, but I was Stephen's girlfriend in Paris. My name is Marisale Haloran. I wanted to call and warn you."

"Warn me about what?" Alicia's heart began to pound.

"Stephen was released from jail last week and after threatening me last night, he purchased tickets for the States. He wanted to get back together with me and raise our child. When I said no, he flew into a rage. If my brother hadn't prevented him, he would have beaten me very badly. He's blaming you for everything, and I think he means to punish you." The woman's voice broke with emotion.

Alicia didn't know what to say. She had all but forgotten about her ex-husband. "Did he hurt you or the baby?"

"No, I'm staying with my brother, and he protected me, but I wanted to warn you about Stephen. I'd hate to have him hurt another woman." The woman's voice had grown faint and she began to cry. "He is going to try and hurt you."

"I thought he was serving time for assault."

"He was, but he was released on good behavior."

"I appreciate your calling, and I'm so sorry he put you though this. I only wish the very best for you and your baby."

"Thank you. Please heed my warning. Stephen is completely out of control."

"I'll take precautions. Could you leave me your number in case I need to call you?"

Alicia wrote down the number and thanked the woman again before hanging up. She sat back in her chair and grew more and more upset. Her life with Reed had been going so well, and she had hoped that she would never have to deal with Stephen again. She sighed and dialed the telephone. She would have to tell Reed right away, along with Maddy and Bet. It would destroy her if Stephen harmed any of her family.

"Reed."

"Honey, it's Alicia."

"Hi, sweetie, how's your day going?"

"It was going great until I had a telephone call from Stephen's ex-girlfriend in Paris. She called to warn me."

"About what?" But Reed knew. Stephen was going to try and harm Alicia. She had hoped that after several months of quiet he had gone away.

"Stephen purchased tickets to the U.S. last night, and she said he's coming after me because he blames me for everything."

Reed understood that Alicia was terrified and humiliated that she had to deal with this again. Her job and work life had finally settled down and now this unwelcome development. "Have you called Maddy and Bet?"

"Not yet. I called you first."

"I'll call them. You don't worry. Stephen isn't going to hurt any of us. I'm going to talk to our lawyer and see what choices we have."

"I don't have enough to get a restraining order against him. He can do whatever he wants." Alicia was terribly frustrated with the legal system. There was little that could be done when an ex-husband stalked an ex-wife. It was next to impossible to get a restraining order unless a physical act of violence had occurred.

"No he can't, honey. Let me deal with this. I need you to tell Jack what's going on. He needs to make sure you're safe at work."

"I will ... and Reed?"

"Yes, honey?"

"I'm sorry."

"Don't you worry, baby. We'll deal with this together. I love you."

"I love you."

"I want you to ask your security guard to walk you to your car tonight and make sure you're safe. Call me when you leave, and I'll meet you at home."

"I don't think that's necessary."

"Humor me, please?"

"Okay, as long as you watch out for yourself."

"No problem. I have a whole crew watching out for me." Reed would love to have Stephen try to get to her. She was itching to tear him apart. She was so angry that he was able to get away with threatening women.

"I'll call you later."

Alicia waited until lunch time to speak with Jack. Not surprisingly, Jack and his wife were becoming very good friends with her and Reed. They had spent several days on the boat sailing and fishing with the boys and had gone out for dinner and a show several times. Reed and Jack had hit it off because both were rabid football fans. They were talking about purchasing season tickets to the Seahawks' games and spent many a Sunday watching pre-season in front of Alicia's flat screen television.

"Alicia, come on in. You wanted to talk to me about something?"

"Yes, thanks, Jack. I hate to disturb you with this, but Stephen may be back in the area. I received a telephone call earlier today, and he's threatened to come after me. He blames me for everything that's happened to him." Alicia tried to keep her voice calm, attempting to curb the fear and anger brewing inside her.

"How can a convicted felon in France come into the United States?" Jack stood up, anger in his voice.

"He's a United States citizen, and he served his sentence."

"How did you find out?"

"His ex-girlfriend called to warn me."

"That was very nice of her. Now, we need to take some precautions. I'm going to add another security guard in the office."

"Jack, that's not necessary. We don't even know for sure that Stephen is really coming to Seattle."

"I'm not going to wait to find out. I want you escorted to and from your car, and I'm going to make sure that the lobby is on full alert to watch out for him."

"Thanks, Jack, I appreciate that."

"Alicia, none of this is your doing. I kick myself every time I think of the fact that I knew he wasn't safe to have around. I overlooked his behavior because he was good at his job. I'll never make that mistake again."

"You didn't know everything about him and neither did I. It's like this whole different person was hidden from all of us."

Jack stepped up to Alicia and placed his hand on her arm, his eyes gentle as he spoke. "What does Reed have to say about this?"

"She's going to take care of it, and I'm not to worry."

"Good. She's more than capable. I can't tell you how much I've enjoyed getting to know you two outside the office setting."

"You just like having someone to watch football and drink beer with," Alicia laughed.

"Absolutely! Now, don't worry. We'll all watch out for him."

"I can't thank you enough."

"You don't need to thank me. What are friends for?"

Alicia spent the rest of her afternoon in her office trying to put this latest development out of her mind. Reed had called her around three to check in and promised to be at their place by five. Alicia was to call when she pulled into the locked parking lot of the condominium. Reed would meet her in the parking garage.

"Ms. Towers, are you ready to go?" Frank, the evening security guard, asked as he poked his head into her office.

"Hi, Frank. Yep, I'm good to go. I appreciate your escorting me to my car." Alicia smiled up at the friendly man. Fred was not someone you would want to mess with. He was big and burly and one of the nicest men Alicia had ever met. Alicia felt very comfortable with him.

"My pleasure. Can I carry your bag for you?"

"No, I've got it, thanks."

Alicia and Frank chatted as they approached Alicia's Mercedes. "Yeah, my eldest just made the dean's list so we're pretty proud of her."

"You should be, Frank. That is quite an accomplishment."

"Yeah, she's a good kid." Frank stopped Alicia with a hand on her arm. "Alicia, stay right here."

Alicia looked up and her breath left her body. The side of her car had been caved in as if someone had hit it with a big hammer. The word *DYKE* had been carved in the paint. She couldn't stifle a cry when she looked at her car.

"Alicia, come with me. We're going back into the building while I call the cops." Frank's voice was all business, his moves quick and deliberate. His past history as a police officer was ingrained, and protecting Alicia was foremost in his mind.

"I need to call Reed." Alicia was so shocked she could barely think as she was rushed back into the locked building. Frank led her to a couch in the lobby and helped her sit down. He went to the desk and dialed nine-one-one, then spoke rapidly to the dispatch operator about what had happened.

"Alicia, why don't you call Reed on your cell phone while we wait?" Frank was worried about Alicia. Her face was pale with shock and horror. It pissed him off that someone had done this to her.

"Hi, honey ..."

"Reed, my car has been damaged."

"Are you okay?" Reed's heart lodged in her throat.

"Yes, Frank walked me to the car and he, he ..."

"Honey, I'm on my way." Reed swore, grabbed her keys, and headed out of their place running down the stairs two at a time to the parking lot. She had heard the terror in Alicia's voice. "Goddamn it!"

Reed hit the parking garage on the run and didn't see the tire iron until it was too late. It glanced off her shoulder. Turning, she met Stephen's rage-filled face as he prepared to hit her again with the deadly weapon.

"You bastard, you won't get away with this!" Reed roared slamming her body into him and taking him to the ground. Both scrambled to get to their feet. Stephen got up first and ran for the door to the street. He was no physical match for Reed. She was much stronger than he was, but his quickness allowed him to get away.

"This isn't over! I'll keep coming after you two until you've paid for what you did to me!" He screamed as he darted out of the parking lot.

Reed struggled to her feet intending to go after him, but he was gone by the time she shot out of the door. "Shit!"

Her shoulder throbbed. She tried to ignore it, climbed into her truck, and slammed it into reverse. She'd deal with Stephen later. She had to get to Alicia.

Two policemen showed up immediately after Frank had called and began to take pictures of Alicia's damaged sports car. She and Frank sat in the lobby waiting for them to come back and ask more questions. Alicia was completely silent, and Frank sat next to her, his large hand clasping Alicia's in support. She was way too pale, and Frank was terribly worried about her.

Reed burst through the lobby door at a dead run, her eyes wild with worry. "Alicia, are you all right?"

Alicia leaped up and immediately saw that Reed was injured. "Oh, my God, he hurt you!"

"Honey, it's nothing. I'll tell the cops about it when they're done with your car. I'm just worried about you, baby."

"He hurt you." Alicia began to sob, deep painful sobs. Reed gripped her tightly, unable to do anything but hold her. Alicia gradually stopped crying and then started to panic. "He's going to hurt Maddy and Bet."

"They're both fine. They're at home worrying about you. Here, call them on my cell phone while I talk to Frank."

Alicia sat back down, her attention focused on calling Maddy. Reed moved slowly over to Frank, her shoulder screaming with pain, speaking quietly to Frank so Alicia wouldn't hear. "Frank, how bad is Alicia's car?"

"Pretty bad, Reed. He caved in the whole driver's side, and it looks like he keyed it with some pretty horrific words."

"How did he get into the garage?"

"It's not that hard. He might have waited until someone left and snuck in. I'll look over the security tapes and find out. You need to get seen by a doctor, Reed. I can tell you're in a lot of pain."

"I need to get Alicia some place safe, and then we'll deal with my shoulder."

"What happened?"

"He was waiting in our parking garage. I think he was lying in wait for Alicia, but when I came to down he jumped out and hit me with a tire iron. I knocked him to the ground, and he was pretty badly scraped up, but he took off running before I could get to him again. He took the tire iron with him."

"You need x-rays to make sure there isn't any serious injury."

"Reed, what happened to you?" Alicia interrupted, stepping between Reed and Frank. "I want to see your shoulder."

"Alicia …"

"Now, Reed!" Alicia was extremely angry that Stephen had gotten to Reed.

Reed sighed and then pulled her tee shirt sleeve up so Alicia could see the swollen and now purple mottling along her upper right arm and shoulder. "It looks worse than it is. He hit me with a tire iron before I could stop him. Then he took off."

"You need to tell the police what happened. He can be arrested for assault," Frank commented. Alicia smoothed Reed's tee shirt down, tears streaming down her face.

"This is entirely my fault."

"Alicia, I don't want you to ever think like that. This is all on Stephen. We'll take care of this, I promise you." Reed cupped Alicia's head with her hand. "It's *his* fault."

"Ms. Towers, we're done with your car. I suggest you call a car repair place and have it towed. There's quite a bit of damage to the inside of the car also. We took the liberty of putting everything from the glove box into this bag. There didn't appear to be anything else in the car." The police officer spoke calmly in an attempt to soothe the extremely distraught woman.

"Thank you, officer. This is my partner, Reed Thomas. My ex-husband not only wrecked my car, he assaulted Reed with a tire iron."

"Ms. Thomas, why don't you tell me what happened?" the officer inquired.

By the time the police were finished asking their questions and Alicia's car had been towed away, both women were exhausted. The incident had taken over two hours. The police issued an all-points bulletin for Stephen's arrest after interviewing both women and taking a picture of Reed's shoulder. They had also taken the tape Frank had provided from the building's security system. Stephen was shown clearly on the tape using his tire iron on Alicia's car. What stunned both women the most was when they saw Stephen open the door of her car and urinate all over the inside, swearing viciously the whole time. Reed knew they were dealing with a seriously mentally ill person, and so did the police. Alicia was just in shock.

"Ms. Thomas we need you to go to Harborview emergency room so you can be checked out. We'll follow you over there because we need the results of your exam for the police report."

"Okay, officer." Reed turned to Alicia. "Do you want me to take you over to Maddy and Bet's first?"

Alicia's eyes lost their vacant look. Her head snapped up, and she spoke. "I'm going with you to the hospital."

Reed knew she had hurt Alicia with her question. She hadn't meant to, but it was obvious that Alicia was not completely herself, and she was worried about her. "I'm sorry, Alicia, I'm going nuts here."

"Let's get you checked out at the hospital and then we'll go over to Maddy and Bet's for the night," she snapped out.

Reed's was taken aback at the cold, curt delivery from Alicia. She didn't know what to do to make her feel any better. "Okay, honey. Frank thanks so much for the help."

"You're welcome, Reed. Alicia, take care."

"Thank you, Frank." Reed took Alicia's hand and led her out to where her truck was parked. Neither woman uttered a word. Reed pulled out onto the busy street and headed to Harborview, a police car directly behind her. Reed's heart hurt worse than her shoulder as she waited for Alicia to speak. She was so afraid that Alicia would walk away from her because of the stress of everything that was going on.

"Reed, do you believe that I love you?" Alicia's voice was soft and full of self doubt. Even though she knew Reed cared about her, she was fearful that she would not want to deal with Alicia and her crazy ex-husband. Who could blame her?

"Yes."

"Do you love me?" Alicia voice broke over the words.

"Completely, and for the rest of my life, you know I love you."

"I'm afraid Stephen is not going away."

"Honey, Stephen will be arrested by the police, and he will go away. The police officer explained the stalking laws in Washington. We have some of the strictest. He'll pay for everything he's done. And he's so obviously a sick man."

"He hurt you."

"Alicia, he was waiting for you, not me. It could have been you. Do you know what your getting hurt would do to me? I'd kill him!"

Reed parked the car and turned to Alicia, her eyes glistening with tears. "I love you more than my life. He won't ever hurt you again."

"Promise me, Reed, that you'll let the police handle this."

"I will, and you promise me that you'll talk to me about your feelings. Don't turn away from me because of Stephen, please?" Reed waited for Alicia to respond, her eyes dark with worry.

"I promise." Alicia kissed Reed softly and then climbed out of the truck. Reed slowly got out, and she and Alicia crossed the street to where the police car was. The two officers followed them into the emergency room.

An hour and a half later, Reed and Alicia were allowed to leave. Reed's shoulder and upper arm were terribly bruised, but there was no permanent damage. Ice and heat, along with anti-inflammatory pills, were going to speed the healing process. Alicia had spoken to Maddy several times while Reed was being x-rayed, poked, and prodded. They were expecting Alicia and Reed to stay with them. They had gone to Reed and Alicia's place and picked up some things they would need.

Reed pulled into Maddy's driveway and wasn't surprised to see her shoot out the front door with Bet right behind her. Maddy and Alicia met in a hug, clinging together as they cried. Bet went to Reed and slowly wrapped her arms around her. "How are you doing, honey?"

"Fine, I'm mostly just exhausted. Let's get Alicia inside and get some food for us. She's running on empty."

"So are you."

Bet ushered the three women into the house, and she and Maddy made grilled cheese sandwiches and soup for Alicia and Reed. Then they kissed the couple goodnight and went to bed. Reed and Alicia went into the downstairs bedroom and looked at one another. Alicia was pale with worry, and Reed was so tired she could barely think.

"Sit," Alicia commanded, as she backed Reed up to the bed. "I want you to let me take care of you. I'm going to take your clothes off, and then I want you to get right into bed.

"I need to clean up."

"I'll get a hot wash cloth so you can wash your face. Then we're both going to bed and getting some sleep. I'm going to take a sick day tomorrow and take care of my car and a few other things. You're going to take the day off and let that arm rest."

"But Alic ..."

"No buts, and then we're going to visit the lawyer and get some security guards back on duty. If Stephen thinks he's going to hurt you again, he's crazier then I thought. I'm not going to let him scare us anymore."

"I love you, Alicia."

"Reed, I love you so much and I need you." Alicia bent and kissed her lover softly, taking strength from their love for each other.

Alicia had Reed in bed within a few minutes, and then she curled up next to her. After sharing a long, gentle kiss, the two women settled down to sleep, five hours after their ordeal had begun.

Chapter Twenty-Six

"That's all we can do?" Alicia asked in disbelief, leaning back in her chair.

"I'm sorry, Alicia. He'll be arrested for stalking you, damaging your car, and for the assault on Reed, but I doubt if he'll serve much jail time." Reed and Alicia's lawyer spoke in a matter-of-fact manner. "He's already breached the restraining order, so that will probably earn him some more jail time."

"He's never going to go away, is he?" Alicia face was a study in desperation.

"We can hope that he gets arrested fairly soon and that he gets a tough judge. Meanwhile, he's under surveillance, and you and Reed are being watched. He won't get to either one of you again."

"What about Maddy and Bet?"

"Since the police have Stephen under surveillance, we'll know if he tries to get to either of them."

"Alicia, they'll be fine." Reed prayed that she was right. Alicia couldn't handle one more person getting hurt by Stephen. "Thanks, Daniel."

"No problem. Why don't you two get out of here now and let me do what I do best."

Alicia and Reed left the lawyer's office and headed for home. They had argued with Bet and Maddy that morning about returning to their loft. They had taken care of Alicia's car, followed up with the police, and met with their lawyer. They were now going to go home and take a nap.

Reed grasped Alicia's hand helping her out of the truck in their parking garage. Both women were on guard as they approached the elevator. As far as they knew, Stephen was nowhere near. He had last been seen at a cheap motel near the airport. This information had been given to the police, but by the time they got there, he was no longer in his motel room. His rental car was still in the parking lot. They also felt more secure knowing someone was watching their place as they rode the elevator up to the third floor.

Reed pulled the key from her pocket and slid it into the deadbolt unlocking their front door. She moved into their loft first and glanced around before Alicia followed her. She was hyper vigilant.

"Honey, why don't I fix us some lunch and then we'll take that well deserved nap?" Alicia asked, sliding her arms around Reed and kissing her back.

"Why don't I help you with lunch?" Reed turned and lifted Alicia in her arms and kissed her softly. "Then we can both enjoy a nice long nap."

Barely an hour had passed before both women were sleeping soundly. Alicia lay partially on top of Reed, Reed's arms around Alicia gently holding her. Alicia's face was tucked against Reed's shoulder, and both women rested comfortably.

Stephen sat quietly at the bus stop waiting. He wanted to laugh out loud as he thought of how he had outwitted the police. They weren't going to catch him, at least not before he exacted his revenge on Alicia. She had ruined his life, and he would make her pay. He would hurt Maddy, her precious sister. The fucking dyke! It would destroy Alicia when he hurt her little sister.

"Hey, Tim, how's your little girl doing?' Maddy inquired, as she walked through the lobby of her building. Tim was one of the lab technicians that worked with Maddy.

"Excellent, she's sitting up and starting to talk! It's so damn cool!" Tim Acer was the proud father of an eight-month-old little girl.

"Lucky you!" Maddy grinned at the besotted young man.

"Are you heading out?"

"Yep, I'm working this weekend, so I thought I'd leave early and spend some time with Bet. She's off shift today, and we're going to catch a movie together."

"Good plan. See you."

"Bye, Tim." Maddy headed across the street to where her motorcycle was parked in the parking garage. The security guard lifted a hand in greeting as Maddy walked past him.

Maddy put her helmet on, flung her leg over her motorcycle, and turned the key in the ignition. She backed the cycle out of the parking stall and then stopped to zip her leather jacket. Bet insisted she wear the jacket for protection whenever she rode her bike. Maddy was very careful when she rode her motorcycle. She pulled up to the security guard station and prepared to pull out onto the road. In her peripheral vision, she caught a flash of something coming at her, and instinct caused her to accelerate quickly. Stephen was enraged, swinging the tire iron that missed Maddy by inches. The security guard was out of his shack and on top of him in seconds, flattening him to the ground, smashing his face against the pavement. The guard had Stephen completely subdued in seconds. Maddy pulled her bike over and ran back to assist the guard fumbling to get her cell phone out of her jacket pocket.

"I'm calling the police!"

"Maddy, are you okay?"

"Yes, he didn't hit me. Are you okay?"

"Yes, but I'm going to keep this idiot here on the ground until the police get here. He's a raving lunatic!" The guard had Stephen's arms pinned behind his back, and Stephen struggled on the ground cursing and ranting. The guard knew exactly who Stephen was because he had been warned by the Seattle police and asked to be watching for him.

"I'm going to kill you, you fucking bitch! You and that slut sister of yours are going to pay!"

"No, you're going to pay for everything! I'm going to file charges against you for assault and whatever else the police can think of. And Alicia has turned over all the computer files from your computer that proves you were collecting porn. Did you think you were going to get away with any of this shit? You'll pay dearly for to the trouble you've caused her. You'll rot in jail!"

"Maddy, the police are here." The security guard hauled Stephen to his feet and turned to meet the police officer. "This piece of shit tried to hit this woman with that tire iron. There's a warrant out for his arrest, and I was told to watch out for him."

Maddy relayed all the information she knew about Stephen after they loaded him into the back of the patrol car. Another police car pulled in ten minutes later, and the security guard and Maddy repeated their stories. By that time, both officers were aware of who Stephen was and had confirmed that he was wanted on several charges. Maddy called Bet and left her a message before calling Alicia at home.

"Alicia, it's Maddy."

"Hi, honey, what's up?" Alicia picked up the receiver and spoke quietly so as not to wake Reed.

"Stephen has been arrested."

"What happened?"

"He tried to attack me here at work, and the security guard nabbed him. The police have him in handcuffs, and he's going to jail. They're charging him with at least another assault charge."

"Are you okay?"

"Yep, not a scratch! That bastard tried to hit me with a tire iron!" Maddy was just plain pissed off!

"God, Maddy, I'm so glad he didn't hurt you."

"I'm fine, but Stephen isn't. He's going to jail for a very long time."

Alicia began to cry, and Reed took the telephone from her. "Maddy, it's Reed. Can we do anything?"

"Nope, I've given my statement to the police, and they said I could go home. They're taking Stephen to the downtown jail. I asked the officers if he was going to be able to get out on bail, and they didn't think so. You might want your lawyer to follow up with that. I don't want him released for any reason. He's a crazy bastard."

"I'll call him as soon as we hang up. I'm glad he didn't hurt you. Have you talked to Bet?"

"Yep, she's waiting at home. I'm going there now."

"How about if Alicia and I come over to your place for a little bit, she needs to see you and know you're all right."

"Sure Reed. Everything's going to be okay. Stephen's going to jail or a mental hospital for a long time."

"Let's hope so. See you shortly."

"Okay."

"Honey, let's get dressed and go over to Maddy's."

"Reed, he could have hurt Maddy badly." Alicia began to cry.

Reed sighed and pulled Alicia against her chest. Alicia had been through so much and she was so strong about everything, but events were taking their toll on her. "But he didn't, baby, and the police are going to lock him up for a long time."

"You really think so?"

"I know so." Reed prayed she was right. In actuality, she wasn't sure that Stephen wouldn't try to kill one of them if he had the opportunity. That thought scared her witless.

Thirty minutes later Reed pulled her truck into Maddy's driveway and the two of them walked quickly up to the front door. Reed smiled as Maddy flew into Alicia's arms as soon as they entered their home. Reed met Bet with a hug and closed their front door. "I'm glad she's okay."

"So am I. The police just called, and he's not going to be released on bail. They convinced the arraigning judge that he was dangerous, and the judge ordered him to remain in prison until his trial. They're charging him with three counts of assault, stalking, and malicious destruction of private property. He could get as much as five years if they find him guilty."

"There are way too many witnesses and a lot of evidence against him. He'll be going to jail. But he may be able to plea bargain if he offers to get help. According to our lawyer, he can get a couple of years off his sentence if he agrees to get counseling."

"You're kidding!" Bet's eyes flashed with anger.

"No." Reed looked down at Bet and sighed. "I just want him in jail and for this to be over for Alicia. She's been through too damn much."

Bet heard Reed's voice break and she reached up to her hug her tightly. "So have you, honey."

"Hey, does anyone want a beer?" Maddy asked her arm slung around Alicia's waist.

"I could use one," Reed responded, her dark eyes on her girlfriend. Alicia's own eyes were clear as she gazed back at Reed, love radiating from her. Reed smiled back at her as her heart settled in her chest. As long as she and Alicia were together, nothing could get to either of them.

"Good—come on, let's go outside and enjoy our evening. Isn't life great?" Maddy grinned and headed for the refrigerator. Bet smiled and followed her girl-friend. Nothing put Maddy off her toes for long.

The four women sat in the darkening evening drawing emotional strength from each other and visited quietly. Discussion of Stephen was studiously avoided.

"Bet, tell them about your new job," Maddy suggested.

"Well, I fly to Washington D.C. in two weeks for a ten day training course, and then I come back and help Seattle put together their domestic terrorism unit. It will be my task to put the department together by mid-September."

"Wow that sounds like a huge job!" Alicia responded.

"It is. She's going to have a staff of forty-five people to manage." Maddy was extremely proud of her partner.

"I get to work a regular shift, too. I'm now on a regular nine-to-five job."

"Where's your office going to be?"

"Downtown Seattle in the Federal Bureau Building for now. We're setting up a new office in Federal Way, but the command center won't be ready until after the first of the year."

"Congratulations, Bet."

"Thanks."

"And the best thing is she's making a huge bunch of money. In fact, I could retire from work and become her sex slave." Maddy grinned at her girlfriend.

"Maddy …" Bet raised her eyebrows.

"What, it's true."

Alicia and Reed laughed, as Maddy reached out and pulled Bet onto her lap and nuzzled her neck affectionately. Alicia reached out and slipped her hand into Reed's as she gazed at her lover of almost five months, five wonderfully glorious months.

Alicia and Reed drove home a little after eleven. Alicia was silent on the drive home but comfortably so, her hand resting gently on Reed's thigh. Reed glanced over and felt her heart settle as she saw her lover's smiling face. "I love you, Alicia."

Alicia turned to smile back at her beautiful girlfriend, her eyes alight with emotion. "I adore you."

"So when do you want to have a baby?"

"We haven't been together that long. Don't you want to wait a little while?"

"Why? We love each other and we want children."

"I'm still afraid Stephen will hurt one of us. If I get pregnant, he'll become even more enraged." Alicia uttered her worst fears.

Reed waited until she pulled into their parking garage before turning to face Alicia. "You think your becoming pregnant will make Stephen even crazier?"

"Yes. He went nuts when his girlfriend told him he wouldn't have any contact with his child."

"Then we'll wait until he's found guilty and put in jail. Then we'll get pregnant." Reed bent her head and kissed Alicia softly, her lips gently caressing her mouth.

"That sounds perfect," Alicia whispered against Reed's mouth. "I suggest we take this upstairs and celebrate."

"What a wonderful idea!" Reed slid out of her truck and came around and grasped Alicia's hand tightly in her own.

"Hey, bitches!"

Reed whirled around to find Stephen standing next to a cement post. In his hand was a gun pointed directly at them. Reed shoved Alicia behind her trying to shield her from the deranged man.

"You thought you were safe from me, but you were wrong! I'm going to enjoy killing you both, but I want to make *you* suffer, Alicia. I'm going to kill your dyke girlfriend right in front of your eyes!" Stephen slurred his words as he spoke, his eyes feral in the darkness.

"No, Stephen, you want me, not Reed. I'm the one who turned you in." Alicia stepped in front of Reed fighting to get past Reed's strong arms.

"Get out of the way, bitch. I'll take care of you in my own good time. Your dyke lover is going to go first." Stephen raised the gun and moved to get a better angle on them. Reed struggled to put Alicia behind her as he closed in.

"Reed, let me go," Alicia whispered, her eyes overflowing with tears.

"No, Alicia." Reed physically overpowered Alicia and turned her body so that she was shielded as much as possible.

"What a touching scene. She's trying to protect you, and she's going to pay with her life. You think you're so smart, but you're not smart enough. I'll always be one step ahead of you. Maybe I'll just kill your dyke lover and let you suffer for the rest of your life. That would be payback for ruining my life."

"You're wrong," Reed responded. "You ruined your own life. You're sick, and you'll suffer for everything that you've done. You didn't deserve Alicia."

"And you do? You're the one who's sick, sleeping with another woman. I should have killed you the first time I saw you, but now I'm glad I waited because Alicia will be destroyed by your death."

Alicia continued to push against Reed's strength, her breath coming in sobs as tears rolled down her face. She couldn't let Reed be shot. "No, let me go! Reed, let me go!"

Reed surrounded Alicia with her arms and held her tightly against her. "I love you, Alicia. I always will."

A noise behind Stephen made him turn and jerk the gun away from the two women. "Police, put your hands up!"

Reed shoved Alicia down beneath her onto the garage floor as Stephen swung the gun back around toward them. Unbelievably, there was no gunfire. Only the sounds of a scuffle and grunts of pain could be heard. And then several voices began all at once.

"Handcuff him and get him out of here, and check out the two women."

"Are you okay?" A police officer went to his knees next to Reed as she moved off Alicia.

"Alicia, are you okay?" Reed found it hard to speak she was so rattled.

Alicia sat up, her face awash with tears. "I'm fine, I'm ..." She burst into sobs as Reed gathered her tightly to her chest. Reed held on as she, too, began to cry.

"Ladies, let's get you up off the cement to some place more comfortable." The police officer assisted Alicia and Reed to stand up.

It took over an hour for them to get everything wrapped up. Stephen had been accidentally released from jail. His paperwork had been mixed up with another inmate's who was being released on bail. The police hadn't realized their error until shortly before reaching Alicia's to notify her of his mistaken release. The police unit had stumbled upon Stephen just as he was preparing to shoot Reed.

"Thank you, Officer Brook." Alicia shook his hand as he prepared to leave.

"You're very welcome. I'll be on my way."

Reed remained silent as she and Alicia rode the elevator up to their loft. She was dreading Alicia's anger.

"You stood between me and the gun!" Alicia whirled on her lover, fury on her face. "He was going to shoot you!"

"I ..." Reed was shocked at how furious Alicia was.

"You were going to let him shoot you!"

"Alicia, I ..."

"I want you to leave!"

Reed's head snapped up. "I couldn't let him hurt you."

"You were going to let him shoot you."

Reed began to cry. "I love you. I will always protect you with my life."

"I need you to leave!" Alicia's eyes were pale ice as she screamed at Reed.

"Alicia, please ..."

"Leave!"

Reed couldn't believe she was being kicked out. She was devastated. She turned away from Alicia and moved toward the door. If Alicia hadn't sobbed at that moment, Reed would have left.

"Why?" She turned back to Alicia and waited, her face streaked with tears.

Alicia was hysterical. "He's going to keep trying to hurt you because of me."

Reed rushed to Alicia and wrapped her arms around her as she spoke. "I can't leave you, and I won't let him hurt either of us."

Alicia's arms locked around Reed, and she whimpered against her neck. "I can't let him hurt you."

"Alicia, honey, look at me, please baby." Reed cried while she waited until Alicia's wounded eyes looked back at her. "He didn't hurt me, and I would die if he did anything to you. I love you, baby, no matter what."

Reed kissed Alicia releasing a flood of emotion and then picked her up in her arms cradling her against her chest and moving with her into their bedroom. "Shush, baby, we're both okay. We're fine."

"He was going to take you away from me. You're the only thing I want in my life, and he would have taken you away." Alicia was inconsolable as she sobbed against Reed.

Reed could barely understand Alicia, she was so distraught. Reed placed her gently on the bed and lay down next to her pulling her tightly against her body.

"It's okay baby, he's going to be in jail for a very long time. He can't hurt us anymore."

"He could get away again."

"No, baby, he won't. We're safe now."

Alicia's sobs slowed down until at last she grew quiet, still held tightly in Reed's arms. Reed couldn't keep her own tears from sliding down her face. "I love you, Reed. I'm sorry I told you to leave."

"It's okay, baby. I understand." Reed buried her face against Alicia's trying to stop her own tears. She was still reeling from Alicia telling her to get out. The angry words had torn a huge hole in her heart.

"Reed, look at me, please." Alicia's looked at Reed's tear stained face. "I love you. I just want you safe."

"I can't leave you." Reed started to cry, her heart no longer able to hold it all in.

"I know, honey, and I don't want you to leave. I need you." Alicia held Reed tightly to her. She had wounded Reed deeply, and she had only wanted to protect her. "I love you, Reed, more than my own life."

Finally, the women dropped into a restless sleep, their hearts still sore. It would take a good deal of healing before either of them would get over their traumatic night.

Chapter Twenty-Seven

Alicia and Reed's life came nearly to a standstill as they prepared for Stephen's trial. They were both going to be witnesses for the prosecution, as was Maddy. The entire ordeal had taken over their lives, and both Alicia and Reed were finding it difficult to handle. For several months they did little else but go to work. Reed had immersed herself in her jobs, and Alicia had become quiet and nervous. Even their lovemaking had slowly tapered off. Both women struggled to overcome the emotional beating they were taking. Reed was hoping that after the trial they would be able to recover. She couldn't visualize any other outcome. It would destroy her if she and Alicia didn't survive this tribulation.

"Alicia, are you ready?" Reed asked, as she waited for Alicia to gather her things before leaving for court. Reed couldn't help noticing the red eyes and the dark circles under her eyes. Alicia hadn't slept well for weeks.

"Yes." Alicia looked up into Reed's concerned eyes and almost collapsed. She loved her so much, and she was desperately afraid of losing her. Every time Alicia looked at Reed, she was reminded of that fact, and it was slowly killing her. "I love you, Reed."

Reed sucked in her breath and gathered Alicia to her. "I love you too, baby."

Alicia wrapped her arms around Reed and clung to her. She wasn't sure how much longer Reed would be in her life. Reed hadn't touched her as a lover for weeks. It was obvious she didn't want her any more. Alicia was broken inside thinking about losing the one relationship in her life that had made her whole.

Reed breathed in Alicia's scent and almost cried she was so overwhelmed. She didn't know what to do about their relationship. Alicia was so wounded and distant. Reed didn't want to make any demands upon her while she was so vulnerable, but she missed touching her, loving her. She was afraid Alicia didn't want to be with her any more. Who could blame her after what she had gone through?

"We'd better go." Reed slowly released Alicia.

Alicia stared up at Reed and then pulled her down to kiss her gently. "I'm sorry, Reed."

Reed placed her hands against Alicia's face and whispered softly to her wounded lover. "None of this is your fault. We will get through all of this."

Alicia tried to hear Reed, but her heart was too filled with pain and hurt to believe her. Reed would leave her eventually, and Alicia knew she would be destroyed.

"Let's go." Alicia turned and picked up her purse. Reed followed her out of the loft in silence. They would meet Bet and Maddy at the courthouse.

The trial unfolded pretty much as all four women had expected. Stephen was dressed in a suit and looked for all intents and purposes to be a normal business-man sitting docilely next to his lawyer. There were no outward signs of the luna-tic that had stalked his ex-wife and her family. The prosecutor had prepared all of them before the trial. He had been very clear that Stephen was going to try and lay the blame for his actions on Alicia. There were too many witnesses to his erratic behavior for Stephen to deny what he had done. He was also claiming that he was a manic depressive and had gotten a local doctor to provide evidence of his condition. He'd even gone so far as to state that, while on medication, Stephen was a threat to no one. He recommended counseling. Even the prosecu-tor was concerned about the possibility that Stephen would get off.

Maddy and Reed's testimony had been taken before lunch and had gone rela-tively smoothly. Alicia was scheduled to be interrogated right after the lunch break.

"Alicia, remember what I told you. Stephen's lawyer is going to be attacking you. He's going to try to make it look like you contributed to Stephen's prob-lems. He'll say things that are upsetting, and you can't let him get to you."

"I remember," Alicia responded to the prosecutor. "I'll respond briefly, answer only what is asked of me, and keep the emotion out of my responses."

Reed held Alicia's hand firmly. Alicia was way too pale, and her hand was cold. Reed wasn't at all sure that Alicia could stand up to another battering. Alicia turned to Reed and spoke softly to her. "I'm going to be fine."

"I know you will," Reed responded, trying to keep her own voice calm.

"All right then, everyone, it's time."

First Maddy and then Bet hugged Alicia tightly, and then Reed gathered her in her arms. "I'm so proud of you."

Alicia closed her eyes momentarily and listened to Reed's heartbeat. "He won't ever hurt any of you again."

Alicia pulled away, her eyes locked on Reed's for a moment, and then she entered the courtroom. Reed's eyes filled with tears as she followed her into the bench behind the prosecutor. She knew Alicia was going to be attacked, at least verbally, and there was nothing she could do about it.

"The prosecution calls Alicia Towers to the stand."

Alicia was sworn in, and she sat down and looked out at the courtroom. Stephen's smiling face was the first thing she saw. He looked smug and down-right happy. It made her shiver thinking of how evil he was.

The prosecutor skillfully walked Alicia through all of his questions, slowly building up the story of Stephen's stalking behavior. It took well over an hour, but Alicia answered every question clearly, and it was evident at the end of her testimony that Stephen had systematically harassed and threatened her. No one in the courtroom could question that fact.

The defense attorney started off by speaking softly to Alicia about her relation-ship and marriage to Stephen. At first, the questions were innocuous and were easy to answer. Then suddenly, he unleashed his attack.

"Ms. Towers, is it true that you stopped sleeping with your husband after four months of marriage?"

"Yes, I …"

"You moved out of the bedroom and told him not to touch you?"

"Yes, that's true. I had found…."

"It was at this time that your husband developed a relationship with someone at work after you had rejected him?"

"He slept with several of the women at work."

"You wouldn't sleep with your own husband?"

"I found pornography on his computer …"

"Objection, your honor, no evidence has been provided to support this allega-tion." The judge had ruled that the files Alicia had taken from Stephen's com-puter could not be used as evidence against him. This ruling was a big blow to the prosecution.

"Sustained. Please answer the question."

"I refused to sleep with my husband."

"When he asked you for a divorce, why didn't you agree to it?"

"Stephen didn't ask me for a divorce, I asked him."

"Isn't it true that you didn't want a divorce because of what it would do to your image at work?"

"No, that isn't true. Stephen threatened that if I divorced him he would make me pay."

"Isn't it true that you were having an affair with a lesbian before your divorce from Stephen?"

Alicia was stunned by the question. "Of course not!"

"Isn't it also true that you were using your husband to keep a pristine image while you carried on behind his back with Reed Thomas, your lover?"

"I didn't meet Reed until after the divorce. I was not having an affair with anyone."

"Isn't it also true that you flaunted this relationship in your husband's face until he finally divorced you?"

Alicia was completely overwhelmed. "I never had a relationship with anyone while I was married, I ..."

"Including your husband, with whom you refused to sleep with even through he wanted to save the relationship. That is until you had an affair with another woman."

"That is untrue!"

"Your husband granted you the divorce even though he still loved you."

"Stephen didn't love me! He used me to get ahead in business. He even tried to keep me from getting a promotion."

"You didn't really want to be with him and flaunted your lesbian relationship at work to his colleagues and friends."

"That is not true, I ..."

"It got to the point that Stephen couldn't come into the office without your indiscretions being thrown in his face."

"He had a fiancée who was expecting his child. We had no contact at work."

"That was until you called her and lied to her about Stephen causing her to break up with him and destroying his relationship."

"But I never called her. She called me to warn me ..."

"You never notified the police that Stephen was into pornography. There is no evidence that he was doing anything illegal, and yet you told his wife-to-be that he was into sex with young girls."

Reed was ready to jump up and strangle the defense attorney as he systematically bludgeoned Alicia with his questions. Maddy sat next to her shaking with rage, holding tightly to Bet's hand to keep from crying out with fury. Alicia looked ragged as she responded to statement after statement.

"He's making it out to be Alicia's fault," Reed hissed, struggling to keep from crying. Maddy grabbed Reed's hand and squeezed as she cried silently for her sister.

"I could kill Stephen for what he is doing," Maddy whispered, her eyes full of fury.

"I never called Stephen's fiancé. She called me to warn ..."

"Isn't it true that you are living with your lesbian lover?"

"Yes, I ..."

"And isn't it true that everyone at your office knows this?"

"Yes, I ..."

"Didn't you also call Stephen into your office to gloat about this and make sure he knew that you were living with the woman who broke up your marriage?"

"My relationship didn't start until after my divorce."

"Answer the question. Didn't you call Stephen into your office to tell him about this relationship?"

"Yes ..."

"Weren't you also aware that your husband had a problem with homosexuality and that he found it unacceptable?"

"Yes, he made it very clear he didn't like my sister's homosexuality."

"And you also knew this would hurt him deeply, especially when he was also struggling with depression and the failure of his marriage?"

"Stephen didn't have any noticeable depression during our marriage."

"He kept this to himself in order not to worry you."

"He didn't have any medical problems while we were married." Alicia was furious at the defense lawyer's questions.

"How would you know since you spent several nights a week at your sister's home having an affair with a woman?"

Alicia blew up. "I did stay at my sister's home because I couldn't stand to look at a man who thought having sex with underage girls was acceptable. I was not having an affair!"

"There is no evidence of this pornography you claim to have seen."

"Stephen took his computer when he moved out." Alicia knew she couldn't talk about the files she had copied.

"Do you deny having a relationship with a woman?"

"No, I do not deny my relationship with Reed Thomas."

"You live with her in the same home you lived with your ex-husband?"

"Yes, we live together."

"And you don't call that flaunting your unhealthy relationship in your husband's face?"

"There is nothing unhealthy about my relationship with Reed. Stephen and I were divorced before my relationship with Reed began."

"Even though Stephen begged and pleaded for you to give her up and come back to him you still continued this affair?"

"Stephen is crazy. He didn't beg or plead for anything. He threatened to kill Reed and my sister."

"No more questions for this witness, your honor."

"Does the prosecution have any rebuttal questions?"

"Yes, your honor."

"Fine, then proceed."

"Alicia, were you in contact with Stephen outside of work after your divorce?"

"No."

"Did Stephen at any time ask you to get back together with him?"

"No."

"Did you at any time ever see Stephen act depressed or ill?"

"No."

"No further questions."

"Your honor, at this time, the defense would like to recall Madeline Towers."

Alicia moved slowly back to her seat next to Reed. She trembled as she sat down. Reed waited for Alicia to take her hand, but Alicia sat with her hands clenched in her lap. She never looked up at Reed. Reed felt her heart ache, as she felt her lover pulling farther away from her. She felt sick to her stomach at the thought that she and Alicia might not be together when this ordeal was all over.

Maddy stood up and with a quick glance at her own lover she walked up to the front of the courtroom for the second time. She was reminded that she had already been sworn in and seated once more. She had no idea what the defense was going to ask her, but after seeing what they had done to Alicia she was prepared for just about anything.

"Ms. Towers, is it true that your sister came to your home one evening after finding out her husband was seeing another woman?"

"Yes, she had caught him having sex with his secretary in his office."

"Hadn't your sister been spending several nights a week over at your home?"

"Yes, Alicia did spend the night at our home once or twice a week."

"Isn't it true that you are a homosexual?"

"Yes."

"And that you have homosexuals in your home from time to time?"

"Yes."

"Isn't it true that your sister met her current lover at your home?"

"Yes, about five months ago ..."

"Isn't it also true that you went to your brother-in-law's office and threatened to kill him if he didn't divorce your sister and move out?"

"I didn't threaten to kill him, I ..."

"And isn't it true that you made the secretary quit her job?"

"I didn't make her quit."

"Isn't it also true that you hated your brother-in-law?"

"I hated what he did to my sister."

"And you threatened his life more than once?"

"I told him to leave her alone. He was screwing around and hurting her."

"At the same time your sister was having an affair with a woman?"

"My sister didn't have an affair with anyone while she was married."

"Isn't she living with her woman lover?"

"Yes, but …"

"Isn't that what you always wanted?"

Maddy's eyes bored into the lawyer's face. "I only want my sister to be happy and not terrified that her ex-husband is going to kill her."

"And you accomplished this by threatening him into leaving your sister."

"I didn't …"

"I have no more questions for this witness."

"Prosecution, do you have any rebuttal questions?"

"I have one question, your honor. Maddy, do you have any knowledge of your sister having an affair with anyone during her marriage to Stephen?"

"No, my sister would never do that."

"Thank you, no further questions."

Three other character witnesses were paraded in front of the jury as Stephen's lawyer attempted to portray him as a man completely broken over his ex-wife's infidelity and his medical depression. By the time Stephen was called to the stand, Alicia was ready to throw up. The courtroom was not getting the impression that Stephen was the crazy, out-of-control lunatic that he really was. In fact, she imagined that several people on the jury were beginning to feel sorry for him.

Stephen sat quietly in the witness box waiting for his lawyer to begin. Almost immediately, his lawyer began to paint a picture of a life very different from reality. Stephen admitted to hiding his medical condition from his new wife, not wanting to worry her. He categorically denied any involvement with pornography and launched into a defense of his hatred of homosexuality that would have made Jerry Falwell proud. He was a traditionalist and believed in family and marriage. His heart had been broken when his wife had admitted her affair with a woman.

Alicia watched as her ex-husband lied over and over on the witness stand. She was helpless to do anything but listen to the ramblings of his twisted mind. She was beyond shocked at how everything was being played out to support his loss of rationality over his ex-wife's homosexuality. She thought this kind of drama could never happen in real life, only on television. Stephen admitted to trying to hurt his wife, Reed, and Maddy. He had "lost it" after finding out that Alicia had moved into their former home with Reed. Stephen had tears in his eyes as he recounted Alicia telling him about it at work and throwing it in his face. He actually started to cry when he stated that his fiancé had been convinced by Alicia's lies to break up with him. Alicia knew that Stephen's incarceration in France was not going to be able to be discussed during this trial. It amazed her that the court system was in such disarray that past behavior couldn't be used to prove a pattern of abuse and stalking. She was completely in shock at the end of his testimony.

The prosecutor began to question Stephen. "Isn't it true that you attacked Reed Thomas with a tire iron intending to hurt her?"

"She had taken my wife away from me."

"Isn't it also true that you attacked Madeline Towers?"

"She helped to destroy my marriage with her unhealthy homosexuality."

"Didn't you also threaten to kill your ex-wife?"

"I was distraught after finding out she had moved a lesbian into our home. I loved my wife, and she left me for a dyke!" Stephen's facade was beginning to crack.

"Isn't it also true that your wife couldn't abide your touch after she found pictures on your computer of older men having sex with underage girls?"

"That is a lie to cover up her affair with a lesbian!"

"Isn't it also true that you had sex with women at your office?"

"I had a relationship with a woman when my wife rejected me and refused to divorce me."

"Isn't it also true that your fiancé in Paris broke up with you because you threatened her?"

"She was told lies by Alicia."

"Didn't you also try to keep your wife, whom you professed to love, from getting a promotion?"

"She should have spent more time at home taking care of her husband where she belonged!" The prosecutor had been waiting for a break in Stephen's demeanor. He continued to chip away at Stephen's false front.

"You don't think women should work?"

"Not when they have a husband to take care of them. They should stay home and support their husband. It's what a good wife should do."

"Was Alicia a good wife when you married her?"

"I was going to make her into a good wife. She needed to learn what that meant, but she wouldn't do what I asked." Stephen's eyes were glassy while he ranted, and his lawyer was looking increasingly uncomfortable the longer he spoke.

"I would imagine being a lesbian was not acceptable."

"It's aberrant, and all homosexuals should be destroyed. They are sick and should be eliminated! I can't have an ex-wife who's a dyke! She needed to be destroyed along with her sister!" Stephen's voice was a shriek. The jury's faces mirrored the shock that appeared on almost everyone's face in the courtroom.

"No more questions, your honor." The prosecutor walked slowly back to his desk and sat down. He had revealed to the jury the real Stephen. There was no question that he was a lunatic.

The jury took less than thirty minutes to come back with a guilty verdict. Stephen would receive sentencing later that week, but considering all the charges, his prison sentence would be many years. As he was pronounced guilty, his face became distorted with rage, and he turned to Alicia and screamed.

"I will kill you and your sick dyke of a lover! This is entirely your fault. You will pay for everything!"

Stephen was dragged out of the courtroom in handcuffs still screaming in fury. Alicia trembled as she watched her ex-husband morph into a raving animal. She was completely overwhelmed by what a monster he had become, and once again thought of how she had brought him to her family and put them in danger. She didn't say a word when the prosecutor congratulated her, and she allowed Reed to lead her out of the courtroom.

Maddy and Bet hugged her tightly and promised to call her that evening, and then Reed bundled her into the truck and made the silent drive home. It wasn't until they entered their loft that Alicia spoke.

"He is so evil, and I never saw it," she whispered, as Reed led her into the bedroom and gently sat her on the side of the bed.

"No one saw it, baby."

"But I brought him into the family and put everyone in danger." Alicia could barely speak she was so emotionally drained.

"You didn't do a thing. This was all Stephen. He's going to prison where he belongs. He's out of your life."

"He'll eventually get out and come to hurt you and Maddy. He'll never, ever go away."

Reed picked Alicia up and cradled her on her lap. Alicia sobbed out her frustration. Reed cried with her. She could not console her and just held her tightly until she fell asleep, and then Reed tucked her gently in bed.

"Maddy, she is completely destroyed by all of this. She thinks he's going to keep coming after us. I don't know what to do. She's closing up everything inside herself. I can't get her to talk to me about anything. She won't even touch me." Reed's voice broke as she confided to Maddy.

"Give her some time, Reed. She needs time to recuperate."

"I hope you're right," answered Reed.

"Tell her I called and that I love her."

"I will."

Alicia woke up around eight o'clock and found Reed lying in bed next to her reading. She almost cried when she saw her lover's eyes so full of concern for her. "Are you hungry? Would you like me to fix you something to eat?"

"No, thanks, I'm fine."

"Maddy called earlier and said she loves you and to call her."

"I'll call her tomorrow." Alicia rolled over and went back to sleep.

Reed felt the breach between them ever widening.

Chapter Twenty-Eight

"Reed, look at me," Bet requested, looking compassionately at her best friend. Something was terribly wrong. Reed had been spending quite a bit of time away from Alicia and the loft. She was trying to give her some space. Periodically, she showed up at Bet and Maddy's place looking lost and heartbroken.

"I'm fine, Bet," Reed sighed.

"What is going on?"

"The night Stephen tried to kill us Alicia told me to leave." Reed's voice cracked as she spoke, and her eyes filled with tears.

"Reed, Alicia was terrified that Stephen was going to kill you."

"I know that, but she screamed at me to leave."

"You know she loves you."

"Yes."

"But you're still worried about it?"

Reed looked over to Bet and her breath stopped in her chest for a moment. "I came so close to losing her, and now she's completely closed me out."

Bet wrapped her arms around Reed as she cried. Her shoulders were shaking, and she sobbed uncontrollably against Bet's shoulder.

Maddy watched from the kitchen for a few moments and then went to get her keys. "Bet, I'll be back."

Bet looked up at girlfriend and nodded her head. She knew where Maddy was going. It was time to do something about Alicia and Reed. The trial had been over for a full month, and things were not improving. Alicia hadn't spent one night at Maddy and Bet's home. She had closed herself off from everyone and everything.

"Maddy, what are you doing here?" Alicia was surprised to see her sister at her office. She and Bet usually spent their Saturdays together when they were both off work.

"I need to talk to you." Maddy strode into her office and sat down on the chair in front of Alicia's desk.

"Sure. What's wrong, honey?"

"You tell me. You haven't spent one night with Bet and me. You've completely shut yourself off from Reed and your family.

"What do you mean?"

"What is going on with you and Reed?"

Alicia paled at the question. "Nothing is wrong." Except that she and Reed had not made love in weeks, and they weren't even speaking. Reed spent very little time at the loft, and Alicia didn't know what to do about it. She was terrified that her relationship with Reed had been too damaged to survive.

"Reed is heartbroken, and you haven't called me once in five days."

Alicia looked ashen after hearing Reed's name. "God, Maddy, I love Reed so much, and I can't forget that she put her body between me and Stephen's gun. She could have been killed! He's going to get out of jail and try to kill her again!"

"She wasn't hurt, and she was trying to protect you. Are you going to destroy this relationship because there's a tiny possibility that she might get hurt?"

"She'll always try to protect me."

"That's what people do when they love each other. You would do the same thing for her. I would protect Bet with my life. She loves you, Alicia."

"I don't know what to do, and I can't talk to her about it."

"Do you want to be with Reed?"

"More than anything."

"Then apologize to her."

"Apologize? For what? I can't make all this up to her."

"For telling her to leave."

"I did apologize."

"Then get down on your knees and tell her again. She's hurting, Alicia, badly."

Alicia began to weep and Maddy went to her and put an arm around her. "I know things have been tough for you, but you can't let this go any longer. Thinking you want her to leave is slowly killing her. If you no longer want to be with her, then tell her, but don't leave her in limbo."

"I don't want her to leave. I love her. But every time I close my eyes I see her standing between me and the gun. Stephen is going to eventually get out of jail and he *will* try to kill her. It scares me to death that he might hurt any of you. I don't know what to do about anything."

"Tell her that, but don't keep things from her. Talk to her about what you are feeling and let her tell you how she's feeling. She's as terrified as you are."

The truth of Maddy's words hit Alicia with an almost physical impact. She suddenly knew that she had to talk to Reed without any further delay, and that she owed apologies to Maddy and Bet for shutting them out of her life for such a long time. "God Maddy, I'm sorry. I have been so scared. I've got to make things right again!"

"Come on. Let's go find Reed. You need to tell her what's going on. Just talk to her, honey."

Reed was sitting alone in Maddy's back yard when Alicia stepped out of the back door. She looked so alone and so sad it made Alicia want to cry.

"Reed …"

"Alicia, is everything okay?" Reed stood up, her face mirroring the concern she felt. She saw the tears on her face.

"I need to talk to you."

"Okay, honey." For several weeks, Reed had been living with the nightmare that Alicia was going to break up with her.

Alicia went up to her and knelt in front of her placing her hands against Reed's face. "I'm sorry I hurt you when I told you to leave. I wish I could take it back. I need you, Reed. I need all of you in my life. I miss touching you and loving you."

Reed's face was awash with tears. "I miss you so much. I don't know what to do, Alicia."

"Every time I close my eyes, I see you stepping between me and Stephen's gun. It still fills me with horror. It would kill me if something happened to you."

"I know, baby." Reed gently cradled Alicia's head in her hands. "I feel the same way about you. I'm so afraid Stephen will get out and hurt you again."

"Will you please forgive me?" Alicia whispered, looking up into Reed's dark eyes.

"There is nothing to forgive. I love you. I know this has been so difficult for you, and I'm trying not to pressure you."

"Reed, I miss us. I need to make love with you. Being together will help us to heal."

"Oh, God, Alicia, I've been so lonely these past few weeks."

"You won't be any more. Please take me to our new house and let me love you."

Reed stood up and gently lifted Alicia up into her arms. "Let's go home."

Bet and Maddy watched as Reed carried Alicia toward her truck. They smiled as Reed lifted her lover onto the seat and kissed her gently before closing the door. They were going to be okay. They would heal each other with love.

Chapter Twenty-Nine

"Alicia, its Reed."

"Hi, honey, what's up?" Five months had passed since their encounter with Stephen in the parking garage, and they were finally putting it behind them. He had been sentenced to eight years at McNeil Island Penitentiary for attempted murder, assault, and harassment. Alicia and Reed had healed slowly. They were learning to express their fears and deal with them. They were beginning to feel secure again.

"The police called the house." Reed had been working at home while Alicia was at a late meeting.

"What?" Alicia prepared herself for the worst. What if Stephen had escaped?

"Stephen is dead," Reed blurted out. She was still surprised by the information.

"What do you mean he's dead?"

"He was killed in an altercation with another inmate. He was stabbed to death."

Alicia didn't know what to say. Even after he had been sentenced, he had continued to threaten her and Reed. "I'm sorry he was killed, but I'm relieved he won't be in our lives any more."

Reed understood her very well. "I'm sorry, baby."

"It's finally really over."

"Yes."

"I'm going to come right home."

"I'll be here."

"I love you, Reed."

"I love you, baby."

Maybe now she and Reed could think about the future, about children. Alicia had been so afraid of bringing a child into the world with Stephen still threatening them. She could now let her worries go. Alicia turned off the light in her office and closed the door. She was going to ask Reed that evening if she still wanted a child. Both of them had wanted to become parents before Stephen disrupted their lives.

Reed heard Alicia's key in the door and went to greet her.

"Hi, baby."

"Reed ..." Alicia slid into her arms meeting her lips with a kiss. "I ..."

"Do ..." They both tried to speak at the same time. "You go first."

"I want a baby with you."

Reed's dimples grew deeper in her cheeks. She picked Alicia up in her arms and joyfully spun around. "I thought you'd never ask."

Reed carried Alicia into the bedroom and dropped her on top of the bed. "I suggest we get to work on it right away."

"Reed, you do know you can't get me pregnant this way," Alicia giggled. Reed began to strip off her clothes.

"Of course, but it's a nice thought, don't you think? We'll go to the doctor next week and make it official."

"I love you."

"Isn't that just perfect? Because I absolutely adore you," Reed promised nuzzling Alicia's neck with her lips.

"I want you naked," Alicia demanded, as she struggled to get Reed's tee shirt off.

"I'll do it." Reed stood up and pulled off her shirt. Her muscular shoulders and arms were smooth, her breasts full and asking to be touched. She slid out of her jeans and pushed her red briefs down her long thighs.

Alicia's ice blue eyes grew hot watching her lover shed herself of her clothes. "God, you are so beautiful."

"I'm glad you think so," Reed responded, covering Alicia's body with her own, her hips pushing Alicia's thighs apart. Soft skin settled upon soft skin, breasts pressed against breasts. They sighed as their bodies recognized each other.

"Let's make a baby," Alicia whispered. Her fingertips teased Reed's nipples.

"I thought you'd never ask," Reed responded. Her mouth surrounded Alicia's right nipple, and she sucked long and hard.

"Oh, God ..." Alicia cried out, her hands molding the firm back of her lover to her. Then they slid over her tight buttocks and pulled them close.

Reed could feel the heat from Alicia's wet center. She slid against her stomach and rocked harder against her. "More," she demanded.

Alicia hooked her heels behind Reed's thighs and pushed her hips up into Reed feeling in a most physical way how much they both needed each other. "Harder."

Reed's hips churned against Alicia's center until she began to shake, her hands clutching Reed to her. "I'm coming."

"Oh, God … I can't hold it any longer." Reed arched her back as her hips slammed tightly against Alicia's, and they both cried out in pleasure.

Alicia's hands fell to the bed, and Reed slumped onto Alicia's body. She was still shuddering.

"Again," Reed whispered. She reached down and slid her fingers deeply into Alicia and began to stroke her. Over and over she entered Alicia's body, and Alicia felt another orgasm build.

"Reed, oh please …" she trembled while Reed drove her up again.

"I know baby, I know." Reed felt Alicia's body tighten around her fingers and knew she was close. One more deep stroke and Alicia exploded, her body shuddering as her orgasm chased through her body. Reed cried out with her own pleasure and slid next to Alicia.

Alicia turned into her and curled herself over Reed's body needing to be close. They were both trying to catch their breath.

"Well, do you think we were successful?" Reed asked with a grin. She looked up into Alicia's sparkling eyes.

"I don't know. We should probably do that several more times to make sure." Alicia responded with her own grin and moved down Reed's body with her lips. She needed to taste her lover.

"I'm all for that," Reed whispered and then groaned as Alicia sucked on her clitoris. "Oh my God …"

Chapter Thirty

"Ahoy, Captain, permission to come aboard," Maddy yelled, as she and Bet prepared to climb onto the deck. The ever-present skull and crossbones flag flapped in the breeze. Reed made sure she got a new one every time the flag became ragged. It had become a part of her life with Alicia. *The Wind Warrior* was their very own pirate ship.

"Get your butts down here," Alicia called from the door of the galley.

"Where's Reed?"

"She ran to the store for some last minute items."

"Let's have a look at our niece."

"She's in on the bunk sleeping." Alicia smiled, hugging Bet and Maddy hello. "Don't wake her up or she won't sleep tonight."

Maddy and Bet crowded into the little cabin and feasted their eyes on the tiny little girl that lay between two pillows on the bunk. Her rump was stuck up in the air as she slept on her stomach. Her hair curled wildly around her head in blond red wisps. She was almost six months old and a happy, healthy little girl. Alicia had delivered her in less than four hours after a completely unnerved Reed drove her to the hospital late one evening. Alicia had chosen to deliver their child by natural childbirth over Reed's strenuous objections. Both Maddy and Bet had been in attendance, and Reed had helped Alicia deliver a healthy six-pound, eighteen-inch long baby girl. Her entry into the world had been a moment none of the women would ever forget. Reed cried like a baby when Alicia had delivered their little girl.

"Hello, little Olivia. God, she is so pretty, Alicia."

"She's beautiful." Reed stepped up behind them. "She looks just like her mother."

"And she has a personality just like you—stubborn as hell." Alicia laughed and slid an arm around Reed's waist hugging her affectionately. "Let's get this boat moving."

The four women trooped up on deck, and Reed prepared to motor the sailboat out of the marina. This was the fourth time they had sailed with Olivia on the boat. Reed had purchased a life jacket for the tiny child. This time they were going to be on the water for three nights. They planned on fishing, eating, and relaxing. They might be a small family, but they were as close as any family could be after having gone through so much together in the last four years. They had healed from the frightening ordeal, but they could never forget how close they had come to tragedy. It made them appreciate their lives in ways they had never dreamed of.

They cleared the marina breakwater, and Alicia unfurled the sails. Soon they were shooting across the Sound under a brisk wind. They set sail for Blake Island, a favorite spot of Reed's and Alicia's since it reminded them of when they had fallen in love with each other four years earlier. A lot had happened in those four years. Alicia was Senior Vice-President of Operations for her company, and Reed's construction firm was turning away business. The company was booming. They had finished building their home two years earlier and were now safely ensconced in their place on the banks of Lake Sammamish. They also had happily dealt with Alicia's pregnancy before the birth of their little girl. Life was just about perfect.

"Who wants a beer?" Maddy called, as she headed down the stairs to the galley.

"Get one for Bet and Reed. I'm alcohol free for a couple more months while I'm breast feeding."

"Olivia's growing like a weed," Bet commented. She watched Reed and Alicia lean comfortably against each other at the helm of the boat.

"Yes, she is. It's about time for us to think about another one." Alicia grinned at Reed.

"Another one?" Maddy squealed, handing a beer to her girlfriend and Reed.

"One more is in our future plans, but we're going to wait a little bit longer." Reed hugged Alicia. They were looking forward to another child.

"Just a little bit," Alicia whispered. "Go get the poles out."

Reed kissed her again and then went to the cabinet and retrieved the fishing poles. "Come on, Maddy, let's bait these puppies. I want to eat fresh caught salmon tonight."

"First one to catch a fish gets out of the dinner dishes!"

"You're on!"

Reed looked up at Alicia in that moment and placed her hand over her heart. She could remember that very first day on the boat when she had looked up at Alicia and fallen in love, deeply and completely in love. Alicia's silver blue eyes sparkled back at Reed, and she spoke softly to her. "I love you."

Reed's eyes spoke for her as she stared back at the only woman she would ever love. The wail of their daughter interrupted the moment, and Reed's face lit up.

"I'll go get her," Reed called to Alicia.

"Bring her up here so I can feed her."

Reed stepped into the small cabin, bent over the bunk, and picked up the wiggling bundle.

"Olivia, what's all this noise? You're going to scare the fish." Reed cradled her against her chest and nuzzled her neck, drawing a giggle from her daughter.

Reed changed Olivia, snagged a blanket and carried the now fully awake little girl up to her mother. Reed took over the helm as Alicia settled in a chair to feed Olivia. Reed's heart always filled with emotion when she watched Alicia with their daughter.

Twenty minutes later a contented little baby sat on her aunt Bet's knee while the three other women baited their lines and started to fish. It was a glorious day, and Alicia leaned back into Reed and sighed.

"Our life is perfect," she whispered, as Reed slid an arm around her waist. "When I met you my life was transformed."

"So was mine. We just needed to find the right kind of love."

"We found it."

"Yes, we did, and we're going to savor it."

"You are the right kind of love for me … now and forever."

The End

978-0-595-47642-8
0-595-47642-2

Printed in the United Kingdom by
Lightning Source UK Ltd., Milton Keynes
142051UK00001B/298/P